Praise for

The Fairy⇢Tale
MATCHMAKER

"Full of fun and whimsy, *The Fairy-Tale Matchmaker* is a delightful romp through a truly unique fairy-tale world!"
—Jessica Day George, *New York Times* bestselling author of the Tuesdays at the Castle series

"In an engaging start to a new series, Baker creates a whole world with fairies, brownies, ogres, and more that is so accessible readers feel they could join it if only they could find the portal. Cory's struggles . . . will resonate with readers, especially fans of Jessica Day George and Gail Carson Levine."
—*Booklist*

"A funny yet sweet ride through the challenging task of finding where one belongs. . . . Radiates humor and creativity."
—*School Library Journal*

"A fun romp through classic children's fractured fairy tales."
—*Library Media Connection*

"Baker's fans will easily relate to Cory's struggle to define her own path and identity."
—*Publishers Weekly*

"Loyal fans of Baker's other books will appreciate this lighthearted search for one's true self."
—*Kirkus Reviews*

BOOKS BY E. D. BAKER

The *Fairy* → *Tale* MATCHMAKER

E. D. BAKER

BLOOMSBURY
NEW YORK   LONDON   OXFORD   NEW DELHI   SYDNEY

First published in the United States of America in October 2014
by Bloomsbury Children's Books
Paperback edition published in October 2015
www.bloomsbury.com

Bloomsbury is a registered trademark of Bloomsbury Publishing Plc

For information about permission to reproduce selections from this book, write to
Permissions, Bloomsbury Children's Books, 1385 Broadway, New York, New York 10018
Bloomsbury books may be purchased for business or promotional use. For information on
bulk purchases please contact Macmillan Corporate and Premium Sales Department at
specialmarkets@macmillan.com

The Library of Congress has cataloged the hardcover edition as follows:
Baker, E. D.
The fairy-tale matchmaker / by E. D. Baker.
pages   cm
Summary: Defying her mother's wishes and the Tooth Fairy Guild, Cory quits
her tooth fairy training to explore such things as babysitting an adventurous
Humpty Dumpty and helping Suzy organize her seashells by the seashore
until, at last, Cory discovers a power she never knew she had.
ISBN 978-1-61963-140-3 (hardcover) • ISBN 978-1-61963-141-0 (e-book)
[1. Tooth Fairy—Fiction. 2. Fairies—Fiction. 3. Characters in literature—Fiction.
4. Dating services—Fiction. 5. Ability—Fiction.] I. Title.
PZ7.B17005Fam 2014   [Fic]—dc23   2014005607

ISBN 978-1-61963-800-6 (paperback)

Book design by Ellice Lee
Typeset by Westchester Book Composition
Printed and bound in the U.S.A. by Thomson-Shore Inc., Dexter, Michigan
2 4 6 8 10 9 7 5 3 1

All papers used by Bloomsbury Publishing, Inc., are natural, recyclable products
made from wood grown in well-managed forests. The manufacturing processes
conform to the environmental regulations of the country of origin.

This book is dedicated to David Robinson,
a wonderful friend as well as the best stand-in for
Santa Claus I ever met, and to my dear friend
Dorian Robinson, our Mrs. Claus.

⫸→

The
Fairy Tale
MATCHMAKER

CHAPTER

1

Cory crouched on the windowsill, waiting for her eyes to adjust to the dim light in the room. She could hear the child's slow, even breathing, so she was certain that he was asleep. Using the lessons she'd learned during her internship in the Tooth Fairy Guild, she made a map in her mind of everything in the bedroom. The bed was against the wall to her right, the nightstand was on the far side, the rocking chair was against the wall to her left, and the dresser was beside the window. A stuffed animal lay on the bed, and the boy was curled up on his side, facing away from the nightstand.

Good, thought Cory. If the parents had put his tooth on the nightstand, there was less chance that she'd wake him if he was facing away when she took the tooth. If it was on the pillow . . . well, that was a different story.

Cory flew to the nightstand, hoping his parents had set the tooth there, where it would be easy to grab. The butterfly-like wings she had when she was tiny created a flickering light when they beat fast enough to keep her airborne, lighting her way as she searched for the tooth. It was rumored that once in a while, the light woke a child, but that had never happened to Cory.

Darting over the surface of the nightstand, Cory searched for the tooth, but it wasn't there, which meant it was either under the pillow or beside it. She saw it then, lying next to the pillow, inches from the child's cheek. Holding her breath, she flew down and reached for the tooth. Suddenly, a flash of movement caught her eye and what she had thought was a stuffed animal sprang at her. Stifling an involuntary shriek, she darted out of the creature's path as it landed where she had been an instant before. The creature bounded after her, jumping from the mattress to the child's head to the pillow to the other side of the bed.

The little boy woke up screaming. Cory heard shouting in a room somewhere in the apartment. She flew to the curtain, hiding in its folds as feet thudded down the hallway and the door burst open. There was a click and the ceiling light went on. Cory peeked around the edge of the curtain, her wings still and her light no longer shining. A disheveled-looking man and woman had hurried into the room. While the woman pulled the covers off the still-screaming boy, the man stood by the bed, looking around the room as if expecting to find an intruder.

As the boy quieted, the story finally came out. Something horrible had landed on his head.

"I told you we shouldn't let him keep the ferret in his room!" the woman told the man in an accusing voice. "It got out of its cage again. Close the door before it gets out of the room and we have to search the whole apartment."

"If it hasn't already," grumbled the man as he shut the door.

Cory ducked her head behind the curtain when the man glanced at the window. She could hear him moving around the room, searching for the ferret.

"Look, it's going to be light out soon. I have to get up in an hour," the man said.

The little boy scrambled to his knees and pointed at the floor, shouting, "There he is!"

Cory felt the curtains move as the ferret launched himself at them. *It must have seen me when I peeked out*, she thought, trying not to budge. The curtains jerked, almost revealing Cory. There was a shout and a small squeak.

"Blast it. The thing bit me!" said the man.

The footsteps receded. The cage door creaked open, then slammed shut. A metallic rasping sound told her that the latch had been closed.

"There," said the man. "He's in his cage. Can we go back to bed now for the fifty-seven minutes we have left before it's time to get up?"

"You go. I'll be along in a minute," the woman said as she tucked the covers around the little boy again.

Cory peeked out from behind the curtain. She waited as the mother calmed her son, murmuring in a quiet voice until his breathing became slow and even again. After the woman kissed his cheek, turned out the light, and left the room, Cory continued to wait. When she was sure it was safe, she flew back to where she had last seen the tooth. Just as she had feared, it was gone. Someone had knocked it off the bed, which meant that it had to be on the floor. The father had walked all around the room, so it had probably been ground into the carpet. Somehow the night had just gone from bad to worse.

Cory flew to where she thought the tooth might have landed and began to look around, but it was nowhere to be seen. She could hear the ferret in its cage, scrabbling to get out. *Great*, she thought, *something else to worry about.*

After searching the surface of the carpet for the

tooth, Cory decided that it was time to go deeper. *It's got to be here somewhere,* she thought as she shoved her arms into the pile carpet. Maybe it was over this way . . .

Cory, a tooth-fairy-in-training, had been collecting teeth by herself for over a month. Of all the bad nights she had lived through, this had to be the worst. She groaned as she thought about her evening, then froze and held her breath until she was sure that the child hadn't heard her. When he didn't stir, Cory continued burrowing through the carpet.

Her first stop that night had been at the home of a little girl who had a bad cold and couldn't fall asleep. Cory had waited for the longest time until she knew it was safe to start searching for the tooth. At the next house she'd had to lure a cat off the bed so she could look under the pillow. Then there was the little boy who'd fallen asleep with his tooth clutched in his fist. And now this!

Cory clenched her teeth, something every tooth fairy knew you should never do. But this was so frustrating! She should have been on to the next house long before this. In fact, she was so far behind she didn't think she'd catch up that night. Touching something sticky that felt like a piece of old gummy worm, she changed direction. It was amazing what was hidden in the depths of people's carpets that looked so clean from above.

When an insect half as big as her fist scurried across her bare leg, Cory shuddered. Apparently, there were other things hidden in this rug besides candy and a tooth! She was about to crawl out of the carpet to take another look from above when her hand closed on something cold and hard. It felt like . . . Yes! She'd found it!

Delighted, Cory tucked her prize into her collecting bag. After crawling free of the carpet, she pulled a coin out of her gift bag and spread her wings. She had almost reached the nightstand beside the bed when a car honked just outside the window. The boy rubbed his eyes and sat up, facing the door. "Mommy!" he cried.

In a flash, Cory dropped the coin onto the pillow and darted to the window. Flitting behind the curtain, she pressed one hand against the cold glass and, in the softest voice she could manage, whispered the secret fairy words that would allow her to pass through: "Letame passame."

The glass seemed to dissolve under her hand and she floated through as if there was nothing in front of her. A moment later, Cory stood on the window ledge, wondering if she had time to go to the next house. She decided against it when the man at the newsstand on the corner opened the grate that covered his stand at night. The city was waking up, which meant that it was time for her to go home. Although it wasn't light out yet, it would be soon, and she was supposed to be out of the human world long before then.

"I hate this job," Cory muttered as she darted away from the window ledge and down the street.

The passage to her world was only a few blocks away, but the last few blocks always seemed the longest. She hid behind a lamppost when a police car drove past, not wanting the humans to see the flickering light of her wings. When it had gone by, she sped to the corner, pausing to see if there were any humans on the next street. The lights were on in the coffee shop, and she could already see people at the counter. She had to hurry before there were more people around.

"Mother promised that being a tooth fairy would be exciting and fun and rewarding. Maybe it is for her," Cory grumbled, "but I can think of a hundred other things I'd rather do."

Darting around a trash can, Cory turned into the alley between the Chinese restaurant and the flower shop. Long ago, this passage to the land of the fey stood in an open field between two majestic oaks. The oaks were still there because the passage's magic made even the most ardent developer feel compelled to leave them alone, but they were hidden now, tucked away in a small courtyard that the neighboring buildings shared. The alley was an incidental route into the courtyard, with a stone wall at the end that blocked most people from seeing anything except the trees' upper branches. But the fey knew about it and used it even more than the stray cats that lived in the neighborhood.

Cory was partway down the alley when the dogs saw her. The leader was a mongrel with two broken teeth and mangy bald patches in its fur, but its eyes were still good and it lunged at her when she was thinking more about how much she hated her job than about what was going on around her. Startled when the dog's teeth grazed her foot, she shrieked and beat her wings in a frenzy, nearly flying into the side of a Dumpster. The pack of dogs came after her then, barking and snarling and snapping at her when they drew close enough.

Cory was momentarily deafened when the lead dog barked so close behind her that its smelly breath washed over her. Terrified, she glanced back and didn't see the box until she was already in it. She turned around, her wings brushing the cardboard, flitting to the side when the lead dog thrust its head into the box. Saliva splattered her when the dog barked again. Cory set her hand on the cardboard, prepared to say the secret fairy words so she could pass through it if she had to, but just then she heard the sound of a scuffle and the dog jerked backward with a yelp.

Cory held her breath as the dogs tore out of the alley. When everything grew quiet, she peeked out of the box and saw a hulking figure dressed all in black.

This is worse than the dogs, Cory thought when she saw the man towering over her. He stood over seven feet tall with rough, craggy features and long, snarled black hair. One of his eyes was swollen shut and his bottom lip was cut and bleeding. Cory's heart was racing, but as she looked at the man, a breeze blew past, carrying the man's scent to her. He smelled like dirt and wet moss, just like some fey might smell, and it made her look past his scary face and *see* him.

"Blue, is that you?" she asked, emerging from the box.

"Hi, Cory," he replied in a rough, gravelly voice.

Relieved, Cory fluttered closer. "What are you doing here?" she asked. Johnny Blue was her boyfriend's best friend. Although she didn't know him very well, she did know that she didn't need to be afraid.

"Walker had an extra-heavy load tonight and he asked me to help. We should hurry. It'll be light soon."

"I know. You're right. I just want to say thank you. For taking care of those dogs, I mean."

The big man grinned at her, looking even more frightening than before. "You're welcome." His cracked lip started to bleed more heavily and he patted at his mouth with a big, beefy hand.

"Here," she said, taking a handkerchief from her pocket. She dropped the tiny speck of fabric and he caught it. The moment it touched his hand, it grew into a piece of cloth the size a human could use.

"See you around," Cory said as Blue patted his mouth. She turned back to wave before darting over the top of the wall into the courtyard. Glancing down, she saw that one of her slippers was torn, probably from the dog's tooth. *Thank goodness the Boogie Man saved me*, she thought.

CHAPTER

2

*C*ory emptied her sack of teeth into the tooth counter and closed her eyes. This had been one of the worst collecting nights of her very short career, and she didn't need to see the results to know that she'd brought back a paltry number of teeth.

Ping! The number four appeared on the counter, confirming just how disappointing Cory's evening had been. She watched as the scale dumped the teeth into the tooth washer and the transparent lid closed with a muffled thump. Water gushed through a narrow reed into the clay bowl, mixing with tooth-washing powder. When it reached a line in the bowl, the water shut off and the little container began to roll back and forth on its rounded side, swishing the teeth like a mouth full of mouthwash. The little teeth clicked as they tumbled inside the swirling liquid, but the sound was too quiet. *It would be louder if there were more teeth*, Cory thought. *I'm not going to make much for that.*

A painful knot formed in her stomach. More than anything, Cory wanted a job where she could really help people. When she'd realized that being a tooth fairy wasn't that kind of job, she'd decided to stick with it long enough to save some money. She and her mother didn't get along very well, and Cory looked forward to moving out. Someday she hoped to save enough to get her own place, even if she had to share it with a roommate. Then she could get the kind of job she wanted and make a difference in people's lives. At the rate she was earning money now, however, that might never happen. She was going to be stuck in a job she hated, living and arguing with her mother for the rest of her life!

"Whatcha doin'?" asked a flickering light as it fluttered through the open window.

"Hi, Daisy," she said, glancing at her friend. "I just got home. I always take care of the teeth first thing." Flying to the middle of the room, Cory landed on the floor, where she had plenty of space. Light shimmered around her as her gossamer wings disappeared and she returned to her normal, human size.

"I can't stay long; I'm on my way to work," Daisy said,

hovering near Cory's left ear. "I just stopped by to tell you that tonight's rehearsal has been canceled. Skippy has a flock meeting and Olot's got a sore throat. He won a roaring contest last night."

"Good for him. Bad for us," said Cory with a rueful smile.

Daisy fluttered closer to Cory. "You don't look too good. What's wrong?"

"I had a bad night. That's all," Cory said.

"Tell me about it," said her friend.

"You had a bad night, too?"

"No, not at all. I mean I think you should tell me about it. I've been taking a correspondence course in empathy and they say it helps to talk about your woes. Sort of carhartic. Go ahead. I can count it as homework."

"I think you mean cathartic, and I didn't know flower fairies took empathy classes."

"It's continuing education. I thought it would be interesting. Go on. I'm listening. We have to practice being good listeners."

Cory shrugged. "There isn't much to say. I had a lousy night doing a job I hate."

"I'm lucky," said Daisy. "I grew up knowing that I was going to be a flower fairy, just like my parents and grandparents. I love my job and can't imagine doing anything else. Tending flowers and helping them grow have to be the most rewarding things a fairy could do. It's a lot of fun, too."

"My mother has been telling me that I had to be a tooth fairy for as long as I can remember, and I still hate it."

"At least you work the same hours as Walker."

"That's probably the only good thing about this job," said Cory. "The job itself is next to useless. I collect teeth! What good is that doing anyone? Sure, witches used them in potions years ago, and some fairies made jewelry out of them, but hardly anyone needs them anymore. The only thing I want to do is help people and I'm sure not doing that now! Can you think of a more useless job than being a tooth fairy? And as far as jobs go, I make less than you do and I work longer hours and I have to go to the human world to do it. At least you get to stay in the land of the fey and work normal hours and have a job that means something."

"Being a tooth fairy is one of the few jobs that lets you visit the human world," said Daisy. "I know a lot of fairies who would love to see it."

"Then let them! The human world is dirty and smelly and dangerous. I have to constantly hide so I don't frighten the children or let the adults know that we exist. The animals there have no experience with fairies so they don't respect us and half of them want to eat us.

I'd much rather stay in the land of the fey, where I don't have to hide and I can actually talk to people."

"I like humans," said Daisy. "One of my favorite old boyfriends was a human. He wasn't one of those newcomers that a crazy wizard brought over illegally either. His ancestors came when the old fairy queen first lured humans to our world. Humans multiply like mosquitoes in a witch's swamp and now they're one of the biggest minorities around. Most of them are nice enough, but I can't imagine living in a world where there was only one species. Think about it—humans are all pretty much alike with the same number of limbs and heads and digestive systems. Here you have fairies and dwarves and elves and gnomes and ogres and satyrs."

"I know!" Cory replied. "I like variety, but the work of a tooth fairy is pretty much the same from one day to the next. All we do is collect human teeth!"

"If you hate it so much, why don't you quit? There are a lot of other things you could be doing."

"That's a good question, and I've been wondering it myself a lot lately," said Cory. "If I had a cobblestone for every time I was close to quitting I could pave the road from my house to yours. Say, if I quit and I was no longer working nights, I wouldn't have to sleep during the day and could start doing things with my friends. I've been dying to go swimming in the lake. Would you go with me on your next day off? Or we could go bowling at Thunder Alley or—"

Daisy shook her head. "I already told Nimzy that I'd come watch him race on my next day off."

"Who is Nimzy?" Cory asked.

"Nimzy Crod is my new boyfriend. I'm sure I told you about him. He races solar cycles on the semi-amateur circuit. He's the best racer there is; he told me so himself. One of these days he's going to start winning. I just know it!"

"I thought you were seeing Zigfreed," said Cory. "What happened to him?"

"I caught him looking in the mirror one time too many. Never date a boy who is prettier than you are and won't let you forget it."

Cory sighed. Daisy went through boyfriends faster than some flower fairies changed their gowns. If only Cory could have a vision that would show her the right person for Daisy.

A lot of Cory's classmates had come into their powers and abilities when they were in Junior Fey School. Flower fairies were suddenly able to make flowers grow, goblin children could speak in any language, and brownies conveyed magic into the things they made with their hands. When Cory was in Junior Fey School, she started having blurry visions of couples. Occasionally, she saw her friends. Sometimes she saw people she didn't know. Usually the vision was so out of focus that she couldn't tell who they were. Along with these "visions" came the feeling that the people she saw were supposed to be together. The one time she told this to two of her friends, they thought she was crazy and laughed at her. Since then, she hadn't told anyone about her visions.

The finch in the nest on the mantel chirped six times before settling back on her eggs. "Oh, no!" cried Daisy. "It's six o'clock! I'm going to be late for work! Who knew being empathetic would take so long. I'll see you at the next rehearsal!"

"Bye," Cory called as her friend darted out the window.

Another *ping!* drew Cory's gaze to the woven reed basket on the shelf by the door. Two envelopes appeared in the basket, both bearing the flying-tooth insignia of the Tooth Fairy Guild. One would tell her the amount she'd earned for the previous day's collection; the other would be for her mother. Confident that her haul from the night before would be better than this night's, Cory ripped open her envelope. The knot in her stomach grew more painful. Even though she'd collected over twice as many teeth the night before, the guild had paid her very little, which meant that the teeth she'd just collected would bring her almost nothing.

"I can't do this anymore," Cory muttered.

Her mother, Delphinium, was a tooth fairy herself. She had promised Cory that being a tooth fairy was the most fulfilling job a fairy could hold and that the prestige of being a member of the Tooth Fairy Guild, or TFG as most people called it, would more than make up for the lousy hours. Unfortunately, Cory didn't find the job at all fulfilling. She'd told her mother that rewarding children for losing their teeth didn't really help anyone. And if there was prestige, Cory had yet to notice it. Because of the awful hours she had to work, Cory had almost no social life. She worked when everyone else had off, and had off when her friends were at work. The only good thing about the job was that her hours matched those of her boyfriend, Walker, a sandman-in-training. If she quit her job, that was really the only thing she was going to miss.

Cory had started her internship with her mother as soon as she graduated from Junior Fey School. It had been long and boring, with random moments of sheer terror when a cat chased her or a child came close to finding her. Even though she had mastered everything the guild had to teach, including the supersecret tricks of the tooth-fairy trade, none of it had made her any better at her job or like it any more.

Cory had told her mother countless times how much she disliked the job and that she wanted to quit, but all that had done was start arguments that no one seemed to win. After promising her mother that she would give the job a chance, she had stayed with it far longer than she wanted to and given it her best—until now. No matter what her mother said, Cory wasn't going to dedicate her life to a job she hated where she wouldn't even earn as much as a first-year flower fairy. Now, after all her hard work following the decrees of the TFG and trying to meet her mother's expectations, Cory had had enough. She couldn't face one more night looking for children's teeth.

The finch on the mantel chirped softly. It was a quarter past six; her mother would be home soon. If Cory was going to resign, she had to do it now before her mother could start lecturing her. Snatching a fresh leaf from her mother's desk, Cory broke off the end of an ink-plant stem and wrote her letter of resignation.

I quit!
Sincerely,
Corialis Feathering

Tucking the letter in an envelope, Cory wrote TFG on the outside and set it in the woven basket. She knew that she was in for the biggest argument of her life.

CHAPTER
3

*C*ory's mother was lugging a heavy tooth bag when she flew through the window. After dropping the bag on the table, she fluttered to the middle of the room. The air shimmered and she returned to her normal size, just a little shorter than her daughter.

Cory sighed. She didn't want to have this conversation now, but she didn't have any choice if she wanted to tell her mother before the TFG announced that Cory had quit. It was going to be doubly hard because even ordinary conversations with her mother had been strained ever since Cory started working on her own. The two fairies agreed on very little, and they weren't anything alike, from the way they thought to the way they looked. Other than having the same delicate, pointed ears, they didn't have much in common. Delphinium's hair was the same blue as the flower she was named after, like most people born into a flower-fairy family. Cory had dark chocolate–colored hair, which was unusual among fairies. Like the rest of her family, Delphinium had leaf-green eyes. Cory's eyes were turquoise blue, the same shade as the eyes of the father she had never known.

"Mother, I . . . ," Cory began.

Ping! Another letter bearing the TFG insignia appeared in the basket, only this time the flying tooth was bright red.

"Just a minute, Cory. I have an urgent message," said her mother as she reached for the envelope.

Cory watched in disbelief while her mother ripped the envelope open. The TFG couldn't possibly have notified her already! But when her mother raised her head to glare at her, Cory knew that that was exactly what they had done.

"You quit!" Delphinium said in a horrified voice. "How could you do that? No one quits the Tooth Fairy Guild! We've talked about this before! Being a member of the TFG is a lifelong commitment."

"And I've told you that I want to quit I don't know how many times, but I always let you talk me out of it. This time is different, Mother. I'm not meant to be a tooth fairy. I don't like it the way you do. Flying around at night collecting teeth is not how I want to spend the rest of my life. I want to do something that matters, something that will make a real difference, something that will help people. Collecting teeth isn't at all what you said it would be, and I am not going to do it anymore."

"But the job . . . The prestige . . . Being a tooth fairy is one of the most exalted jobs a fairy can hope to earn! Most fairies can only dream of belonging to the TFG!"

"Maybe," said Cory. "But it's not my dream. Honestly, Mother, I've given the job a chance like I told you I would, but I can't just—"

Her mother's eyes had narrowed when her glance fell on the tooth washer that had already finished cleaning Cory's collection. "How many did you get?" she interrupted, lifting the lid and peering inside. "Four! You got only four teeth in an entire night!"

Cory winced as her mother's voice grew shriller. "I had a bad night."

"You must not have tried!" Delphinium cried, throwing her hands in the air in exasperation. "You collected more teeth your very first night out!"

"I'm no good at it, Mother. I'll certainly never be as good as you."

Delphinium pulled one of the mushroom-shaped stools out from under the table and sat down with a groan. "Good or bad, the Tooth Fairy Guild will never let you quit. You've gone through all the levels of training. You've learned everything they have to teach you. If you were going to quit, you should have done it before you reached the third level and learned their most guarded secrets. No one outside of the special guilds is supposed to know how to go from our world to the humans', or pass through solid objects when the job requires it. I was so certain that you would learn to love the job, I just didn't want to see you throw your life away on some second-rate job as a flower fairy."

"I never wanted to be a tooth fairy, Mother. If only you had listened to me!"

Delphinium slapped the table so loudly that Noodles, Cory's pet woodchuck, woke in his basket in the corner, blinking up at them with his big, brown eyes. "Oh, I listened to you, all right! I've heard nothing but complaints from you, even though I did my very best teaching you everything I know, but have you ever thanked me or shown any sort of appreciation? I don't know why I ever bothered. But there's only one thing you can do now," she said, getting to her feet. "You have to take a new leaf and write to the guild, telling them that it was a mistake and you didn't really mean to quit." Her back was stiff as she strode to her desk and took out a fresh leaf, thrusting it at Cory.

"I'm not doing that!" Cory said, backing away from her mother. "I'm glad I quit and I'm not going to take it back. I'll see you later. I can't talk to you when you're like this."

"When I'm like what?" her mother called after her as Cory stalked out the front door.

Cory was furious. When her basic tooth-fairy training was over and Cory still didn't like it, Delphinium had told her that she'd enjoy it once she'd learned all there was to learn. And now that Cory had learned every-thing, Delphinium had the nerve to say that it was too late to quit, that Cory should have left the guild sooner. As far as Cory was concerned, saying that prestige was more important than how much one liked a job or how fulfilling one found it didn't make it true.

Delphinium had once said that most people didn't like what they did for a living, and that Cory was naive to think that she could ever have a job that she enjoyed. But Delphinium loved the job and had declared count-less times that it was the job she had dreamed of when she was a little girl. For her to say that most people didn't like their jobs didn't make sense. Where did she think Cory had gotten the idea that she could love a job, if not from watching her?

Cory had been wandering for nearly an hour when she

realized that she had walked in a big loop and was near her uncle's house. Her uncle, Micah, was her mother's brother and was nothing like Delphinium. Both of their parents were flower fairies, but Delphinium was all about appearances and climbing the fairy ladder, while Micah dressed like a flower fairy, acted like a flower fairy, and had taught at the Junior Fey School since before Cory was born.

"I wonder if he's left for work yet," Cory murmured, and turned toward her uncle's house. If anyone could give her good advice, it would be her uncle Micah.

He was there still, seated at his kitchen table with a cup of berry juice and a plate of cold, roasted parsnips and potatoes in front of him. His pet squirrel, Flicket, sat on the table, gnawing a walnut and dribbling pieces of shell.

"Uncle Micah, is it okay if I come in?" Cory said through the open window.

Her uncle glanced up from passing another walnut to the squirrel and smiled. "Cory! Of course you can come in. You're always welcome here. You know that. Are you hungry? Have you eaten breakfast yet? Or would you call it dinner since I assume you'll be going to bed soon?"

"I'm too upset to eat," Cory said as she came through the door. She shooed a blue jay off a mushroom stool and took a seat at the table. "I just had another argument with Mother. I quit my job at the TFG today."

"Ah," said Micah. "Then your mother must be upset, too. Oh, don't get me wrong. I know how much you disliked the job, so I think you did the right thing, but I can also see how your mother would be unhappy. Everyone knows how highly she thinks of the TFG."

"She wants me to tell them that I made a mistake and don't really want to quit. I'm not going to do it, but I know she's going to keep after me until I give in. I dread going home just to have the same argument all over again."

Micah picked up his cup of berry juice and fished out a bit of walnut shell before taking a sip. "You can always stay here with me while you look for another job. I have a guest room if you want it."

"Are you sure? Because I'd much rather stay here than face my mother."

"I wouldn't say it if I didn't mean it."

"Would you mind if I brought Noodles?" Cory asked. "He and Mother don't really get along."

"The more the merrier," said Micah. "You know I like animals."

"In that case, can I move in tonight? I'd like to wait to get my stuff when Mother goes to work."

"Tonight would be fine. I have to leave in a few

minutes, so make yourself at home. The guest bed is already made up if you want to get some sleep."

"That sounds perfect," Cory told him. "But do you think I could have something to eat first? My appetite just came back."

CHAPTER

4

Cory had a flying dream, which wasn't unusual for a fairy. But in this dream she was soaring high above the clouds, which fairies never did. She woke suddenly and sat up, wondering why she felt so free, when she remembered that she had quit the TFG and never had to collect another tooth. Feeling as if she had shed a great weight, she sprang out of bed and spread her arms wide, twirling on her toes.

When she glanced outside, she saw children walking home from school. That meant it was late afternoon and Walker would be up now. If she left soon, she could ask him to help her get her things from her mother's before he went to work.

Walker lived in the north end of town with his older brother, who was also a sandman. They came from a long line of sandmen, another prestigious guild in the fairy world. Cory and Walker had met when they were in Junior Fey School, and both were on the path to careers in the guilds. Even then Cory had wondered if that was one of the things that Walker had liked about her; he often said that he was going to be an important person someday and that he expected his wife to be, too.

They had dated since they graduated from Junior Fey School. A lot of people thought they would be together forever, but Cory wasn't so sure. She liked him well enough, but she wasn't in love with him, not the way she thought two people should be.

It didn't take long for Cory to shrink to flower-fairy size and fly to Walker's house. He was outside with his brother, Sandy, polishing the glass covering his house that gave it a dreamlike quality as it reflected the sky and clouds above. Like many of the wealthier fey, the brothers wanted the exterior of their home to hint at their trade.

Cory had just turned back to her normal size when Sandy noticed her walking toward the house. Wadding up a dripping, soapy rag, he threw it at Walker, hitting him with a *sploot!*

"Hey!" Walker shouted, glaring at his brother. "What was that for?"

"You have company," Sandy told him, grinning at Cory. "How are you doing, Cory?"

"Really good, thanks," she replied. "Walker, can I drag you away for a minute? I need to talk."

"Go on," Sandy told him. "We're almost finished here."

Walker grinned as he climbed down the ladder and dropped his rag into the bucket. "I'm glad you came by," he told Cory as he led the way to the back of the house. "I hate cleaning glass. I've been telling Sandy we should hire someone, but he's too cheap to consider it." He took a seat on the garden bench and gestured for Cory to join him. "What's up? You don't usually come around this time of day. Shouldn't you be getting ready for work? Some of those little kids go to bed pretty early."

"I'm not going to work. That's one of the reasons I wanted to see you. I resigned from the guild today. I'm free now! I can do whatever I want."

"If this is a joke, it's not very funny," Walker said, his brow knitting together in a frown. "The guild was your life!"

"No, it wasn't. Or at least I didn't want it to be. You know how miserable I've been collecting teeth! Or haven't you been listening when I talk to you?"

"Of course I've been listening," Walker said, sounding irritated. "But I thought it was just beginner's whining. Everyone complains about a job when they first start. Most people try to stick it out, though—not give up when the going gets hard. I thought the guild was a lifetime commitment."

Cory was getting angry. This wasn't at all the sympathetic response she'd expected from her boyfriend. "Now you sound like my mother. I thought you had more faith in me than that."

Hearing the tone in Cory's voice, Walker put up his hands as if to stop a charging unicorn. "No need to get all riled up! I do have faith in you, Sweet Pea. I'm sure you're doing what you feel is right for you. But you do realize that whatever job you get now, we probably won't have the same work hours."

"I know, but I just can't do this anymore. This isn't the right job for me. I've known it since the beginning, but no one would listen. My mother wants me to tell the guild that I didn't mean it when I told them I was quitting, but that isn't going to happen. I know she isn't going to let up on me, so I'm moving out tonight. I was hoping you could come help me get my things."

Walker shook his head. "Sorry, I can't tonight. I have to be at work early. I have a special meeting with my supervisor."

"Tomorrow night then?" Cory asked.

"I can't. I have a meeting then, too."

"Then I guess I'll have to do it without you," she said, disappointed and more than a little angry. She didn't understand why he had meetings now; he'd never had to go in for early meetings before.

Daisy still lived with her parents, whose cottage was only six away from Delphinium's. When Cory turned up on her doorstep, Daisy was happy to see her. She was even happier when she heard that Cory had quit her job.

"You finally did it! I knew that job was all wrong for you. It was making you miserable and it was only going to get worse. I never could understand why your mother made you stay with something you disliked so much. What did she say when you told her you'd quit?"

"I didn't tell her. The Tooth Fairy Guild notified her before I had the chance. She was furious, of course. She tried to make me tell the guild that I'd made a mistake and wasn't really quitting."

"Which you refused to do, I hope," said Daisy.

"Uh-huh," said Cory. "I left and ended up at my uncle Micah's house. He offered me a room there; I'm moving my stuff tonight while Mother is at work. I was wondering if you would help me."

"I told Nimzy that I'd hang out with him later, but I have some time right now. Let me get my shoes on. Do you need boxes or anything?"

"A couple, I guess. I'm not getting everything. Just the stuff I need the most. And Noodles. I can't abandon him."

"I don't know why not," Daisy said. "I'd leave the little monster behind."

Cory laughed as she followed her friend into the house. "You say that only because he doesn't like you."

"He doesn't like *anyone* but you," said Daisy, rummaging through a closet. "Are three boxes enough? We can use my daisy cart to haul them."

"Three should be fine," Cory said, taking the boxes from her friend. "I can go back to get the rest another day."

"My cart is in the backyard. I'll meet you around front in a minute."

While Cory hauled the boxes out the front door, Daisy went to fetch the cart. It was a small cart meant to hold bouquets of daisies, but flower fairies often used their carts for other things, like bringing home groceries, giving small children rides, and collecting twigs from the yard after a storm.

Fairies flew everywhere when they were small, but their full-size bodies were too heavy for their frail wings to lift them. Small fairies couldn't carry heavy objects, which meant that they had to be big and walk if they were carrying an object that weighed more than a few ounces. Most flower fairies used a cart when they needed to haul away dead flowers or plants that were being transplanted. Sometimes there were so many carts on the paths that traffic jams were common. Although it was annoying for fairies in a hurry, it was a pretty sight with the carts decorated in the owners' special designs. Every inch of Daisy's wooden cart was carved with daisies painted a bright, sunny yellow. The flowers looked so real that one almost expected their petals to ruffle in the wind.

"Here we are!" Daisy sang out as she rounded the corner of the house. "Just put the boxes in the cart and we'll be on our way."

"Thank you so much for doing this," Cory told her as she arranged the boxes on the wooden floor. "You're a very big help. I asked Walker to help, but he said he's got a meeting tonight."

Daisy snorted, then covered her mouth with her hand. "That Walker is a busy boy."

"He said he has a meeting tomorrow night, too," Cory said as they started down the path that led between the houses.

"I just bet he does," said Daisy. "Did you tell him that you quit?"

"I did, but he wasn't very supportive. He agreed with Mother that I shouldn't have done it."

"Pfft!" Daisy said. "That shows what he knows! Cory, there's something I should tell you about Walker . . ."

"Oh, no!" Cory cried. "Not again! Noodles has one of Mother's good shoes!" She pointed at the window where the woodchuck was peeking out at them with a dainty pink slipper dangling from his mouth. "Can you take this around back?" she asked, relinquishing the handle of the cart to her friend. She didn't stay to hear Daisy's reply, but ran to the front door and darted into the house. The woodchuck had a guilty look on his face when he dropped the slipper onto her hand. It was slobbery, but she didn't see any tooth marks on it.

"Mother must have left the door to her bedroom open," she told Daisy, who was carrying in the boxes. "Noodles doesn't like Mother and chews up her things every chance he gets." She bent down to scratch Noodles between his ears and smiled when he made a soft chirring sound. Glancing up at Daisy, Cory added, "Most of the stuff I need is in my bedroom."

The pudgy woodchuck waddled down the hall behind Cory and plopped down on his bed when they reached her room. He watched through half-closed eyes while Cory took armloads of clothes off the shelves lining one wall. Daisy helped her pack them into boxes, then waited while Cory collected the woodchuck's toys. When Cory shooed Noodles off the fluffy pillow he used for a bed, she picked it up and spotted a ragged hole in the carpet.

"Oh, dear, I forgot about that," she said. "Here, help me move the flower rug. Mother's mad enough at me as it is. She'd be even madder if she saw this."

"Did Noodles do that?" asked Daisy as she helped drag a small rug shaped like a delphinium blossom over the hole.

Cory nodded. "He chews everything if he doesn't have his toys. Let's put these in the cart. Then I need to write my mother a note. I don't want to argue with her, but I don't want her to worry, either."

While Daisy carried the rest of the boxes outside, Cory went into the main room to get a leaf from her mother's desk. She already knew what she was going to say.

Dear Mother,
     Don't worry. I'm fine. Staying with Uncle Micah.
No, I'm not sorry I resigned!
                              Love,
                              Cory

She was laying the leaf on the desk when she heard a *ping!* Turning to the woven reed basket, she saw an envelope appear bearing the red flying-tooth insignia.

Her name stood out below the insignia in thick red letters. A stack of envelopes sat beside the basket; the one on the top bore her name in red as well.

"Those are probably all for me," she muttered. "I don't need to read them to know what they say. Let's go, Noodles," she said to the woodchuck, who was sitting on her foot. "We've spent too much time here already."

CHAPTER
5

Cory was eating breakfast with her uncle the next morning when he handed her *The Fey Express* opened to the help-wanted ads. "I thought you might want to look through these. An idle fairy is an unhappy fairy."

"I thought I'd take a day to rest before I started looking for a job," Cory said, holding the paper as if it might bite.

"You already did," said Micah. "Yesterday. Today is the day you start looking. I glanced through it before you got out of bed. There are a few in there that I thought you might find interesting. You don't have to decide on a new career right away, but you should have a job while you decide what it is you really want to do.

Unless you've already decided?" he added, raising one eyebrow.

Cory shook her head. "I have no idea what I should do. All I know is what I *don't* want to do."

"Then maybe one of these will inspire you. Take a look. It can't hurt." He glanced down at the woodchuck sleeping on his foot. "Pardon me, Noodles, but I have to get ready for work."

"He likes you," Cory said as the drowsy woodchuck rolled off Micah's foot and went back to sleep.

"Most animals do," her uncle replied. He pushed his mushroom-shaped stool back from the table. "Good luck with the job hunt. Oh, before I forget, here are some leaves and an ink stick. You might want to make a list."

"Thanks," Cory said, not very sincerely. She sighed as she moved her nearly finished bowl of mashed berries and cooked oats out of the way. Glancing at the front page, she noticed an article about Santa Claus. He had been speaking at the Looking Forward to Christmas Conference and the paparazzi had mobbed the hotel where the conference was being held. A picture showed the old elf looking angry and upset as a crowd of satyrs and dwarves surrounded him, shoving Mrs. Claus and his assistant elves aside.

"Poor Santa," Cory murmured. "He never gets a moment's peace."

Turning the paper over, she studied the help-wanted ads. The first ad to catch her eye read:

HELP WANTED
Must be creative, careful, and have steady hands. If interested, contact P. Cottontail at 1 Bunny Trail.

"I bet they're looking for an assistant egg dyer," she told Noodles, even though he was still asleep. "I knew a girl in Junior Fey School who did that after she graduated. It's a seasonal job, so it doesn't last long. From what I heard, she went from one seasonal job to another. I'd rather find something that would last more than a few weeks. Wait. What's this? It looks interesting."

A NEW AND EXCITING FAIRY GUILD!
On-the-job training, fun, rewarding, great pay, great benefits! Contact Fuzz for Life to learn more.

"I wonder what they want me to do," she said. "What do you say, Noodles? Should we find out?" She glanced down at the woodchuck, who was now sleeping on his back with his paws in the air. Grunting in his sleep, he waved one paw.

"You think so, too, huh?" said Cory. "Then let's do it!"

Taking one of the leaves her uncle had given her, she wrote, *Who are you?* After addressing it to Fuzz for Life, she set it in the woven reed basket on the shelf by the door. It vanished, and less than a minute later a nice crisp envelope appeared. Inside was a leaf bearing the words The Belly Button Lint Guild.

"Ugh!" said Cory. "Forget that! Collecting belly button lint would be worse than collecting teeth." After throwing the leaf into the trash, she made a big, dark X through the ad.

"All right," she said, sitting back on her mushroom stool, "What else is there?" Running her eyes down the column, she noticed that most of the jobs required that she show up in person. "At least the weather is good," she muttered, and reached for a clean leaf to start her list. After reading them all, only three jobs interested her. She copied them down word for word on her leaf, and decided to go to the closest one first. Wall Road was at the edge of town. If she flew, it should take her just a few minutes to get there.

The leaf was light enough that she could shrink it

and take it with her. She read the first ad over again as she flew.

HELP WANTED

Must be able to lift heavy weights, be compassionate, patient, and know first aid. Apply in person to D. Dumpty at 100 Wall Rd.

Cory didn't really want to lift heavy weights, but the job sounded intriguing and she wanted to see what it involved.

Wall Road was a pretty little street with only a few houses, all on the same side of the road. A high stone wall ran along the other side, with a rolling, clover-filled meadow just beyond it. Sweet-faced cows grazed in the meadow, nibbling the clover and drinking from the sparkling stream that ran from one end of the meadow to the other.

One hundred Wall Road was the last house on the street. It was a cream-colored, squat little house with bowed walls and an oval door. Wisteria vines covered the house, dripping fragrant purple clusters of blossoms down its sides. The scent was intoxicating when Cory was tiny, but became more muted when she returned to her human size.

After checking the address one last time, Cory

knocked on the door. Nearly a minute went by before a short, egg-shaped woman answered. Her skin was pale, but she wore so much makeup that she didn't look real. Big, round circles of red colored her cheeks and the swipes of bright blue on her eyelids matched her eyes. Some of her red lipstick had come off on her small, baby-size teeth.

"Are you here about the ad?" she asked, sounding hopeful. When Cory nodded, the woman's smile grew so wide that her face seemed to split in two. "Marvelous! Then come right in. I'm Doris Dumpty and my son's name is Humpty. He's in his bedroom. I'll have him come meet you." Turning halfway around, the woman shouted, "Humpty! Your new babysitter is here!"

"Babysitter?" said Cory as she followed the woman down a short hallway. "I didn't know that was what you wanted."

"But the ad was perfectly clear," the woman said, leading the way into the brightest room Cory had ever seen. Everything was yellow, from the furniture to the rugs to the paint on the walls and ceiling. Even the doorknobs were yellow. "I need someone to watch Humpty while I go visit my ailing mother. Her mind is a bit scrambled lately. If I don't go see her, she'll hatch a new plan to escape from the nursing home and get lost again."

"But I don't think I . . . ," Cory began.

"Oh, good! Here's my beautiful boy!" Mrs. Dumpty said as a boy skipped into the room, gave her a quick look, and climbed on one of the overstuffed chairs, taking a seat on the back. The shorts and T-shirt he was wearing showed off the bandage on one of his spindly legs and scars on his thin little arms. Narrow at the hips and shoulders, he was wide around the middle and his skin was even paler than his mother's. Cory couldn't help but think that he looked like an egg wearing clothes with another egg balanced on top for a head.

Doris Dumpty sighed. "Humpty! How many times have I told you not to climb on the furniture? Sit on the seat, please!"

Humpty scowled as he slid down the back of the chair, but his scowl disappeared when he looked up at Cory. "Do you like to climb?" he asked.

"That depends on what we're climbing," she replied.

"No climbing!" his mother said as the boy squirmed off the chair. "I'll be gone for only a few hours, but he is not allowed to climb, no matter what he says. My little Humpty is a fragile boy and gets hurt easily. Here's a list of emergency numbers," she said, handing a leaf to Cory. "My husband, RJ, is the first one you should call if there's ever a real emergency. Now be good, Humpty. Listen to Miss . . . What is your name?"

"Cory. Don't you want to—"

"Be a good boy, Humpty, and listen to Cory. Mother loves you," she said, planting a kiss on the top of his head.

"But, Mrs. Dumpty, you don't know . . ."

"I'm sure you two will be just fine. Good-bye, my little darling," she said, twiddling her fingers at her son even as she hurried to the door.

The moment the door closed behind his mother, Humpty took hold of Cory's hand and pulled her toward the hallway. "Let's go outside. We can play hide-and-seek. You're it!" he cried as they stepped onto the grass. "Face the wall and count to five billion."

"I don't think this is a good idea," said Cory as he turned her toward the house. He let go of her hand and scampered off, but instead of counting she turned back to protest. The boy was already gone. "Humpty! Where are you?" she called. She heard giggling, but she couldn't tell where it came from, so she cupped her hands around her mouth and shouted, "Humpty, I'm not playing this game!" The only reply was another rash of giggling.

"He's close enough that I can still hear him, and he likes to climb," Cory muttered to herself and began to look in the trees. She started with the trees closest to the house, then searched the ones by the road. When she couldn't find him from the ground, she became tiny and flew into the trees, inspecting them more closely.

She finally found him hidden behind a leafy branch, high in an old oak tree.

"Gotcha!" she said, tapping him lightly.

"You're a fairy!" said Humpty. "I've never had a fairy babysitter before. Hey, didn't you say you weren't going to play this game?"

"I did indeed. And didn't your mother tell you to listen to me?"

Humpty nodded. "I always listen to my babysitters. That's how I know where you are when you're looking for me."

"How many babysitters have you had?" asked Cory.

Humpty shrugged. "A new one every week. Nobody ever wants to come back."

"Uh-huh," said Cory, wondering what she'd gotten herself into.

"Want to race?" Humpty asked her. Before she could answer, he was running across the street as fast as his spindly legs could carry him.

"Humpty, no!" Cory cried as he started to climb the wall that bordered the road. Although he didn't look very strong, the little boy was fast and he'd reached the top before Cory was halfway there. Turning small again, she darted to the top and became big as soon as she landed. "Your mother said that you weren't supposed to climb!" she said, peering at the ground, which seemed far away.

"I know," said Humpty. "It's quiet up here and I like to watch the cows. I wish I could fly, but I don't have wings like you."

"It is very pretty," Cory told him as she looked out over the meadow.

Humpty sighed. "My mother always says it's not safe. She's never been up here. She doesn't know what it's like. Things always look different from up high."

"If going up high is what you want, maybe we can find a way that you can be safe and happy. Let's go inside and see if we can't figure something out."

"You won't tell my mother that I came up here?" asked Humpty.

"Not if you don't," said Cory. "Sometimes a mother is happier if she doesn't know everything."

Cory held her breath as the boy scrambled down the wall. He flashed her an endearing grin when he reached the ground, and she found herself smiling back at him. Maybe this job wouldn't be so bad after all.

When Mrs. Dumpty came home a few hours later, she found her son curled up in the top of the linen closet with every pillow in the house piled on the floor below him. Cory was seated beside the pillows, reading a story out loud. Seeing the expression on the woman's face, Cory was sure that she was angry.

"Well, I never!" declared Mrs. Dumpty. "All my pillows! Even the good ones out of the parlor!"

"I'm sorry," Cory began. "It was the only thing I could think of that would . . ."

"What a marvelous idea!" said Mrs. Dumpty. "I wish I'd come up with that!"

"Then you don't mind about the pillows?" asked Cory.

"Not at all!" the woman gushed as Cory got to her feet. "Can you come back next week at the same time?"

"Sure," Cory replied as Mrs. Dumpty handed her some money. "See you next week, Humpty."

"See ya," said the little boy.

Once Cory was outside, she stuffed the money in one pocket and took her notes out of the other. The next job was farther out in the country, but it wouldn't take long to get there. Cory read the ad three times as she flew, trying to figure out what kind of job Mrs. McDonald wanted done.

HELP WANTED

Must be quick, observant, and good with a carving knife. Apply in person to Mrs. McDonald at the Dell.

Cory thought she was quick and observant, but she had never used a carving knife. Did they want her to carve wood? She had carved a piece of soap into the shape of a butterfly in art class, but she'd never made anything out of wood.

As Cory flew above the trees, she noticed that the number of houses dwindled while the farms grew larger. She knew where the Dell was located, having seen the farm sign when out flying with Daisy. When she finally reached it, she saw large fields and a big, red barn behind a tidy white house. Landing at the doorstep of the farmhouse, she had just returned to her human size when the door slammed open and an elderly woman peered out at her. "What do you want?" the old woman asked.

"I came about the job," said Cory. "Mrs. McDonald advertised for . . ."

"I'm Mrs. McDonald! I know exactly what I need! Are you any good with a knife?"

"What do you need me to do?" asked Cory.

"Pest control!" said the old woman. "Get rid of the three blind mice that keep chasing me. I already cut off their tails with a carving knife and now I need someone to finish the job. The little vermin won't leave me alone! They follow me everywhere I go."

Movement behind the woman caught Cory's eye. Three tailless mice were nibbling a half-eaten peach pie in the middle of the kitchen table.

"If you want the job, get in here and take care of the

mice before I change my mind about you!" the old woman snapped.

"I'm not sure I want to . . . ," Cory began, but Mrs. McDonald was already dragging her into the kitchen and shoving the knife in her hands.

"A couple of good whacks ought to do it," Mrs. McDonald declared. "Just take care of those mice before they get away. I'll find a box to put the bodies in."

While the old woman shuffled out of the room, Cory studied the mice. They looked odd without their tails, and she could tell they were blind by the way they stared straight ahead, regardless of what they were doing. One of them stopped eating long enough to scrub his tiny face with his paws, wiping away some crumbs.

"You're so cute!" Cory exclaimed. She felt sorry for them. They had learned how to survive even though they were blind. It didn't seem right to kill them.

"Did you whack them yet?" Mrs. McDonald asked as she came back into the room. She was carrying a shoe box, which gave Cory an idea.

"I just need the box," Cory said, reaching for it.

A teakettle on the stove began to shake and whistle as steam poured from the spout. Mrs McDonald hurried to turn off the burner. While the old woman wasn't looking, Cory held the box under the edge of the table and used the knife to whack the table on the far side of the pie. Startled, the mice turned away from the sound and ran straight for the box. Using the flat of the blade, Cory pushed them over the edge and into the box, clapping the lid on to keep them inside.

"All done!" she declared. "These mice aren't going to bother you again."

"Thank goodness!" cried Mrs. McDonald. "Here," she said, handing Cory some money. "Take them outside and get rid of them."

Cory smiled. "It will be my pleasure!"

Holding the lid on the box, Cory hurried out to the lane that ran past the house and peeked under the lid. The mice seemed so small and helpless that she couldn't bring herself to let them go. She'd have to take them home for now, which meant that she wasn't going to be able to fly. Even if she shrank the box and the mice, they would be too heavy to carry when she was small. She'd just have to call the pedal-bus and hope that one was coming out this way.

Like most of the fey who lived in town, Cory always carried a token for the pedal-bus. There were nearly twenty buses zipping through town and around the suburbs now, but two fairies and a brownie had started the business with only one pedal-bus just the year before.

Although the first few buses had been magic-propelled, keeping the magic at full strength was costly when non-fairies were operating it, so most of the buses used a little magic and a lot of pedaling.

The buses looked much like the bicycles that Cory had seen in the human world, only these seated twelve people, with one operator in the front and one in the back. The passengers sat in the middle with baskets for their belongings. Everyone had to pedal, but because the bus was magically enhanced, it went much faster than pedaling alone would have made it go. There was magic in the seats as well, so a brownie only a foot tall could ride with an ogre topping eight feet.

Knowing that there were more buses the closer one went to town, Cory started walking in that direction even as she took the token out of her pocket. She rubbed the token with her thumb while declaring her destination—her uncle's address. After tucking it back in her pocket, she continued walking; the token would tell the operators where to pick her up.

Only a few minutes later she heard the ringing of the bus's bells. A bearded goblin wearing a patch over one eye was sitting in the front operator's position while a slender male elf with a long ponytail was seated in the back. Most the seats in between were filled with nymphs dressed in the clothes of their trade; bark for tree nymphs and water lilies for water nymphs. The only seats available were right behind the goblin, who scowled when Cory took her seat and placed the box in the basket in front of her.

"Aren't you ready yet?" he grumped, although she hadn't taken any time at all.

"All set," she said, and put her feet on the pedals.

Everyone pushed down on the pedals at once and the next moment they were flying down the road. Cory thought they were probably moving as fast as she could fly. If they hadn't had to stop now and then to let a passenger off or pick up someone new she would have been home in minutes. As it was, she was there in less than an hour, paying the goblin with a coin when she got off.

Cory watched the departing bus until they had driven out of sight before heading up her uncle's walk. After taking the box to her bedroom, she let Noodles outside for a few minutes, then put him back in her room. The moment she was out the front door, she made herself small again.

Cory wasn't far from the address on Curdsin Way and was glad she had saved it for last. She knew Marjorie Muffet, the person who had written the last help-wanted ad, having met her at her friend Apple Blossom's birthday party years before. Cory had seen Marjorie a few times over the years, and thought she was nice. If their paths had crossed a little more often, she might have called her a friend.

Cory had never been to Marjorie's house before, but when she finally found the address, she thought the little cottage suited her perfectly. Miss Muffet lived in a cute little cottage with a white picket fence. Pink roses covered the arbor that stood at the gate, with more pink roses planted along the inside of the entire fence and lining the walkway that led to the front door. A patch of black-eyed Susans surrounded a FOR SALE sign in the middle of the front lawn. The sign was weathered, as if it had been there a long time.

Cory read the newspaper ad once more as her feet touched the ground.

HELP WANTED

Must be fearless, have large shoes and a strong stomach. Apply in person to Miss Muffet at 22 Curdsin Way.

Her shoes weren't exactly large, but she did have a strong stomach and she'd proven herself to be pretty fearless as a tooth fairy. *Maybe the shoes aren't that important*, she thought, heading for the gate.

Cory had just stepped through the arbor when she noticed that Marjorie was seated on a carved bench nestled in a corner of the garden. Wearing a pink ging-ham dress and a white ruffled apron, she was intent on the pages of an oversize book.

"Hi, Marjorie!" Cory called.

The girl glanced up. She looked puzzled at first, but her expression brightened when she recognized Cory. "Cory Feathering! What are you doing in this part of town?"

"Looking for a job," Cory said as she walked toward the bench. "I saw your ad in the paper."

"Apple Blossom told me that you were training to be a tooth fairy. Didn't that work out?"

"I was almost finished with my training, except I quit a few days ago. That's why I need to find a job." Cory felt a flush of embarrassment over admitting that she'd walked away from such a prestigious career. Saying it like this made her sound like a failure, something she hadn't felt before.

"I'm sure there's a story behind that!" said Marjorie. "But I'm not going to pry. Come sit beside me and I'll tell you about the job, then you can tell me if you still want it. I have spiders, you see. They're not poisonous, but they are obnoxious. My house is full of them. I've tried putting out spider traps so I can release them in the wild, and bait that makes them turn green, fall over, and twitch so they'll want to leave and not come back, but neither the traps nor the bait do the job. Every day I have more spiders than the day before and I'm getting quite desperate. It bothered me so much that I put my house up for sale, but no one is interested. To tell the truth, I hate killing anything, but lately I've resorted to stomping on them. Unfortunately, I have tiny feet and it doesn't do anything except make them mad. That's why I need someone with large feet."

"How big are these spiders?" asked Cory. She had already glanced down at Marjorie's feet, which were indeed very tiny, but then Marjorie was so petite that the top of her head barely reached Cory's shoulder. Cory suddenly recalled that Marjorie had been called Little Miss Muffet when they were younger. Ordinary spiders might seem huge to someone so small.

"Come inside and I'll show you," Marjorie said, standing up. She set the book on the bench, but changed her mind and picked it up again. "This is a very useful book. I refer to it often."

Cory glanced at the cover as they walked toward the house. The title, *What Mother Goose Didn't Want You to Know,* sounded intriguing. She nearly bumped into Marjorie when the girl opened the front door and stopped to peek inside.

"I don't see any yet," Marjorie said, tiptoeing across

the threshold. "It won't be long before they show up, though. Look! There's one now!"

A spider as big as Cory's hand with her fingers spread wide was sauntering across the woven sea-grass carpet in the main room. Cory shuddered. She'd never liked spiders, but had never been particularly afraid of them—until now. Taking a step back, she wondered how anyone would think of stomping on something so big when suddenly the spider jumped, landing on the wall beside her. In a heartbeat, Miss Muffet swung her book, smacking the spider so that it fell to the floor, stunned.

"Wow! That was impressive!" exclaimed Cory.

"I told you this was a useful book," Marjorie said with a grin. Pulling a pair of cooking tongs from the pocket of her apron, she plucked the spider off the floor and carried it out the door. With the tongs held at arm's length, she marched to the middle of her yard and set the spider down. Returning to Cory's side, she pointed at the spider and said, "Now watch."

The words had scarcely left her lips when a crow landed on the ground beside the spider, tilted its head to one side to get a better look, then snapped up the spider and swallowed it in one gulp.

"They must be tasty," Marjorie explained. "The birds really seem to like them."

"I have one question," Cory said as the crow flew off. "Why do you want to hire someone to stomp the spiders? It looks as if you're handling it well yourself."

"I usually do, except I'm tired of them jumping on me in the middle of the night or landing on the table when I'm eating. I've given up eating curds and whey, although they used to be my favorite food. I haven't been able to stomach them ever since a spider landed in a bowl while I was eating. At first I found the spiders intimidating, but now they're just an annoyance. I want them to be gone, even if I have to pay someone to take care of them for me. Are you interested in the job?"

"I'm sorry," said Cory. "But I don't think I'd make a good spider stomper. My feet are much too small to stomp one of your spiders."

"I didn't think you'd want the job. But at least we got to see each other again," said Marjorie.

Cory nodded. "Now that I'm no longer working at night and don't have to sleep during the day, I'll actually be able to see my friends."

Marjorie smiled. "I'd like that! And maybe we can go somewhere that doesn't have things jumping out at you."

"I'm sure I can find a place like that!" Cory said with a laugh.

≫→

Cory told her uncle about her day at dinner that night. He seemed interested, especially when she mentioned the spiders in Marjorie's house. "How big did you say they were?" he asked.

"As big as my hand," Cory said, holding up her hand and spreading her fingers wide.

"I don't know if this will work or not, but I have an idea that might do the trick. There's a spray made from chrysanthemums that I've used to get rid of insects. It's worked well for me, but then I've never tried it on such big spiders. I have some in the garden shed if you want to try it."

"I would! Thank you!" Cory told him. "I think that at this point, Marjorie will try just about anything."

CHAPTER
6

The next morning, Micah was already making breakfast when Noodles followed Cory into the kitchen. "Someone sent you a message," Micah said, gesturing to an envelope propped against Cory's plate.

"Was it my mother?" asked Cory.

Micah shook his head. "It wasn't her handwriting."

"Good," Cory said, taking her seat at the table. "Because I really don't want to read what she has to say."

Let's have dinner together tonight.
Nimzy is a jerk and my parents are
making me crazy. You pick the place.
Daisy

Because of the hours she'd had to work as a tooth fairy, Cory hadn't gone out at night with a friend in a very long time. Although she knew that Daisy wouldn't get her message until the flower fairy returned from work, she wrote back to her saying, Everything Leaks at 7:00. She was about to put it in the basket when she stopped and asked her uncle, "Do you have any special plans for tonight? Do you mind if I go out with Daisy?"

"Go right ahead. Noodles, Flicket, and I will be fine, won't we, boys?" Micah said as he dropped a handful of lettuce leaves in the woodchuck's bowl. Flicket was nearly finished with a pile of nuts.

"Thanks!" Cory said, dropping the message into the basket. She was determined to make her stay with her uncle work out. If he hadn't offered to let her live with him, she didn't know where she would have gone. Until her mother accepted that Cory was not meant to be a tooth fairy, she wasn't sure she wanted to talk to Delphinium again. The way things stood now, she wasn't sure that would ever happen.

Cory began to slather crushed berries on a piece of toast. The morning newspaper was on the table, so she glanced at the front page as she took a sip of juice. There was another picture of Santa Claus, only this time he was standing beside one of his elves; they both looked very unhappy.

"Apparently, one of Santa's elves punched a reporter in the nose," said her uncle.

"It was probably one of those paparazzi who always follow them around," Cory replied. Noodles grunted as he munched his lettuce.

She opened the paper to the help-wanted section and glanced down the column. "The ads are all the same as yesterday," she said, then noticed that one was missing. The ad from P. Cottontail wasn't there.

"I should have applied there while I had the chance. I don't know what I'm going to do if I can't get a job," she told her uncle. "Mother will probably tell me I should have thought of that before I quit the TFG. All I know is that I *don't* want to collect teeth. I want to help people. I just don't know how."

The woodchuck came over, a piece of lettuce sticking out of his mouth. He stretched out on her foot and closed his eyes while he chewed.

"You're so lucky, Noodles. You don't have to worry about your future. You know I'll always be here for you." The woodchuck grumbled when she rubbed his back with her other foot, but he didn't stop eating.

Cory turned to the next page. There were ads for used carts, reconditioned magic wands, and one for axes that could cut through anything from a ripe tomato to a solid oak door. A giant was selling a toothbrush—barely used.

Cory pointed the ad out to her uncle. "That's just gross," she said. "It doesn't say much for his hygiene."

Her uncle swallowed his last bite of toast. "Or that of the person who buys it," he said. "Sorry, but I have to run. I have some students coming in early for extra help this morning. I'll see you this afternoon. Noodles, it's just going to be you, me, and Flicket for dinner tonight, so think about what you'd like to eat. I know—how about lettuce!" he said with a chuckle.

Cory waved good-bye as her uncle left the kitchen. She didn't have very many relatives, but he'd always been her favorite, partly because he was the only one with a sense of humor. When she heard the front door close, she turned back to the ads. A few people had listed houses for sale. Below that were ads placed by people looking for things.

WANTED
A flying broom built for two. Must have seat belts and good brakes.
WANTED
Unicorn halter for smaller unicorn. Prefer silver with gold trim.
WANTED
Hairbrush for giant. New or used.

"Look, Noodles, it's the same giant who's selling his toothbrush," she said after checking the contact information.

WANTED
Three-bedroom house. Must be cozy and have nice garden. No sties, please!

WANTED
Gingerbread cottage with large oven. Secluded area preferred.

"I didn't see anything interesting today," she told the animals. "I suppose I could go try out Uncle Micah's idea on Marjorie's spiders."

Flicket flicked his tail, dropped the last empty shell, and scurried out the open window. Noodles snorted and rubbed his jaw against Cory's ankle, his eyes still closed. Edging her foot from beneath the sleeping woodchuck's head, she went into the main room to send a message.

Dear Marjorie,
    Can I come visit you this morning?
I have something I want to try on the
spiders.

                Cory

She was tapping her foot, wondering if she was wasting her time, when she heard a *ping!* and a reply landed in the basket.

> *Sure! Come on over!*
> *Marjorie*

Cory was still reading Marjorie's note when a message from her mother arrived.

Cory, we need to talk. You can't just walk away from the JFG. Family is very important to me, and I had hoped that being a tooth fairy would become a family tradition. We all have to make sacrifices and do things that we don't want to do, so don't be so selfish. If you are worried about the amount you are making for collecting teeth, you must know that the tooth market is down right now and will be going back up soon. I'm sure of it. You'll also get better at collecting with practice.

If you don't return to the JFG, have you thought of what you might do instead? There isn't a lot out there for a fairy without the right kind of formal training. I want to sit down and discuss this . . .

Cory had read more than enough. Crumpling the message into a ball, she tossed it into the garbage basket and went back into the kitchen to get Noodles. While she was out, the woodchuck was going to stay in her bedroom along with his chew toys. She didn't want her uncle to have any reason to ask her to leave.

Marjorie was waiting for Cory when she arrived. She was seated on the garden bench again with a large book in her hand and a small table bearing two pink tulip cups beside her. This time she was thumbing through *A Tour of Fairy Gardens*. Spider-size smudges stained the cover.

"Oh, good, you're here!" Marjorie exclaimed when Cory returned to her human size. "Come sit down. Would you like some mint lemonade? The mint is from my garden. I'm so glad you came. I have a lot to tell you. First of all, I know you don't really want the job I offered you, but I think you should take it."

"Have the spiders gotten worse since yesterday?" Cory asked, sitting down with one of the tulip cups in her hand.

"Oh, no, nothing like that. It's just that I've received an anonymous message telling me not to hire you. It said that you were still under obligation to the Tooth Fairy Guild and weren't free to pursue another career. I got so mad when I read it! I think what they're doing is underhanded and sneaky. We can't.let the big guilds dictate how we live our lives! That's why I think you really should become my spider stomper. I know your feet aren't much bigger than mine, but we can figure something out."

"I really appreciate the offer, but to tell the truth, I already have something else in mind. My uncle recommended a spray we can use on the spiders. He's not sure it will work, but it's worth a try."

"I saw a huge one in the kitchen this morning," said Marjorie.

"The bigger the better!" Cory replied. "If it works on a really big one, we'll know that it'll work on any of them."

Marjorie led her to the back door that opened into a bright, sunny kitchen with yellow walls and white cupboards. A spider the size of a small dog squatted on the kitchen table, turning to look at them when they entered the room.

Cory dug into her pocket for the small bottle of spray that she'd taken from her uncle's shed. If this worked, she'd come back with a bigger bottle.

"Have your book ready in case this doesn't work," Cory told Marjorie.

Darting toward the table, Cory squirted the liquid on the spider, nearly stumbling over her own feet backing away when it looked as if the creature was about to jump on her. Instead of jumping, however, the spider twitched, shook itself, staggered to the edge of the table, and fell off. Cory held her breath while the spider lay still, but a moment later it was back on its feet, limping out of the kitchen.

Suddenly, Marjorie sneezed so explosively that Cory jumped, startled. She began to worry when the poor girl couldn't stop sneezing. When Marjorie finally stopped, she was so weak that she had to sit down. Taking a lace handkerchief from her pocket, she patted her streaming eyes dry and said, "Even if it had worked, I don't think we could have used that spray in here."

"I guess not," Cory said with a sigh. "We'll just have to think of something else. Say, I'm going to meet a friend for dinner tonight. Why don't you join us? It should be fun."

"I'd love to!" said Marjorie. "Do you know how long it's been since I ate out with friends? It's been ... so long that I can't remember when. See, I knew something good would come out of that ad!"

Another note from her mother was waiting for Cory when she returned to her uncle Micah's house. She threw it away without reading it. After letting Noodles snuffle around the yard and nibble grass, she took him back inside. The woodchuck was rattling his food dish when

Cory began to make them each a salad for lunch; hers had dressing and his didn't.

Noodles was restless again after lunch, so she clipped his leash on his collar and took him for a walk around the neighborhood. They met a few other people walking their pets. A tall, thin genie walking a six-foot-long iguana introduced himself as Salazar, Micah's next-door neighbor. A squat, little woman waddling behind her wild boar stopped long enough to say hello before her boar dragged her down the street. A girl with catlike eyes was walking a spotted leopard. When both the girl and the cat eyed Noodles hungrily, Cory decided it was time to go back to the house. Even so, she liked that there was such an interesting mix of people in her uncle's neighborhood. Most of her mother's neighbors were fairies. From what she understood, the majority of the neighborhoods in the town were made up of one kind of person or another, like fairies or genies or humans, with or without magic. Only a few neighborhoods had a mixture like her uncle's.

By the time they reached the house, Micah was there, sitting on the front porch with a cup of cider in his hand and Flicket the squirrel on his shoulder. "How was your day?" he asked, leaning down to pet Noodles. Flicket chattered at the woodchuck, flicking his bushy tail up and down.

Cory brushed birdseed off the other chair before sitting down. "I tried your spray on the spiders. It made Marjorie sneeze a lot, and when I say a lot I mean I thought she was going to pass out from lack of air."

"That's not good," said Micah.

"I know," Cory replied. "I'll just have to keep looking for something that will work."

An hour later, Cory was wearing a short turquoise dress the same color as her eyes. Her uncle even told her how nice she looked as she was on her way out the door. She couldn't remember her mother ever giving her a compliment.

Daisy was waiting by the door when Cory arrived at the restaurant. "What do you think?" Cory said after greeting her friend. "I've never been here before but I heard that the food is good and the atmosphere is even better."

"It looks great so far," Daisy said as a handsome satyr approached them. "Table for two," she told the waiter.

"Make that three," said Cory. "I asked Marjorie Muffet to join us. I hope you don't mind."

"Not at all," Daisy said over her shoulder as they followed the waiter to their table. "I always liked Marjorie."

"So, why did you say Nimzy is a jerk?" Cory asked her as they took their seats.

Daisy waited until the waiter had given them their menus and trotted away before answering.

"He left for an out-of-town race and didn't tell me until the last minute. I spend all my free time with him, and he can't even tell me that he's going to be away." Daisy pursed her lips and shrugged. "Boys! I don't know why I bother!"

Marjorie walked in just as Cory was about to mention how unthinking Walker could be. Instead she waved to her friend and gestured for her to join them. On any other girl, the pale, pink sleeveless dress with the darker pink bow tied in the back might have made her look like a child, but Marjorie looked soft and pretty and very grown-up.

"That's Little Miss Muffet?" Daisy whispered to Cory.

Marjorie smiled her thanks at the waiter, who looked slightly stunned and didn't leave until she turned away. "Hi, ladies!" she said to Cory and Daisy. "I'm sorry I'm late. It took me forever to decide what to wear. I saw some people setting up on the stage when I was coming in. I didn't know there was going to be music!"

"Neither did I," said Cory. "I wonder who it is."

The waiter came back then and the girls all ordered

salad. They had nearly finished eating their dinner when Cory noticed that Daisy had grown very quiet and was staring at someone across the room. "What is it?" Cory asked, turning to look behind her. When she saw him, she felt as if someone had punched her.

"Who are you looking at?" Marjorie asked, turning to look as well. "Is it that handsome fairy kissing the girl with the long blond hair? He looks like he should be someone famous. Do you know who he is?"

Cory swallowed and nodded. "That's Walker. My ex-boyfriend."

Marjorie frowned. "You look upset. Did you break up recently?"

"Like, two seconds ago," said Daisy. "She just learned what a cheating glob of pond scum he is. I'm so sorry you had to learn it this way, Cory." Daisy leaned across the table and patted Cory's fisted hand. "I heard what he was doing, and I wanted to tell you. I was going to the other day, but then you saw Noodles eating your mother's shoe."

"You know, girls," Marjorie said with a bright smile on her face, "ditching deadweight is never a bad thing."

Cory had been with Walker since Junior Fey School and had never thought about going out with anyone else. Although she hadn't been madly in love with him, she had always assumed that he was faithful and it hurt to find out that he wasn't. She'd known that he wasn't happy she'd quit the guild, but she'd thought they could weather anything. For a moment she wondered if he was seeing someone else because he was angry with her, but then she realized that that couldn't be the reason. If Daisy knew about it, it must have been going on for a while. Marjorie was right. Walker was deadweight. She didn't need him. She didn't need her mother, either. She didn't need anyone but her friends and her uncle and Noodles. Tears prickled behind her eyes and she had to fight not to run from the restaurant.

"Look, the band is about to start," Daisy said.

Cory was too caught up in her own misery to pay attention to the band, but after they had played for a few minutes, the music finally got through to her. It was a blues band and the trumpeter was exceptional. She noticed the rapt expressions on her friends' faces before she turned around. When she did, her own jaw dropped. The musician playing the trumpet was Johnny Blue, the same person who had saved her from the dogs the morning of her last collection.

Cory studied Johnny Blue's face while he played. His eyes were closed and his cheeks were puffed out as he blew life into his song. It was obvious that he was lost in his music and that, at that moment, nothing else mattered to him. In the human world he might have been considered ugly, but not in the fey world, where full-blooded trolls were so hideous that they could frighten their own mothers. Cory had always thought Johnny Blue had an interesting face. Now, despite his puffed-out cheeks, Cory thought he looked almost handsome in a craggy-faced, big-featured sort of way.

No one talked while the musicians played, but the moment they stopped for a break, Daisy turned to Cory and said, "That's why Walker is here! He came to see Blue!"

"I bet you're right," Cory admitted. "They've been best friends for years. Blue even filled in for Walker the other night. Walker is a sandman," she explained to Marjorie. "They call Blue the Boogie Man, so I always thought he went to the human world to scare little children."

"He is scary looking enough," said Daisy. "But he sure does know how to boogie! He's the best trumpet player I've ever heard! I don't know why we never heard him play before."

"I'd love to meet him," Marjorie said. "I think he has an intriguing face. Is he seeing anyone?"

"Not that I know of," said Cory.

"Do you think you could introduce me to him?" Marjorie asked. "Most of the people in my neighborhood are old. I never get to meet anyone who doesn't have white hair or walk with a cane."

"Sure," said Cory. "We might as well do it now before they start playing again. They should be finished with their break soon."

Blue was just coming out of the manager's office when Cory reached the hallway. He looked surprised to see her, and when he glanced toward Walker, she understood why. "I didn't know you played the trumpet," she said. She didn't want to talk about Walker now, not when the pain was so fresh, but from the look on Blue's face, she couldn't help but feel that he had known all along and felt sorry for her. The last thing she wanted was Walker's best friend's sympathy. "We all thought you sounded fantastic! You've met Daisy before, haven't you? And this is our friend Marjorie."

"Hi!" said Daisy.

"It's nice to meet you," Marjorie said, extending her hand to Blue.

Blue's irregular features twisted into a smile as he took Marjorie's hand in his. When Cory's stomach started to feel queasy, she wondered if she might have gotten food poisoning. "I think I need to go home now," she told her friends. "I'd love to stay and hear your next set," she said to Blue, "but I think something I ate isn't agreeing with me. Daisy and I are in a band, too. It's called Zephyr. We'll be playing at Sprats' Friday night. It would be great if you could come see us."

Marjorie nodded. "I'll be there!"

Cory was turning to go when she glanced at Blue again. He was looking at her and seemed almost sad, but the moment passed and he turned back to Marjorie, who was talking and still holding his hand. Cory's stomach lurched as she started for the door, hoping that she wasn't coming down with something.

CHAPTER

7

*Y*ou got another message," her uncle said the next morning. "You might want to read this one."

Micah had witnessed her throw out two unread messages from her mother when she returned home from dinner the night before, so she wasn't surprised he thought that she'd throw out another. This one wasn't from her mother, however. It was an official notice from the TFG.

"It's a list of all the rules and regulations I'll be breaking if I resign. They're offering me the chance to come back without a blemish on my record if I do it now," Cory told him after reading it. "I think this is a very important piece of information and I must treat it with the respect it is due." Crumpling the message into a ball, she tossed it in the garbage.

"You can't do that indefinitely," her uncle told her with a shake of his head. "Sooner or later you're going to have to empty the garbage."

"I'll make that one of my official duties around here," Cory said with a smile.

Micah drank the last of his juice and set his cup on the table. "I'm going to be later than usual tonight. I have a planning meeting with the rest of my department."

"Then I probably won't be here when you get home," said Cory. "My band is rehearsing at Olot's."

Ping! Another message appeared in the woven basket. Cory opened it even though it was from her mother.

Cory,
  You are making an enormous mistake. I am telling you this only because I love you. It upsets me terribly that you have not responded to my other messages, which leads me to believe that you are as stubborn as your grandfather. I wish that you and I could . . .

Cory had read enough, and her mother's note joined the others in the garbage. There wasn't any point in reading them, because they all said the same thing. Except, what did her mother mean about Cory's grandfather? Delphinium and Micah's father was the only grandfather Cory had ever known, and he was a big mushball when it came to his wife. He did everything she asked, saying it was the only way to promote marital harmony. He was a lot of things, but no one could call him stubborn. Cory didn't mention this to either Micah or Noodles, however. Her uncle was headed out the door and didn't have time to listen, while Noodles was cleaning himself in a highly personal way.

After feeding Noodles and eating her own breakfast, Cory looked through the ads and found two that interested her. The first house was only a few streets away.

WANTED

Individual with patience, strong lungs, and a big heart to help with occasional babysitting for large family. Must pass interview. Contact Gladys at 2345 North Shore Rd.

The other was halfway across town.

WANTED

Person to mow lawns. Job will last all summer and includes three houses. Lawn mower provided. If interested, contact A. Porcine at 123 Cozynest Lane.

After sending messages to both people, Cory cleaned up the kitchen, fed the mice, and took out the trash from the garbage basket. When she walked Noodles to the yard, he didn't want to come back in, so she got a later start than she'd intended.

Apparently, she had given up being a tooth fairy so she could spend her summer babysitting and mowing lawns. Cory hoped her mother didn't hear about this.

The woman who had answered Cory's message lived near a large lake at the south edge of town. Although Cory had heard of the house before, she'd never actually seen it. "So this is the house that looks like a shoe," she murmured, looking up at the house from the street. She thought it looked more like a boot than a shoe with its high leather sides and thick edging around the bottom that could have been a sole. If it hadn't been for the front door in the toe and the windows at random intervals in the walls, it wouldn't have looked like a house at all.

Cory stood by the road for a moment, trying to see what a home buyer might notice. The grass was a little long, the shrubbery overgrown. Swings hung from the branches of an old oak in the side yard, while another tree supported a dilapidated tree house.

"Hello! Are you Cory?" called a voice. A little woman

who couldn't have been more than four feet tall stood just inside the open door.

"I am," Cory said, heading up the stone path.

"I'm Gladys!" said the woman. "Won't you come in?"

Cory stepped across the threshold into a room lined with chairs and sofas. It looked comfortable enough, but the furniture was crowded so closely together that there was almost no space to walk.

"What an interesting house. How long have you lived here?" Cory asked as the woman closed the door.

"Twenty-six years. My husband and I bought it when we first got married. It's a good house and has served us well. This is the main room," said Gladys. "We have a lot of children, so we needed lots of seats if we all wanted to be together."

"How many children do you have?"

"Forty-three," the old woman said, sounding tired. "That includes four sets of twins and one set of triplets. Only eleven still live at home. Make that twelve. One just moved back in. Come along. The kitchen is this way."

A narrow hall led to the kitchen, where a big maple table dominated the room. Chairs were crammed so tightly around the table that Cory didn't see how anyone could pull them out to sit down. The room would have looked large if it wasn't so full of furniture.

"Would you like some tea?" the woman asked as she took some cups from the cupboard.

"Uh, sure," said Cory.

"Have a seat," Gladys told her, still facing the counter.

Cory took hold of the closest chair and pulled. The two chairs on either side moved with it, so she had to push and pull all three chairs until she could get one out. She sat down and couldn't help but notice that the chair seat was sticky.

"Here you go," Gladys said, handing her a chipped cup full of slightly warm tea. "Now, I want to hear all about you. How long have you been babysitting?" She pulled out a chair on the other side of the table and sat down.

"I just started, actually," said Cory.

"What's the largest number of children you've watched at once?"

"Uh, one," said Cory.

"That will do. Learn through experience, I always say." At the sound of a loud thud somewhere overhead, Gladys sighed and said, "That would be my son Tom Tom. Shortly after he graduated from school, he was arrested for stealing a pig. He just got out of jail. Can you believe the boy found a job already? He works the strangest hours, though. I'd ask him to watch his brothers and sisters when he's home, except I know he'd just yell at them and lock himself in his room. Of all my children, he's the most like his father. But then again, he's the only one I birthed. The rest were all adopted, thanks to my husband. You don't know who my husband is, do you?"

"I'm sorry, I don't," said Cory. "Should I?"

"No, I suppose not. It's just that most people do. My husband used to be known as the Pied Piper. He was a young musician when I met him, but he had a way with music. We were married for five years before we had Tom Tom. We wanted more after that, but eventually we realized that wasn't going to happen. Marvin, my husband, knew how much I wanted them, so he got it into his head that he was going to get them for me. He went to the human world and used his pipe to lead the children here. I did want more children, but I meant one or two! Then he was arrested and went to prison. The authorities left the children here with me. They couldn't go back to the human world, and somebody had to raise them. I did the best I could by myself."

"You raised forty-three children by yourself?" Cory asked, incredulous.

Gladys nodded. "Of course, they were all different ages when they got here, from little tykes up to teenagers. The older ones helped me with the younger ones. The ones that were old enough to work got odd jobs to help buy groceries. We made do, but it wasn't easy. So that's my situation. What do you think?" Gladys said, leaning forward in her chair. "Are you interested in babysitting my children? It wouldn't be very often—just when school is out and I have to work."

"Sure," Cory said slowly. "Although I have to tell you up front that I intend to find a career. I'm not going to be able to babysit for long."

"Oh, that's all right!" said Gladys. "I might not need you for long. A few of my older children are having a hard time making it on their own. Any one of them could move back any day and they're all more responsible than Tom Tom. I just wanted to find someone who could watch the kids for now and knew our story beforehand so she wouldn't run off the first time she helped me out. Thanks for coming by. You'll be hearing from me soon!"

Cory found herself standing on the walk in front of the house, not sure what had just happened. It had felt as if she was interviewing the woman more than that the woman was interviewing her. At least Gladys understood that Cory wasn't going to babysit for long.

But then I don't want to mow lawns forever, either, she thought as she landed facing 123 Cozynest Lane a few minutes later. It was a tidy, little brick house at the end of a dead-end street. A well-trimmed hedge surrounded the house, serving as a background for masses of daisies, dahlias, snapdragons, and zinnias. The grass, however, was quite long, reaching almost to her knees. A short, little man dressed in yellow slacks, a flowered orange-and-pink shirt, and a wide straw hat was bending over the flowers, picking the largest and prettiest.

"Pardon me," Cory said, coming up behind him. "Are you Mr. Porcine?"

The little man straightened suddenly as if startled, and turned to face Cory.

Cory was surprised to see that he was a pig; not that he looked like one, but was an actual pig with a snout holding up a pair of sunglasses and pointed ears poking through slits cut in his hat. She had met dogs who looked and acted like people, as well as cats, monkeys, a blue dinosaur, and even an alligator, but she had never met a pig. Although they were usually animals that had been changed through magic, she had heard that there were some who were descended from such altered animals and acted as normal as any person. When the pig removed his sunglasses to wipe the perspiration from his forehead, she decided that he must be one of these.

"Why do you ask?" said the pig.

"I'm Cory Feathering," she said after a moment's hesitation. "I've come in response to your ad; if you're Mr. Porcine, that is."

The pig flicked a glance toward the front door, before saying, "I'm Mr. Porcine, but I didn't write any ad."

"Didn't you advertise for someone to mow your lawn?"

"No, I didn't."

"But," she said, glancing at the address on the house, "this is the address in the listing."

"What's going on here?" a second pig demanded as he strode across the lawn. He looked a lot like the first one except for his patched shorts, faded T-shirt, and earring in one of his ears.

"This girl said that someone posted an ad for a person to mow his lawn, but it wasn't me," said the first pig. "We wouldn't do that, would we, Bertie?"

"Of course not! I find this highly suspicious. Why would you say we had placed an ad when we clearly did not? Is this some sort of trick? Why would anyone do such a thing, unless . . . Who sent you? Why are you really here? Is this some ploy you've concocted to snoop around? We don't take kindly to snooping!" The pig moved toward her in a threatening sort of way.

"Uh," said Cory, taking a step back, "I think there's been some sort of mistake. I came here to work, not snoop." She thought it was curious that while Bertie looked angry, his brother looked frightened. "Good day, gentlemen. I'm sorry to have bothered you." She was about to leave when the front door to the little brick house opened.

"What's all the ruckus?" said yet another pig. This pig was more conservatively dressed than the others in tan slacks and a white shirt. He wore metal-framed glasses on his piggy snout and he smelled of after-shave.

"This girl is sniffing around, asking nosy questions," said the pig named Bertie. "She made up some story about answering an advertisement."

Cory sighed. "Someone named A. Porcine wrote a help-wanted ad for a person to mow his lawn."

"I'm Alphonse Porcine," said the pig in the suit. "I wrote the advertisement. I purchased a lawn mower last week, but I found that I was unable to push it myself. You'll have to excuse my brothers. They're a little jumpy around strangers. They don't get out much," he said, giving the other two pigs a meaningful look. Turning back to Cory, he continued. "So, if you are interested, I could use your help. I need you to mow this yard as well as the yards on either side of mine. They belong to my brothers, who also cannot work my mower."

"Oh, sure," Cory said, glancing at the other two houses. "I can do that."

Cory had just seen a house that looked like a boot, so she didn't think that the house made of straw or the house made of twigs was odd. They both had big yards, however, so she paid more attention to the grass she'd have to mow, trying to estimate how long it was going to take her.

"Would you like to start now?" asked Alphonse. "The mower is around back."

The other two pigs followed them to the shed behind the house and watched while their brother took out the mower and showed Cory how to use it. Cory could see why the pig couldn't manage the mower; he was so short that he couldn't see over the handlebar and he'd have to push with his arms above his head. What she couldn't understand was why he'd bought it in the first place.

Alphonse puffed and grunted as he pulled it out of the shed. "I saw a smaller version at the shop. I was very impressed . . . that it powers itself with cut grass . . . and has never-need-sharpening blades. The salesman . . . talked me into buying . . . the biggest one they had, although they didn't . . . have any in stock at the time. He said it would . . . cut the mowing time in half. I'm sure . . . it would, if only I could use it. Do you . . . think you could handle it?"

"How do you start it?" Cory asked.

Alphonse plucked a few blades of grass and sprinkled them into a recessed cup in the top of the mower. There was a soft hum and a light went on. The mower vibrated and moved a few inches forward. Cory took the mower from the pig and started pushing. It was hard at first because the grass was so tall, but after she'd pushed it a few feet, the light grew brighter, the hum grew louder, and the mower rolled through the grass easily, leaving a clean-cut swath behind. All Cory had to do was steer.

"Just push the red button to turn it off," Alphonse told her, gesturing to a place on the handle.

"I can do this!" said Cory, thinking it wouldn't take long at all.

"Good!" said Alphonse. "Then I'll leave you to it." Cory was aiming the mower to the edge of the yard when he turned to his brother and said, "So, Roger. Were you picking my flowers again? Bertie, we have to talk about the way you act with strangers . . ."

CHAPTER
8

*I*t took only a few hours for Cory to mow the three little pigs' lawns. When she finished, Alphonse paid her well and asked her to come back the following week. Cory flew home to find that her uncle was still at work. She took Noodles out, threw away yet another threatening message from the TFG, and went to her room to change her clothes. She was pulling a soft yellow shirt with fluttery sleeves over her head when she noticed an old blue shirt that had been mixed in with the rest of the clothes. The shirt had belonged to Walker back when they were in Junior Fey School, and he'd given it to her when they went swimming one day and the weather had turned cold.

Seeing the shirt brought back the hurt and anger

that she'd felt when she saw him with that girl. He was cheating on her and thought he was getting away with it! Walker was a lowlife, a lying worm that didn't deserve her as a girlfriend! No, that wasn't right. He was worse than a worm! He was . . . Cory shook her head. He wasn't worth her time or her tears. Swiping furiously at the damp streaks on her cheeks, she told herself to forget him. When everyone had told them they were the perfect couple, she'd wanted to believe it was true. When her friends wished they had boyfriends like Walker, she'd been happy knowing that he was hers. Apparently, she'd been deceiving herself all along. The real Walker wasn't the person she'd thought she was dating. That person would never have done something like this!

"Marjorie was right," Cory told herself. "It's time for a new start."

Opening her closet door, she took out one of the boxes she'd used to move her things to her uncle's. The blue shirt went in the box first. Rooting through her clothes, she weeded out those that Walker had given her and had once seemed so special. After that she went through the few mementos she'd brought to her uncle's house, and picked out the ones from Walker, like the tooth-shaped toothbrush holder and the saber-toothed-tiger tooth necklace. She hadn't noticed before that aside from his old, used clothes, the only things he'd given her were tooth related.

The box was only half full when she closed the lid. She thought about putting it out with the trash, but decided to leave it on Walker's porch instead. Torn between never wanting to see him again and telling him exactly what she thought of him, she carried the box out of the house and down the street. She was nearly there when she finally decided what she'd do. If she saw him, she'd talk to him. If he wasn't there, she wasn't going to seek him out. It was possible that he knew she'd been at the restaurant last night. Even if he hadn't seen her, someone might have told him afterward. Somehow she doubted that he knew. If he had heard, he probably would have been over to see her to tell her some sort of lie. Walker had never liked loose ends.

When Cory finally reached his house, she set the box on the porch and hesitated. Should she ring the bell hanging beside his front door, or leave the box and walk away? If she rang the bell and he didn't come, she would have tried at least. But what if he . . .

And then Walker stepped out. He looked surprised to see her. "Hi! I didn't expect to see you today. What's with the box?"

"I'm returning your things," Cory told him. "I don't want them anymore."

"Why, Sweet Pea?" he asked, looking puzzled. "What's wrong?"

Cory's lips tightened into a thin line. He had the nerve to act like nothing had happened! And for him to call her his old endearment . . . "Don't 'Sweet Pea' me, you lying, two-faced—"

"What are you talking about?" he said.

Cory thought he was still trying to look innocent, but she had seen the flash of understanding in his eyes. "You know exactly what I'm talking about. I saw you last night, kissing another girl."

"Oh, her!" Walker said. "That was nothing. She's my cousin who came to visit."

"Don't lie to me, Walker! At least show me that much respect! I know she's not related to you. I've been to your family reunions! I know everyone in your family and I never met that girl."

"An old friend from school?" he asked as if he doubted she would believe him.

"Be honest, Walker!"

"Fine. She's someone I met at a club one night. It's your fault I'm with her at all, you know. If you hadn't been so busy, you would have been there and I would never have talked to her."

"I was at work, which is where you should have been instead of going to clubs. You worked the same hours I did! Is that why you had Blue fill in for you—so you could go to clubs?"

"I needed a break now and then. I'm not like you. I want to enjoy life, too!"

"So do I!"

"Yeah? Well, I don't know how you're going to do that, now that you've quit the only job you know how to do. When I met you, you had a future. *We* had a future. We were both going to have good jobs and be able to afford whatever we wanted. But now you're unemployed, with no future except mooching off your uncle. You're a deadweight and I'm not going to carry you!"

"Nobody ever asked you to. I don't want anything from you now that I've seen what you're really like. Here's your stuff," Cory said, kicking the box. "Have a good life, Walker!" Turning on her heel, Cory stepped off the porch.

Walker called after her as she strode away, but she ignored him and kept going. Whatever he had to say, she didn't want to hear it.

Cory was in a bad mood when she arrived at her uncle's house, and it only got worse when she saw what Noodles had done. Preoccupied with getting rid of Walker's things, she had forgotten to close the woodchuck in her room with his toys. When she walked through the door, the first thing she saw was Noodles expanding an already large hole in the middle of the main room rug.

"What are you doing?" Cory cried. "I leave you alone for a few minutes and you do this! I should have given you to Walker so you could destroy his house. What is Uncle Micah going to say? Never mind. I know exactly what he'll say. 'Get out, Cory, and take your evil woodchuck with you!' Because of you, we're going to be out on the street before morning!"

Cory sank to the floor. Noodles ambled over to her, a coarse strand of fiber caught between his teeth. She winced when he climbed onto her lap, his pokey feet digging into her. Turning around until he was comfortable, he draped his plump, furry body across her legs and sighed.

Cory idly scratched the woodchuck's head. "There's nothing I can do to fix it, and I certainly can't hide a hole in the middle of the room. I guess I'll just have to buy him a new rug. One this size will probably wipe out my savings. What am I going to do, Noodles? If I don't figure out a way I can help people and make money, too, Walker will be right and I will be a deadweight living off Uncle Micah."

Cory looked up when the finch on the mantel chirped five times. "I have to go soon. I guess I'll leave Uncle Micah a note. I don't really think he'll kick us out, but he won't be happy when he sees this." She cast a rueful glance at the rug as she lifted Noodles off her lap and set him on the floor.

The woodchuck followed her into the kitchen, where she wrote a short note of apology, promising to buy her uncle a new rug. After a moment's thought, she added that she was taking Noodles with her to rehearsal to keep him out of trouble, although it was really so her uncle wouldn't have to see the culprit so soon after learning about the rug.

Grabbing a crunchy nut bar for herself and a stalk of celery for Noodles, Cory clipped a halter on the wood-chuck and started out. Her band, Zephyr, usually prac-ticed in Olot the ogre's cave partly because he had plenty of room, and partly because no one complained about the noise there. Olot's cave was due east and only a short distance past the edge of town. Cory left her drums there and normally flew to rehearsals, but tak-ing the woodchuck with her meant that she had to walk the entire way.

Walking with Noodles wasn't a problem. He could galumph along quite quickly when she wanted to run and amble peacefully when she chose to walk. However, he did like to stop frequently to sniff or taste or sit. It was in this start-and-stop method of travel that they finally left the town behind and entered the foothills where Olot's cave was located.

It was a lovely walk and Cory enjoyed it, except for the last bit where she had to lug Noodles across a rope bridge and up a steep hill to Olot's cave. Like always, Cory was happy when she finally caught sight of the door to the cave half hidden in the side of the hill. It was a massive wooden door, over eight feet tall and more than two feet thick. It would have been nearly impossible for anyone except an ogre to move it Olot hadn't bought special hinges from the dwarves, making it swing wide with the slightest touch—provided you were one of the people allowed to open it. Olot had changed his door after his wedding to Chancy, whom he had met on a walkabout to one of the twelve kingdoms. Chancy, one of the ladies-in-waiting to a truly wicked queen, had fallen in love with him at first sight. Although most people doubted the match would last, Cory was certain they were perfect for each other.

Noodles scratched at the door while Cory raised the heavy knocker shaped like a fist and let it fall. "Who is it?" called a melodious voice.

"It's Cory! Am I the last one again?" she asked as the door opened.

Chancy shook her head, making her soft brown curls

bounce against her shoulders. "Cheeble is running late. He sent a message saying he was stuck in a game of horseshoes and would be here as soon as he could."

Cory nodded. Cheeble the brownie was a professional gambler who specialized in horseshoes, marbles, and jacks. Everyone in the band knew better than to play against him; he played for money and took his work very seriously. If he even thought someone was cheating, the game always ended badly.

"Oh, you brought Noodles! Hi, sweetie!" Chancy said, kneeling in the doorway so she could pet the woodchuck. Behind her, an open hallway ran deep into the hillside, ending in an enormous cavern that Olot and Chancy used as their main room. Cory could see light spilling into the hall from the cavern until a large body blocked the opening.

"Who's at the door?" bellowed Olot, coming down the hallway.

"Look, Cory brought Noodles to see us!" said Chancy.

"Hey, little buddy!" the ogre said, scooping the woodchuck off the floor as if he weighed nothing at all. Noodles squirmed and made the soft chirruping sound he made when he was happy. "Come on in, Cory," the ogre added. "We're almost finished setting up."

"He really loves animals, you know," Chancy told

Cory as they followed Olot and Noodles down the hall. "It's too bad so many of them are terrified of ogres."

"Noodles is very discerning," said Cory. "He can always tell a good person, regardless of his species. He never did like Walker."

"Daisy told me what happened," Chancy said, lowering her voice. "Don't worry, I won't tell anyone."

As they stepped into the cavern, Cory noticed that everyone was gathered around Daisy.

"He was actually kissing her!" Daisy was saying to the three dark-haired nymphs who were Skippy's current girlfriends. "We all saw him, although I wish C—"

"Ahem!" Skippy the satyr said when he saw Cory.

"That's all right," Cory said as Daisy and the three nymphs spun around. "Everyone is going to know soon, anyway. I broke up with Walker today."

"Oh, Cory!" cried Chancy.

"Did you talk to him?" Daisy asked.

"I took him a box of his things. Honestly, I don't know how I stood him for so long. He's such a jerk!"

"Who's a jerk?" Cheeble asked, stomping into the cavern. "Are you talking about me, because if you are . . ."

"We're talking about Cory's boyfriend. They broke up today," said Skippy.

"Are we going to practice or what?" Olot asked, setting Noodles on the floor.

"Are you okay?" Daisy asked as Cory headed toward her drums.

"I'm mad, but I'll be fine. I can't believe I didn't see what he was really like sooner than this. Thinking about him makes me so mad! I've never hit anyone in my whole life, but when he said that it was my fault that he went out with that girl, I just wanted to bop him in the nose!"

"He didn't!" cried Daisy.

Olot picked up his lute and strummed a chord to get their attention. "Ready, everyone?" he asked.

Cory responded with a thump on her drum while Cheeble blew into his ox horn, Skippy tootled his pan pipes, and Daisy clacked her castanets. When the musicians started to play, Chancy picked up Noodles and made herself comfortable on a big overstuffed chair covered with snow-leopard fur—a wedding gift from a yeti. Noodles sniffed the chair with great interest, but the next time Cory glanced his way, the woodchuck was asleep in Chancy's arms.

Cory was still angry at Walker when they started to play, but she relaxed as she became caught up in the music. Even so, she banged the drum extra hard during her solo and everyone agreed that she played better than she ever had before.

After rehearsal, Cory was on her way out the door with Noodles when Daisy joined them.

"Aren't you going to fly home?" Cory asked her as they started down the path.

"I'd rather walk with you," said Daisy. "You're my best friend and I haven't seen much of you lately."

"That's because you're spending all your time with Nimzy."

"I was," said Daisy, "until this afternoon. That's what I wanted to tell you. I'm thinking about breaking up with him. He did it again! This afternoon he went to an out-of-town race and didn't tell me he was going until he was walking out the door. I think he's almost as inconsiderate as Walker. Well, maybe not that bad, but he's not what I need in my life right now. I need someone who wants to be with me and is more considerate of my feelings."

"I think everybody wants that," said Cory.

"Boys! I just don't understand them."

"Maybe you should get a woodchuck like Noodles. He's not hard to figure out and he likes spending time with me."

"I wasn't joking!" Daisy exclaimed.

"I wasn't either," said Cory. "I think I'm giving up on dating, at least for now. It hasn't exactly worked out well for me."

Daisy looked horrified. "I'm not doing anything that drastic! I just don't want to date Nimzy anymore. I'll see you later. I guess I would rather fly than walk."

"I thought she'd never leave," Cory told Noodles as Daisy flew out of sight. "I just broke up with my boyfriend and she wants to talk about *her* dating problems! So much for her lessons in empathy!"

CHAPTER

9

Cory woke the next morning to the crash of glass breaking. Noodles sat up with a snort and shuffled to the door as Cory scrambled out of bed. When she reached the main room, she found her uncle crouched over shattered glass from the window.

"What is it?" she asked. "What happened?"

Micah picked up a large, white object. "Someone hurled a tooth through our window."

Cory took the object from his hands to examine it. Turning it over, she shook her head, saying, "It isn't real. Someone made it out of plaster. And look. There's writing."

Large letters were written in purple on the back of the tooth. "'Once a Tooth Fairy, always a Tooth Fairy,'" read her uncle. "I guess we know who was behind it."

He glanced at the gaping hole in the window, crunching glass under his slippered foot when he stepped closer. "Stay away from here, Cory," he told his niece. "You have bare feet."

Cory shook her head. "I'll put on shoes and clean that up. I can't believe the TFG would stoop so low! I never imagined they'd do something like this. You'd think a big, important guild would be more civilized. I'm really sorry I brought my problems to your house. Maybe I should look for somewhere else to live."

"And take your problems there so you have to deal with them on your own? No, you're family and you're staying right here. If you have a problem, I have a problem. And I don't want this kind of thing to change your mind about going back to the TFG. If anything, it's made me that much happier that you're out of that organization."

"Thank you, Uncle Micah! I was afraid that after what Noodles did last night, you'd want me to leave anyway."

"What, a hole in the rug? I've dealt with worse than that. I let a pair of badgers live here once. You should have seen what they did to the floor! No, I should have known better and made arrangements for Noodles when you first moved in. You can't change an animal's nature just because he's living in your house, but you can make accommodations. Don't you worry about the hole. Although I'd appreciate it if you could call a repairman and stay until the window is fixed. It looks like it's going to rain. We really should call the Fey Law Enforcement Agency, too. Vandalism like this should be reported."

"I'll take care of everything," said Cory. "Don't you have to leave for work soon?"

"I do indeed. I got up early this morning, but now I'll probably be late to work."

"Then hurry," Cory told him. "Just don't forget. Zephyr is playing at Sprats' tonight."

Cory had never sent a message to the Fey Law Enforcement Agency before. She wasn't sure what to say, so she said just what she thought they needed to know.

Please come quickly. Someone has thrown a tooth through our window.

Sincerely, Cory Feathering
Address—576 Maple Lane

She was tempted to clean up the broken glass, but thought the officer should see it first. Leaving the mess where it was, she returned to her bedroom to get dressed and feed the mice before taking Noodles into the kitchen for breakfast. The woodchuck was nibbling radishes when Cory filled a small bowl with cold grain and milk for herself. Settling down at the table with her breakfast, she opened the paper to the want ads and began to read. A new help-wanted ad caught her attention.

NEED ASSISTANCE WITH INVENTORY. Applicants must have good eyesight and opposable thumbs. If interested, contact Suzy at Suzy's Seashell Shop, 6767 Seaside Street.

Cory was circling the ad with an ink stick when there was a knock at the door. She hurried to the main room and opened the door. Seeing a goblin standing on the porch, she let out a small shriek and tried to slam the door in his face. The goblin was quicker than she was, however, and stuck his foot into the opening so that she couldn't close the door all the way.

"Officer Grimble Deeds, responding to a message from a . . ." The goblin looked at the leaf that he held in his hand before continuing. "Miss Cory Feathering. Is that you, miss?"

"It is," Cory said, embarrassed that she had been so rude to the person who had come to help her. "Please come in."

Cory had never spoken to a goblin before, and she

kept casting sideways glances at him as she pointed out the broken glass. He was shorter than Cory, with a bulging forehead and a long, crooked nose. He looked lumpy inside his dark green uniform and one of his feet was longer than the other. His teeth stuck out at odd angles and he smelled like Noodles did when he hadn't been washed for a while. He looked scary enough that if he hadn't been a member of the FLEA, she would never have let him in.

When Cory handed him the tooth, he held it close to his eyes, sniffed it, and gave it a tentative nibble. "This is plaster! I thought you meant a real tooth. I was wondering how anyone could throw a tooth through a window, so I came out myself to see it. If I'd known it wasn't real, I would have sent the officer-in-training. Well, I'm here now," he said, sounding irritated. "You might as well tell me what happened." He whipped an ink stick out of his pocket and looked at her expectantly.

Cory shrugged. "Someone threw it through the front window. That's all I know."

"Uh-huh," he said, writing it down. "And do you have any idea who might have thrown it?"

"I *know* who threw it. Look on the back."

"'Once a Tooth Fairy, always a Tooth Fairy,'" read Officer Deeds. "And that means . . ."

"The Tooth Fairy Guild sent it, of course!" said Cory.

"I was a member and I just quit. This is a warning that I should rejoin the guild or this kind of thing will happen to me."

"What makes you think that? It could just mean what it says—that you are a tooth fairy even after you quit."

"That doesn't make sense!" said Cory. "If they thought I was still a member of the guild, why would they hurl this through my window?"

"You tell me," said the officer.

"I just . . . I can't . . . What?"

"Uh-huh," said the officer, tucking the ink stick and leaf into his pocket. "I'm afraid I can't help you, miss. I need a lot more to go on than this. Contact us if you have any real problems."

Cory watched, openmouthed, as the goblin officer left. Contacting him had been a waste of time. Even if he'd wanted to be helpful, Cory had no idea what he could have done, but he could have been more understanding.

After sending a message to a repairman, Cory cleaned up the broken glass. She had just carried the shards to the trash when a message appeared. The repairman would be at the house as soon as he finished the job he was already working on and had taken his juice and muffin break. While she was waiting for him, a message from Miss Muffet arrived.

Dear Cory,
    I like Johnny Blue, but there was no special magic between us. He seemed very somber after you left. I want to meet someone with a great sense of humor who can make me laugh. Do you know anyone like that?

                   Your friend,
                   Marjorie

Cory doubted the repairman would be arriving soon, so she closed her eyes and did something she hadn't done in a very long time; she tried to *see* who would be right for Marjorie. She'd tried it a few times before, but it had never worked very well. Once in a while she'd get an image that she was *almost* able to make out, if only it was a little less fuzzy. But most of the time, trying to call up a vision didn't do anything except give her a headache.

The best visions usually came with no warning. Her eyesight would go funny, then suddenly she'd see two faces. The few times she'd been able to see one of the faces clearly enough to tell who it was, the other face was too indistinct to be sure, and the most she could do was guess the person's identity from the hair color or the shape of the head. So far, all her guesses had been wrong.

Cory had learned not to trust her guesses or describe her visions to her friends, but the nagging feeling was still there. What if they did mean something? Why would she have them otherwise? Now a friend was asking her for help. Maybe the visions could be useful. Maybe she just had to learn how to interpret them.

Cory made herself relax, but nothing came to her. Without any new knowledge, she sent a message to Miss Muffet saying that she would think about finding her another date.

The repairman came a few minutes later. After showing him the window, she went to the kitchen to clean up. Noodles kept her company as she tidied the room, and followed her to the big, comfy chair where she curled up to watch the repairman replace the glass.

"What broke the window?" the repairman asked as he handed her his bill.

"Someone threw a tooth through it," said Cory, not wanting to tell him the whole story.

≫→

Shortly after the repairman left, Cory headed to Suzy's shop, by the seashore. Although she had to fly into the wind most of the way, she didn't mind because she loved the smell of the salt air and was looking forward to seeing the ocean. When she was young, her mother had taken her to the beach for a vacation one summer. Delphinium hadn't liked the way the sand got into everything, so it was the only time they went, but Cory still remembered it fondly.

Spotting a lighthouse, Cory turned right. She flew above the shoreline, looking for the little cove where Suzy's shop was located. When she finally saw it, she circled once before landing. Suzy had told her that there was more than one building, but she hadn't said how charming they were. The biggest building was a converted seashell with a wide wooden porch on the front. Whatever creature had lived inside the shell had been enormous; it was huge even after Cory returned to her human size and stood next to its milky-white curved wall. The other buildings were set farther back from the water in an uneven row. Made of driftwood with driftwood furniture on their small porches, they had colored, sea-smoothed bits of glass in their windows.

Hearing sounds from the bigger building, Cory walked around to the front and saw that the area under the porch roof was a shop filled with items made from

seashells. There were seashell necklaces, bracelets, ear-
rings, anklets, rings, and brooches. There were seashell
belt buckles, headbands, nose rings, tusk rings, and ten-
tacle bands. Seashell-decorated halters hung on a wall,
while a large table was covered with seashell-decorated
book covers, hats, vases, and lamps.

A green-haired mermaid who had dried off enough to
turn her tail into legs was examining the jewelry. Two
human women were exclaiming over the more unusual
items and had already set aside a pair of lamps to buy.
Cory waited while a selkie carrying a bulging shopping
bag over one arm and his sealskin over the other nodded
to her and stepped off the porch, heading for the ocean.

It wasn't until Cory stepped onto the porch that she
noticed the person behind the counter. She was an older
woman with a slight build and long gray hair hanging loose down her back. The tunic she wore had been
woven in the blues and greens of the sea, and around
her neck strand after strand of seashell necklaces clinked
when she moved.

"Are you Suzy?" Cory asked her.

"I sure am," the woman replied. "I'll be with you in
just a moment."

While Suzy helped the two women decide between
two vases, Cory wandered around the shop. She was
holding a string of shells the same blue as her eyes

when the two women left and Suzy came over to help her.

"That's the last one of those I'm going to make," Suzy told her. "I've quit making jewelry altogether, actually. I plan to close my shop and retire soon."

"Is that why you're doing inventory?" asked Cory.

"You must have seen my help-wanted ad!" said Suzy. "Are you here to apply for the job?"

"Yes, I—"

"Good! You're hired! I'm going to take inventory so I know how much stock I have left. I have a buyer who wants most of it and I'll take the rest with me when I move to Greener Pastures. I'm going halfsies on a cottage there with my sister. Just a minute. I think Algina is almost finished."

Cory waited while the mermaid made her final choice and bought all the jewelry she'd selected. When Algina left, Suzy began to pull down wall-size shutters, closing the shop off from the outside. Cory caught a glimpse of the mermaid stepping into the waves. A moment later, her legs grew together and she disappeared into the water with a swish of her long, scaled tail.

Suzy pulled the last shutter down and turned to Cory. "We'll work in here today and tackle the storage room tomorrow. Here," she said, taking leaves and ink-plant stems from a drawer under the table and handing one of each to Cory. "You start at that side of the room with the lamps. I'll do the jewelry. List how many I have of each color lamp. Tell me when you're finished."

Cory worked diligently throughout the morning, listing everything that wasn't jewelry. At noon, Suzy went through the back door, returning a few minutes later with cooked shrimp rolled up in seaweed. After they'd eaten, Cory started helping Suzy with her list. They finished by late afternoon and Cory left, promising to return the next day.

That night, Cory's band set up at Sprats'. Its owners, Jack Sprat and his wife, Jillian, were known for their fine food both for people who liked fattening treats as well as those on diets. The restaurant had a bar on one side and a dining room on the other. Cory's eyes swept the crowd as she tuned her drums and was surprised to see that every seat was filled. Zephyr had played there before, but never to such a large crowd. Humans and fairies took up most of the tables in the dining area. A group of ogres seated at a table near the stage was getting rowdy. When Cory turned to let Olot know, she saw that he was already watching them.

No one had brought a stool for Cheeble, so they had to wait until a busboy fetched one. While the brownie grumbled about how people always forgot him, Cory studied the crowd. She saw Chancy sitting front and center, like usual. Skippy's three nymphs were with the ogre's wife, giggling and waving at the satyr. Cory had to look twice when she saw the elf whose picture had been in the newspaper for punching a reporter. Marjorie Muffet was seated at a table beside a window, and Johnny Blue was sitting near the group of ogres. Cory was looking at her friends when one of her visions started making everything blurry.

The stool arrived for Cheeble. Olot cleared his throat and said, "All right, everyone. Let's begin."

The vision faded away as Cory reached for her drumsticks. One of the figures might have been Marjorie, but the other was too indistinct to tell. *Maybe it will be clearer next time,* she thought.

The first song they played was "Fairy Spring," one of their most popular songs. It started out slow, but would pick up tempo halfway through. Apparently, the ogres couldn't wait that long.

"That tune's as lively as a dead skunk and stinks just as bad!" shouted one of the ogres.

The other ogres agreed, banging their flagons of watered-down fermented berry juice on the table. Cory shot a glance at the other members of the band. Olot's jaw was set in a grim line, Cheeble and Skippy looked nervous, while Daisy was beginning to look frightened.

They had been heckled before, but never by a group of ogres. At Olot's signal, the band picked up the pace.

"My granny's snoring sounds better than that," shouted another ogre.

"The cats yowling outside my cave sound better than that," a different one hollered.

The ogre who had first called out slammed his flagon on the table so that the juice sloshed over the rim. "Stick 'em in a sack and toss 'em in the river. Get us some musicians who can really play!"

The ogres were laughing and discussing who should go fetch the sack when Johnny Blue pushed back his chair, stood up, and bellowed, "QUIET!"

Cory and her friends stopped playing as everyone in the restaurant turned to look at Johnny. Even the ogres, who she'd always thought didn't respect anyone, seemed to respect Johnny Blue. He was half ogre, and as the best trumpet player around, he brought honor to them all. Instead of getting angry at him, as they would have if anyone else had told them to be quiet, they closed their mouths and settled back in their chairs, waiting to hear what he had to say.

"Play 'Morning Mist'!" Johnny Blue said to Olot, and sat back down.

It was a song that the band members had come up with during a jam session on a quiet morning when they couldn't get together that night. They'd been talking about how beautiful the mist was in the meadow below Olot's cave when, one by one, they began to play. Although it was one of the band's favorite songs, they'd played it in public only once. Evidently, Johnny Blue had been there to hear it.

Cory and her bandmates turned to look at each other. When Olot nodded, they started to play.

Cory's drums beat the pulse of the earth deep beneath the ogre's cave. Skippy's pan pipes were the sleepy birds waking up and greeting the rising sun. Daisy's castanets were insects in the underbrush telling of their night's adventures. Cheeble's ox horn and Olot's lute played the melody of the coming day, drawing everyone together.

As the band played, the ogres listened, their heads tilted to the side, their eyes closed. The nymphs giggled until Chancy shushed them, then they closed their eyes, too, and smiled, just like the ogres and everyone else in the room. There was magic in the song; everyone there could feel it. When it was over, they sighed as if something wonderful had happened.

"That was beautiful," someone whispered, but because it was still so quiet, everyone heard it.

Then someone began to clap, as hard as she could. It was Marjorie, seated off to the side. Soon everyone was clapping, including the ogres, who never, ever clapped for anyone. After that, the band played other songs that they had made up together. And the ogres loved each one. Cory and her friends played "June Bug Jamboree," one of the first songs they'd written as a group. The ogres laughed and swatted at each other, as if the room really was full of june bugs. Then the band played "Storm-Chased Maid," "The Last Flight of Silver Streak," "Heat Lightning," and "Shooting Stars." When they played "Dusk in the Meadow," some of the ogres actually began to cry.

By the time they finished playing, Cory and her band were tired but happy. They had played songs that they enjoyed and made other people happy, too. The people who had been eating dinner when the music started were still there, which meant that there hadn't been tables for anyone else. Late arrivals were standing in the back of the room.

"We'll have more tables next time," the Sprats told Olot as the band put away their instruments.

"That song they played, the 'Morning Mist' song," Cory overheard one restaurant patron tell another, "when I closed my eyes, I felt as if I was in a meadow on a beautiful spring morning. I swear I felt the mist on my cheek and could smell the flowers!"

"I know! Me too!" said her friend as they walked away.

"They were right," Johnny Blue said, coming up

behind her. "That's a great song. I think your band puts magic into your songs when you play like that."

"They're just songs we've written," said Cory. "I'm glad everyone liked them! You know, I was about to go looking for you to say thanks. If it weren't for you, tonight would have been a disaster. Those ogres were about to turn ugly!"

"You mean they weren't already!" Johnny said with a laugh. "Seriously though, you don't need to thank me. I didn't do anything special. You would have turned them around soon enough."

"Hey, Johnny!" shouted one of the ogres standing in the doorway. "Me and the boys want to buy you a berry juice!"

"Listen, you all played really well," Johnny told Cory, Daisy, and Cheeble, who had come over to see him. "I just wanted to congratulate you."

"Johnny!" the ogre called again.

"I've got to go. Someone has to keep an eye on them when they get like this," Johnny told Cory and her friends before heading to the door.

As Cheeble went to talk to Olot, Cory tried to find Daisy in the crowd. She finally spotted her talking at a table of young elves. When Daisy took a seat with them, Cory decided not to interrupt or wait around for her. Feeling oddly alone, Cory left for home.

CHAPTER
10

It was sprinkling off and on when Cory woke the next morning. The sky looked gray and dreary, and she was still tired from being up late the night before. She wished she could stay in bed, but Suzy was expecting her. Crawling out from under the covers, Cory made herself get dressed and staggered into the kitchen, yawning.

"What are your plans for the day?" her uncle asked as he set a cup of juice by her place at the table.

Cory pulled out her mushroom stool and slumped onto it. "I got a job helping a woman named Suzy do inventory. She's selling everything in her seashell shop and moving to Greener Pastures."

"I have a friend who moved there," said Micah. "It's supposed to be a very nice retirement community."

Thunder rumbled and he turned to look out the window. "Drat! I hate flying to work in a thunderstorm. I suppose I'll have to take the pedal-bus. In that case I should go now. The bus always takes longer in bad weather because so many people use it. No one wants to fly in weather like this." Snatching a piece of nut bread from his plate, he gave Cory a quick kiss on her cheek and hurried out.

Cory scowled at the rain as it grew heavier and began pounding at the window. She doubted that the pedal-bus ran all the way to the beach, but if it did it was going to be a long, wet ride.

By the time Cory had eaten her breakfast and was ready to leave, the rain had let up, although the sky was still overcast. Hoping to get to Suzy's before it started raining again, Cory flew as quickly as she could. Drops were just beginning to fall when she stepped onto the porch. Suzy had some of the shutters down to block the rain, but the rest were open to let in the cool air.

"There you are!" said Suzy. "Come on in! We have a lot to do today, but we were so fast yesterday that we might be able to get it all finished. We'll be working in the storage room. You start with the odds and ends and I'll start with the jewelry. That seemed to work well yesterday."

Cory followed Suzy through the house, aware that she was gawking like a tourist. Once past the door to the shop, the seashell house was spacious with curving passages and large rooms where the builder had broken through the shell's dividing walls. The floor would have been slick if it hadn't been covered with gritty sand that gave it traction. It was light inside; everything was white and the shell itself was nearly translucent with a faint pink cast.

"This is beautiful!" said Cory.

"I love it," Suzy said, caressing a wall as if it were alive. "It's going to be hard to leave, but it's time. I'm getting too old to keep the shop going and I need to relax a bit. Collecting the seashells, making my treasures, and selling them takes up all my waking hours and I'd like to try something else for a change. Macramé, maybe, or I might take up the drums. I'd also like to read a book, something I haven't had time for in years. Let's see now . . . You can start with the vases on this shelf while I go through this box of rings."

They had been working for nearly two hours and had made good progress when Cory heard an odd scraping sound. "What was that?" she asked.

"What was what?" asked Suzy.

"Listen! There it is again." Cory looked toward the ceiling. She was sure the sound had come from above.

"That's odd," said Suzy. The noise grew louder as they listened until it seemed to come from all around them. "I don't like the sound of that."

Cory followed Suzy out of the storage room and down the hall to the door leading onto the porch. Suzy opened the door and stopped with a gasp. There were crabs everywhere, climbing on the tables, skittering across the floor, even dangling from the seashell wind chimes.

"Watch out!" Suzy exclaimed, pushing Cory back and slamming the door shut. "I've never seen anything like this before and I've lived here for thirty-two years. Stay here. I'll be right back."

"Shouldn't we close the rest of the shutters?" Cory called after Suzy, who was running down the hall.

"We will!" Suzy shouted over her shoulder.

Cory lost sight of her and was left alone wondering how they could get the porch cleaned off. The crabs were scratching on the door now; Cory even saw the doorknob move. And then Suzy was back, lugging buckets inside a round metal tub with a lid.

"Here," said Suzy, handing her a bucket. "Scoop up as many as you can, but be fast about it. They're speedy little critters."

Crabs tumbled into the hall when Suzy opened the door. While Cory picked them up, Suzy ran onto the porch to collect more. Cory slammed the door shut as soon as she could, then turned and headed for the steps.

"Where are you going?" Suzy asked.

"To dump these in the ocean so I can collect more."

"Don't do that! Put them in here!" Suzy said, poking the metal tub with her foot even as she emptied her own bucket into it. As soon as Cory had added the crabs she'd collected, Suzy clapped the lid on. "Good! Now help me close the shutters."

Crabs were still swarming up the steps when Cory and Suzy started closing the few open shutters. "What are you going to do with all the crabs?" Cory asked.

"Eat them, of course," Suzy said. "I love crab soup and steamed crabs and crab cakes and—"

The crabs froze, making Cory wonder if they had understood what Suzy had said. Suddenly, they began to turn away from the door, climb down the table, and scrabble at the closed shutters. Above them, the noise of scurrying crabs moved to the edges of the porch roof, followed by soft thuds as they hit the sand.

"These are smart crabs!" Cory said as she and Suzy continued to collect them.

"Not really," said Suzy. "If they were, they wouldn't be here in the first place."

It took them the rest of the morning to collect all the crabs that had been trapped on the porch. When they were finished, Suzy took some to her kitchen to steam for lunch. Cory and Suzy returned to work in the storeroom after they'd eaten. It looked as if they really might finish taking inventory that day, until Suzy discovered a stack of boxes she'd forgotten.

"It's getting late," said Suzy. "And it's going to take a few hours to get these done. Would you be able to come back tomorrow?"

"Sure," Cory told her. "Do you think we could have crabs for lunch?"

"Honey, I'm going to be eating crabs for days, and enjoying every minute of it!"

Cory couldn't be sure, but she thought the scratching of the restless crabs in the metal tub sounded louder.

The sun was shining when Cory woke the next morning and the weather promised to be beautiful. As she flew to Suzy's house, Cory thought about how nice it would be to take a dip in the ocean after they finished inventory, or at least wade along the water's edge barefoot. As she neared the cove, the screeching of gulls made her pull up short and flutter in place. A flock of seagulls was circling Suzy's house, screaming and diving at anything that moved. Afraid that a gull could mistake her for a bug when she was tiny and snap her up in its beak, Cory landed a good distance away and returned to her human size.

The gulls spotted her when she was approaching the house and came swooping down at her. Waving her arms in the air to fend them off, she ran as fast as she could across the sand. Suzy had left all the shutters closed except for one. She was standing in the opening, shouting, "Run faster!" when a determined gull tried to peck Cory. "Duck!" Suzy shouted as she lobbed an empty clamshell at the bird.

Cory ducked and the shell hit the gull's head. It swerved, startled, just as Cory darted up onto the porch. Suzy slammed the shutter while Cory caught her breath. "That was close!" Cory said. "Thanks!"

"Closer than you think," said Suzy. "We'll go to the bathing room to clean up your hair."

"What's wrong with my . . . Oh!" Cory said, touching something wet on the back of her head.

Cory grimaced when she thought about what the seagulls had done, and scarcely noticed the rooms they passed through on their way to the bathing room. She tried to see her reflection in the shell-framed mirror while Suzy wiped the worst of the bird droppings out, but she couldn't see much.

"Bend down and stick your head in the sink," Suzy told her.

Cory closed her eyes as warm water doused the back of her head. When she opened them, she took the towel Suzy offered and dried her hair as she looked around the room. It was a cozy room with a huge shell for a bathtub and a smaller one for a sink. Seashells cupped the fairy light on the walls while tiny shells of pale pink, yellow, and orange covered the floor.

"I've never seen anything like this!" Suzy said when Cory handed her the damp towel. "First the crabs yesterday, then the gulls today. I wonder what's making these critters so crazy!

"Last night I looked at the boxes we found," the older woman continued as they walked down the hall. "We should have the inventory finished in no time. I probably could have finished them myself without much trouble, but I'd already asked you to come back, and I do enjoy your company. It makes the job fun having someone to talk to, don't you think?"

Cory agreed. She liked working with Suzy, although she could have done without the encounter with the gulls.

When they reached the storage room, they divided up the boxes and got to work. They finished a few hours later, but Suzy wouldn't let her helper leave until they'd eaten crab cakes for an early lunch. When it was time for Cory to go, Suzy led her onto the porch. The screaming of the gulls was louder there than in the house, and Cory began to wonder if she should stay until the gulls had gone.

She was about to mention this when Suzy took three of the live crabs from the metal tub. "What are those for?" asked Cory.

"They're your ticket out of here," Suzy told her. Opening one of the shutters a crack, she pointed at it, saying, "You go out this way when I tell you to. Just give me a minute."

Cory shrank while Suzy opened the shutter on the opposite side of the porch. Pulling her arm back, the woman hurled the crabs as far as she could. The screaming of the gulls grew deafening as they converged on the three flailing crabs.

"Go!" shouted Suzy.

In an instant, Cory was out the small gap and darting away from the house. She didn't slow down until she was well away from the beach and was sure that she had left the gulls behind. Somehow she didn't think she'd go back anytime soon for a dip in the ocean.

CHAPTER
11

It was early afternoon when Cory reached her uncle's house. She expected to see him outside working in his garden, but no one was there. When she landed on the walkway, she found the muddy paw prints of a large dog heading away from the house toward the street. Following the paw prints back to the house, she discovered that two of her uncle's prize roses had been uprooted. The garden hose lay next to one of the holes, trickling water into the mud. Cory ran to the side of the house to turn off the faucet.

"Who would have done such a thing?" she wondered out loud, although she had a good idea who it might be.

Planning to change into clothes that she wouldn't mind getting dirty, Cory started up the steps and found that the muddy paw prints led all the way to the door.

She shook her head in dismay when she saw mud splattered on the door and the wall on either side. A folded leaf was stuck in one of the bigger globs on the floor. Poorly written in crayon, the note said,

People who tuRn theiR backs on the guild that loves them deseRve what they get.

A scowly face was drawn on the note.

Cory took the note inside and sent a message to the Fey Law Enforcement Agency.

Someone has vandalized our front porch and left a threatening note.

Cory Feathering,
576 Maple Lane

She wasn't looking forward to talking to the goblin officer again, but she didn't see how the FLEA could ignore the continued vandalism. While waiting for him to show up, she changed her clothes and collected a bucket, soap, and a sponge. When she went back outside, Johnny Blue was trudging up the walk, wearing the same dark green uniform that Officer Deeds had worn.

"Cory, are you all right? You sent a message about vandalism," said Johnny.

Cory nodded. "It's right here," she said, pointing at the door. "I didn't know you were an officer for the Fey Law Enforcement Agency."

"Officer-in-training," said Johnny Blue. "I'll finish my training in six months. I hope to become a CI— Culprit Interrogator—next year. In the meantime, they send me out on the jobs that they think aren't worth their time. Sorry, I didn't mean that this   "

"No, I'm sure you're right," Cory said. "Officer Deeds made it plain enough that he felt that way when he was here."

Johnny nodded. "He can be a little gruff. So, why don't you tell me what happened."

"This time or last time?" asked Cory.

"Both," Johnny said.

"Last time, someone threw a tooth through the window. It was a plaster tooth. I can show it to you if you want. I kept it in case Officer Deeds wanted to see it again. Then today I came home and found the door splattered with mud and, well, you can see for yourself," Cory said, gesturing to the door. "Whoever did it got the mud from there." She pointed at the muddy holes where the roses had been.

Johnny nodded and bent down to examine the holes. He wrote something on a leaf, then stood and climbed the steps, stopping to study the paw prints on the way. When he reached the top, he noted the mud on the door and wrote on the leaf for a while.

"You mentioned a threatening note?" he said when he'd finished.

Cory handed him the leaf and watched his face as he read it. He looked grim and far more interested than Officer Deeds had looked.

"May I see that tooth now?" asked Johnny.

Cory led him inside and left him in the main room while she retrieved the tooth from the cupboard. When she handed the tooth to Johnny, he turned it over to study the writing on the back.

"I'm no expert, but I have had a few classes in analyzing handwriting. It looks to me as if the writing on the tooth and the writing on the leaf were done by the same person. He mentions tooth fairies and the guild. Any idea why?"

"I quit the Tooth Fairy Guild a few days ago. They've been trying to make me rejoin, but I've refused. I'm surprised Walker didn't tell you about it," she said, unable to keep a trace of bitterness from her voice.

"I haven't spoken with Walker since the night I saw you on your tooth-fairy run," said Johnny.

"I quit that morning after I got home. I hated the job and I'm never going back. The TFG doesn't seem to understand that."

"And they've been trying to force you back by vandalizing your home?"

"Among other things. I helped a woman named Suzy inventory her merchandise in her store at the beach. Two of the days I worked there, something happened. Yesterday crabs swarmed her house. Today it was seagulls. Suzy said that she'd never seen anything like it. I didn't mention it to her, but I think it was the TFG. Why else would they show up when I did?"

"And Suzy can verify the crabs and gulls?"

Cory nodded. "She filled a tub with crabs. She told me about all the different ways she was going to cook them."

Johnny jotted something else on his leaf. "You're traveling quite a way if you're working for someone at the beach. Why did you go there?"

"A job is a job. Since I left the TFG, I've been trying to find what I really want to do, so I go where the jobs take me."

"And what is it you really want to do?" asked Johnny.

"Help people," she said. "The jobs I take might not be much, but I am helping people."

"That's very admirable, but you should be careful not to put yourself at risk. Flying to the beach and back is a long and potentially dangerous trip, especially when someone is out to harass you."

"I was fine," said Cory.

"This time," said Johnny. "But harassment like this tends to only get worse. Please stay closer to home, Cory. It's the only way the FLEA can help you if you need us."

"The FLEA hasn't done much to help me so far," Cory told him.

"I wasn't on the case before," said Johnny. "If anything else happens, contact me directly."

He took a fresh leaf from his pocket and wrote his name and number on it, handing it to Cory. The look he gave her was still grim, but somehow it made Cory feel better.

After Johnny Blue left, Cory took Noodles with her when she went back outside. The woodchuck followed her around while she replanted the roses and used the garden hose to rinse the mud off the door, the porch, and the walkway.

"Why would someone bring their dog with them to do something like this?" she asked him as she watched the muddy paw prints dissolve. "I would never take you with me if I was slinging mud around." When she glanced at her pet, his fur was caked with mud. There were flat places in the mud under the rose bushes where he had rolled. "Noodles! Sometimes I really do wonder why I keep you!"

Cory grumbled at Noodles the whole time she was giving him a bath and drying him off with an old towel. She had just taken him back inside when she heard the *ping!* of an arriving message.

I'M INTERESTED IN HAVING YOUR BAND PLAY AT MY CAFÉ. COME SEE ME AS SOON AS YOU CAN AT PERFECT PASTRY. IT IS LOCATED AT THE INTERSECTION OF COZY COMFORT LANE AND LAST CALL ALLEY.

JACK HORNER

"As soon as I can is right now," Cory said, tucking the message in her pocket.

Taking a leaf from the stack on the table, Cory wrote a note to her uncle saying that she was back from house-sitting, and had gone to meet Jack Horner at Perfect Pastry. Noodles refused to go into Cory's room, so she dragged him in and slammed the door before he could escape. "I'll probably have to pay for that later," she muttered as she stepped onto the porch and locked the door behind her.

Cory knew where Cozy Comfort Lane was, but she wasn't sure about Last Call Alley. She found the café easily enough, though, because of the picture of a giant basket of pastries above the front door. PERFECT PASTRY was written below in plump gold letters. It looked like a nice little restaurant, but the smell of baked goods wafting from the building alone would have been enough to draw her in.

A young man wearing a white shirt with a halo-crowned éclair embroidered on the pocket approached her as soon as she crossed the threshold. Cory noticed that he was wearing a name tag that bore JOSEF in big, bold letters. "Good afternoon, miss. How many in your party today?" he asked.

"Actually, I'm looking for Jack Horner," said Cory.

"Ah," the young man said. "He's seated at the last table."

Cory glanced toward the back of the room. Most of the tables had two or three people seated at them, but a single man was writing something in a notebook at the last table. After thanking Josef, Cory headed to the back of the room. When she looked around, she noticed the pastry displays behind the counter, the pastries listed on the wall menu, and paintings of pastries decorating the walls.

"May I help you?" Jack Horner asked when Cory paused near his table.

"I'm Cory Feathering. You sent me a message today."

"You were quick!" Jack said, his eyes lighting up. "I'm glad. Please sit down. Would you like something to eat or drink?"

Cory pulled out the chair across from him. "No, thank you," she said. "You mentioned my band in your note."

"I did," Jack said, nodding. "I've heard only good things about Zephyr. You were quite a hit the other night at Sprats'."

"We were lucky enough to play songs that the audience liked," said Cory.

Jack smiled and leaned back in his chair. Steepling his fingers together, he gazed over his fingertips at Cory. "An audience that included a group of ogres. Not an easy audience to please."

"As I said, we were lucky."

"An old friend of mine said that it was more than that. He said that you are very talented, but just don't know it yet."

"You mean my band is very talented, right?" asked Cory.

"Yes, I'm sure that's what he meant."

"If you're really interested in booking us, you'll have to contact Olot. He handles all of that."

"I will," said Jack.

"Your restaurant isn't very big," said Cory. "Where would the band set up?"

"Oh, you wouldn't be playing here. I have another restaurant—the Shady Nook. It has more than enough room for your band."

Cory had heard of the Shady Nook. It was popular among human and fairy kind, but was supposed to be hard to get into, regardless of whether you were a customer wanting to eat or a band wanting to play. Whoever had recommended Zephyr to Jack Horner had done them a real favor. She was about to ask for the name of Jack Horner's friend when the young man who had greeted her at the door came to the back of the room and murmured something to Jack.

"You'll have to excuse me," he said as he got to his feet. "I'm needed in the kitchen. We're having a small pastry emergency."

As Jack slipped through a door into the kitchen, Cory turned to Josef. "I'd like to buy some pastries to go. How are your cream puffs?"

Cory was pleased. Not only was her band doing well and about to get a very desirable engagement, but she had a bag of her uncle's favorite pastries. True, carrying the pastries meant that she couldn't fly, but she could take the pedal-bus and be home almost as soon.

Cory was looking forward to rehearsal that night, when she would tell everyone about her meeting with

Jack Horner. She was thinking about what fun it would be to give them such good news, when suddenly her vision grew fuzzy. She could *see* a woman who might be her friend Marjorie with a slightly taller man with light-colored hair. The vision was too blurry to see features, but Cory thought it might be Jack Horner. It lasted just a moment before the image blurred even more and faded away. Cory could get them together and see if she was right, although maybe she wouldn't mention the vision.

When Cory walked into her uncle's house and handed him the cream puffs, he was delighted. He was even more delighted when she told him about her meeting with Jack Horner.

"It sounds as if your band is finally getting noticed. First Sprats', now the Shady Nook. Who knows, maybe someday you'll be invited to the palace."

"Maybe, but which one? Some kingdoms are better than others."

While her uncle nibbled a cream puff, Cory went to her room to change her clothes. Everything looked fine at first, but then she glanced at the floor under the window and groaned. Noodles had chewed up three pairs of shoes. Now her only wearable shoes were the ones on her feet.

"Oh, Noodles, what am I going to do with you?" she asked as she picked up the pieces.

A soft groan came from under the bed and two misery-filled eyes peered out at her.

"You don't feel well, do you?" she said, hauling him out. He was a large woodchuck and heavy to move, especially when he was limp.

Cory scratched Noodles behind his ears. "I guess I'm not taking you with me tonight. I'll ask Uncle Micah to keep an eye on you. I don't think he'll mind too much. For some reason, he actually seems to like you."

By the time she got Noodles settled on his bed with some peppermint to soothe his stomach and his favorite toy to snuggle, she didn't have much time left to talk to her uncle and grab a bite to eat. After Micah reassured her that he would keep an eye on Noodles, Cory headed for Olot's cave. She was flying over the neighbors' house when movement in their garden made her look down. A large dog was hiding in their shrubs, looking toward her uncle's house. Cory wondered if she should go back to tell her uncle, but then the dog turned and ran off, disappearing into the woods down the street.

That's odd, she thought as she resumed her flight to Olot's cave, but forgot all about it when a passing fairy asked her for directions.

When Cory arrived at the cave, Chancy was laughing as she opened the door. "What's up?" Cory asked, peering down the hall where she could hear more laughter.

"We have a guest who wants to try out for our band," said Chancy. "He's been telling us the funniest stories."

"I didn't know we were looking for a new band member," said Cory.

"We weren't, but Olot says we should listen to him. If he's any good we can include one more."

As they walked down the hall, Cory tried to see the newcomer, but her friends were clustered around him, blocking her view. "What's his name?" Cory asked. The group shifted and she saw him, recognizing him right away. It was the elf who used to work for Santa. Her friends were looking at him as if he was some sort of celebrity.

"His name is Perky," said Chancy. "Come meet him. I think you'll like him, too."

Perky was talking as they entered the room. "Mrs. Claus gave him a very nice set of revised road maps, and he gave her ice-fishing gear. And guess what she gave him for Christmas the next year? A secondhand, never-used set of ice-fishing gear!"

Everyone laughed. When they had quieted down, Cheeble said, "Does Santa hate reporters? I've seen a lot of pictures of him looking angry at them lately."

"He was fine with them until a few years ago when

one asked what his favorite dessert was and he said chocolate mousse," Perky replied. "The reporter misspelled it, calling it chocolate moose. The Society for the Prevention of Cruelty to Forest Creatures got mad at Santa and he got mad at the reporter. That was the last interview he gave. Now he tries to avoid reporters, and the elves try to help him."

"So you punched a reporter because he wanted an interview?" said Skippy.

"I punched him because he made some rude remarks about the Clauses. Santa and his missus are like parents to me. They are to all the elves who work at the North Pole."

"Hi, everyone!" Daisy said as she walked into the room. "Did I miss anything?"

"Good, we're all here!" said Olot. "Let's set up so we can get started."

Cory was disappointed. She'd wanted to tell her friends about her meeting with Jack Horner, but it would have to wait until after rehearsal. While she gave her drums a tentative tattoo to limber up her fingers, she watched Perky, who was setting out an arrangement of bells on a table he had brought with him. From where she stood, she could see sleigh bells, cowbells, and a set of silver bells including one as small as an acorn to one that was bigger than her head.

"Ready?" said Olot. "We're going to start with 'This Old Nest of Mine.' Are you familiar with that one, Perky?"

When the elf nodded, Olot started the song with a strum of his lute.

As they played, Cory paid as much attention to Perky's playing as she did her own. She could tell from their sideways glances that the others were doing the same. The elf was good, she had to admit, and his playing did seem to make a good song even better. Cory was surprised by how deep his voice was when he joined in the part where they all sang. Even Cheeble smiled when he heard it.

When the song was over, Skippy sent the elf a thumbs-up while Cheeble gave him a nod of approval. The next two songs were even better, and by the end of the evening it was obvious that Zephyr had a new member.

Cory hurried to cover her drums so she could talk to Olot before the rest left. "Something happened today that I think everyone should know about," she told the ogre.

Olot raised an eyebrow even as he gestured for the others to come join them. Cory continued when everyone was there. "Jack Horner asked me to meet with him. He likes what he's heard about Zephyr and wants us to play at the Shady Nook."

"Really!" said Skippy. "I like that place. Their food is

fantastic and you won't find a better dance floor any-where."

"You've been able to get in?" said Cheeble. "They've never let me near the door."

"This is great news!" said Chancy. "Imagine, Zephyr playing at the Shady Nook!"

"An old friend of Jack's told him about us," Cory said. "He never did tell me his friend's name."

"I bet it was Johnny Blue," said Daisy. "He really liked our music at Sprats'."

Cory turned to the ogre. "I told Jack that he should talk to you, Olot."

"Good," said Olot. "I'll check our calendar."

"How is your empathy class going?" Cory asked Daisy as they left the cave together a few minutes later.

"Oh, I quit that. Peterby told me a class like that is a waste of my time. He said I should take something with real meaning, like animal rights or tree hugging."

"I hate to ask, but who is Peterby?"

"My new boyfriend. I met him after we played at Sprats'. He's so cute! And very smart. He promotes animal rights. His current mission is to free all captive unicorns."

"I didn't know there were any captive unicorns."

"See how good he is! By the way, I wanted to tell you that I think it's really nice of Johnny Blue to tell people nice things about Zephyr. But I think he likes more than just the music. I've seen the way he looks at you."

"What? Me? I don't think so," said Cory. "He just feels sorry for me because of Walker."

"I don't know . . . ," Daisy said with a mischievous smile.

"Well, I do. He's no more interested in me than I am in him," Cory told her. "Race you to the edge of town!"

"You're on!" said Daisy.

In an instant the two fairies were tiny dots of light tearing over the hillside. It wasn't until she'd let Daisy win and had waved good-bye that Cory thought about what her friend had said. Her and Blue? Not likely! The idea was enough to make her feel queasy. She settled on a leaf until the feeling passed. Apparently, some ideas were just too crazy to think about!

CHAPTER
12

When Cory and Noodles strolled into the kitchen the next morning, Flicket was perched on the table, nibbling a walnut. Cory's uncle had a newspaper open on the table and seemed engrossed in one of the articles. "What are you reading?" Cory asked him.

Her uncle looked up from the paper. "It's about Santa Claus again. It seems the reporters just won't leave him alone. He and Mrs. Claus were on vacation at a hotel. The reporters found out and stormed the hotel looking for him. See—here's a picture of the elves trying to fend off the reporters."

"So the Clauses take the elves on vacation with them," said Cory. "I'm not surprised. Perky did say that the Clauses treat the elves like family. Oh, I forgot to tell you: the elf who punched the reporter in the nose is liv-ing in town. He joined Zephyr last night. He plays the bells and has a very nice baritone."

"That's wonderful!" said Micah. "Joining your band should help him feel like he belongs here."

"What's that picture?" Cory asked, shifting in her seat. The picture showed the couple getting into the famous sleigh.

"That's the Clauses leaving the hotel earlier than planned. That's too bad. I'd be mad if I had to cut my vacation short because someone was pestering me. That's not a very flattering picture of either Santa or Mrs. Claus. They both look tired and worn. I guess that wasn't a very restful vacation." Micah set the paper aside and turned to Cory. "So, what are you doing today?"

"I'm going to put an ad in the paper for odd jobs."

"You don't have any set up already? You really should keep track of them in a notebook or something."

"Good idea. I have an old loose-leaf notebook that I can use. And no, I don't have any jobs lined up, but I hope to soon!"

Cory's uncle left for work while she was eating her breakfast of mashed berries on whole-grain toast. When she was finished, she retrieved her notebook from the bedroom and got to work listing all the jobs she'd done and where she'd performed each one. After that, she wrote her ad and sent it to the paper.

Honest, Hardworking Fairy Willing to Take on Your Odd Jobs. Contact Cory.

"While I'm at it . . . ," she said, and took another leaf from the pile to write a quick message to Marjorie Muffet.

> I've thought of someone else you should meet.
> His name is Jack Horner and he's very nice. Are
> you interested?
>
> Cory

Cory was going over the entries in her notebook when she heard a *ping!* Thinking it was Marjorie, she hurried to the basket. The message was from Gladys, however. She wanted Cory to babysit that day. A moment later, there was another *ping!* and the message Cory had been expecting appeared.

> *Yes, I'm very interested!*
> *Marjorie*

"Good!" said Cory. "Then I have one more message to write."

Jack Horner, I know a young lady who I think you should meet. Do you have the time?
Corialis Feathering

Cory was cleaning up the breakfast dishes when his response arrived in the basket.

YES. BRING YOUR FRIEND TO THE SHADY NOOK TODAY AT 6:00. I'LL BE BRINGING A FRIEND WHO JUST MOVED BACK TO TOWN.
SIGNED,
JACK HORNER

Cory smiled, feeling as if she'd already accomplished something before her day had really begun.

The boy who met Cory at the door of the shoe house stared at her with such distrust in his eyes that she wondered what he thought she'd done wrong. "I'm Cory Feathering," she said, giving him as warm a smile as she could. "Your mother contacted me," she added when he didn't respond. "To babysit?"

"Patrick knows what you're talking about," a girl said, coming up behind the boy. "He just doesn't think we need you here. None of us do. We're old enough to take care of ourselves for one afternoon."

When Cory stepped into the house and shut the door, the boy glared at her before going down the hall.

"Why are you home?" Cory asked the girl. "Isn't this a school day?"

"It was, but they closed our school early. A water nymph came into her powers all of a sudden and flooded the cafeteria. They took her to Junior Fey School right away, but they had to close our school while they cleaned up the water. Did you know that your shoes don't match your outfit?"

Cory nodded. "My pet woodchuck chewed up all my other shoes yesterday. This is all I have till I can go shopping."

The girl's eyes lit up. "I love to shop! Where are you going to go? My favorite stores are at East Side Market. I went there last week with some of my older sisters and they bought me a whole bunch of clothes. They have jobs and share a house, but they come home and take us out to buy us stuff every couple of months. They know that Mom doesn't have much money, so they help out however they can. My name is Heather. Want to see what they bought me? Jamie Linn got me the coolest dress! Mom thinks it's too short, but Jamie Linn says—"

"This is the babysitter?" said a slightly older girl who had just walked into the room. "I thought Mom had gotten some old woman to watch us."

A girl with long brown hair that reached almost to her knees started tugging on Cory's sleeve. "I want to do the lemonade stand today. It's a nice day out and Mom said we could do it the next nice day."

"She meant on a weekend when she was home," said Heather. "We can't do it without an adult here, Mary Alice."

"How many of you are home now?" asked Cory.

"Eight," said the older girl. "James is reading a book, Steven is cleaning his fish tank, and Rory, Joey, and Patrick are probably playing with their miniature fairy warriors. My name is Sarah Beth and that's Mary Alice." She pointed at the younger girl with long brown hair.

"Our big brother Erik is an artist. He made little clay figures for the boys. They like to reenact the big battles of the fairy wars," Heather added. "Joey has the trolls, Rory has the fairy warriors, and Patrick has everybody else."

"I want to do the lemonade stand!" Mary Alice said again.

"I suppose I could help you with the stand if you have everything you need," said Cory. "Do you make it with real lemons?"

"We do," Sarah Beth told her even as Mary Alice latched on to Cory's arm and began to drag her to the kitchen. "Aunt Sally grows lots of things. We help her out on the weekends and holidays and she gives us fresh fruit and vegetables. She has a big greenhouse and grows lemons all year."

"We have a stand and everything," said Mary Alice. "I'll ask the boys to set it up."

"But it's Monday," said Cory. "I don't know how many customers you're going to get."

"Oh, we'll have plenty," said Sarah Beth. "Wander Lake is the most popular fishing spot around, and it's just a block away. People fish in the lake every day and they come past our house to get there from town."

While Sarah Beth, Mary Alice, and Heather made the lemonade, Steven and Rory set the stand up by the street. Cory helped the girls carry the lemonade outside and sat with them while they waited for customers. It wasn't long before they had their first sales to an old man and his son who were arguing over who should ride their donkey. A water-lily fairy hauling her cart stopped for a cup as well. A few minutes later, two round-faced men dressed in identical striped shirts laid their fishing poles on the ground to purchase their cups of lemonade.

Mary Alice had just poured the lemonade for the men when dark clouds appeared overhead and the first fat raindrops fell, splashing on the children's upturned faces.

"That's odd," said one man. "It didn't look like rain a moment ago."

"Maybe we should—" Cory began, but then the rain truly started to fall, pouring from the sky so that they were all drenched in seconds. "Run!" Cory told the children. "I'll bring the lemonade!"

As the children dashed into the house, Cory picked up the pitcher and the bowl of lemons and ran after them. Her hair and clothes were streaming when she finally set everything on the kitchen table.

"Wow!" said Mary Alice, peering out the window at the water pouring from the sky. "That's a lot of rain! And it looks like it's just here at our house. The house across the street still looks dry."

"Look at that!" said Sarah Beth as the clouds disappeared as suddenly as they had arrived. The bright sunlight made the raindrops glisten and sparkle like tiny prisms.

"That's so pretty!" cried Mary Alice. "I'm going back outside."

The girls left the house, skirting the newly formed

puddles. Before they had gone far, however, Heather began to shriek, Mary Alice froze in place, and Sarah Beth started flapping her hands and making odd sounds.

"What is it?" Cory said, running out the door. "What's wrong?"

The three girls were staring at the ground; Cory could see why when she looked down. Every inch of the yard was covered with squirming earthworms writhing over each other, through the grass, over the stone walkway, and the bare patches of mud.

"It's the Tooth Fairy Guild," Cory said through clenched teeth. "They're never going to give up. Well, neither am I!"

"What did you say?" asked Heather.

"Never mind," said Cory. "Stay where you are. I have an idea." She turned to go back inside and found the boys standing behind her, peering out at their sisters. "Boys, I need you to find every empty jar, can, or sturdy box and bring them to me."

"Why?" asked Joey.

"I have a brilliant idea, that's why. Now hurry before the worms are gone."

"Worms!" said James.

"Do you think my fish would eat a worm if I put it in their tank?" Steven said as the boys ran to look for containers.

Cory was still trying to figure out how to get the jars to the girls when the boys returned. "Good!" she said, seeing how much they had brought back. "Each of you choose one of your sisters. Start walking toward her while collecting all the worms in front of you. When you reach your sister, give her a container so she can start picking them up, too. Try not to step on the worms. Joey, you stay with me. We'll start collecting in that direction," Cory said, pointing away from the girls.

"I have squished worm on my shoes!" cried Heather.

"Just don't step on any more," said Cory. "We'll clean your shoes off later."

"Why should we collect worms?" Sarah Beth wailed. "I don't want to touch them. They're gross! Some of them are huge!"

"These worms are worth money, especially the big ones," said Cory. "They're night crawlers. The fishermen who pass by here might buy one cup of lemonade, but they'll buy a lot of worms. If you want to make some money, here's a great way to do it!"

"Oh!" said Heather, looking at the worms as if they might not be disgusting after all. "Maybe I could make enough money for that bracelet I wanted. Quick, James! Hand me that jar!"

The children collected the worms as quickly as they could. The girls picked them up gingerly at first, but the more they collected, the easier it became. After a while it grew into a competition, seeing who could collect the most worms, or the biggest worms, or even the grossest worms before they slipped back into the mud. By the time all the cans and boxes and jars were full, the only worms that Cory could see were the ones that the girls had stepped on as they ran out the door.

The day was hotter now than it had been when they had started selling lemonade. It had already dried out the dead worms as well as the girls' clothes and hair. Cory had everyone put their containers of worms on the lemonade stand, then sent them back to the house to brush their hair and wash their hands. "Leave your shoes outside so I can clean them!" she told the girls.

Steven was the first one to come back out. "I'm going to make a new sign," he announced.

While Cory cleaned the shoes the best she could, Steven found a large leaf and a small jar of paint. WORMS FOR SALE! read the sign when he was finished. He took the lemonade sign down and propped the worm sign up in front of the stand, angling it so people coming toward the lake could see it.

When the stand was ready, Steven sat down beside Cory. They sold the first worms before the girls came back outside. By the time they sold the last worms, the children's mother was walking down the street.

"Thank you so much for watching the children!" she told Cory. "I work in the Clinic for Ailing Fey and I can't take time off when the school closes. How much do I owe you?"

Cory told her a lower rate than she would anyone else. It didn't make sense to help the family raise money, then take it all away. She thought about not taking anything, but they would probably consider it charity and she doubted they would accept it.

The children clustered around as Cory said goodbye to Gladys. "We want you to come back," said Sarah Beth.

"And bring your woodchuck," Heather told her. "I've never seen a pet woodchuck before."

"I will," said Cory. "As soon as your mother needs me again."

"Finally, a babysitter that they actually like!" said Gladys.

That evening Cory flew to the Shady Nook, wearing her blue dress and the new pebble-gray shoes she'd bought on the way home from babysitting. She'd bought a fresh-cream-colored pair as well and had set it high on a shelf in her room where even the most determined wood-chuck couldn't reach.

When Cory stepped into the restaurant, Marjorie

was already there, seated at a table by the window. Marjorie looked up and smiled as Cory took a seat across from her. "Oh, good. You're here! Jack Horner came over and introduced himself when he heard that I was in your party, but he was called away. He said he'd be right back."

"That's fine. It gives us a chance to talk first," said Cory. "How have you been? Are the spiders still as bad?"

"Worse!" said Marjorie. "Oh, it's not like they try to bite me or anything, but they're forever getting into things and stealing my possessions. Why, just this morning one stole my cereal bowl while I was still eating! They're making it nearly impossible for me to get any work done. As soon as I set down an ink stick, they take it!"

Cory thanked the waiter as he filled her glass with water. "I probably should have asked before this, but what kind of work do you do?" she asked when they were alone again.

"I'm a writer," said Marjorie. "I write big books with lots of pictures. You've seen some of them at my house."

"You mean you wrote the books that you use to smash spiders?"

"I did," Marjorie replied. "Although that wasn't why I wrote them, but they do work very well, don't you think? So tell me about yourself. What have you been up to since I saw you last?"

"I've been doing odd jobs like house-sitting, doing inventory, mowing lawns . . . Actually, things would be going pretty well if it weren't for the Tooth Fairy Guild. They keep trying to sabotage my work. Today they made it rain while I was babysitting. Then they had worms come out all over the ground. You should have seen it. There were worms everywhere!"

"So . . . you had to stay inside?"

"Not at all! I had the children collect the worms in jars and sell them to fishermen. They made quite a bit of money."

Marjorie clapped her hands and grinned. "What a good idea! I never would have thought of that!"

Cory glanced up when Jack Horner took one of the empty seats. "Very few fairies would have," he said. "Most would have found it discouraging."

"I got the idea from a former employer named Suzy," Cory told them. "The TFG sent a huge swarm of crabs onto her property while I was there. Suzy filled a tub with the ones she caught so she could eat them later."

"And why is the Tooth Fairy Guild doing this exactly?" Jack Horner asked.

"Because Cory quit being a tooth fairy," said Marjorie. "Apparently, the guild doesn't take rejection well."

Cory wasn't sure she wanted everyone to know what was happening between her and the guild. Telling her friend was one thing, but she regretted sharing the story with someone she barely knew. "Didn't you say that you were going to invite a friend who had just moved back to town?" Cory asked Jack, hoping to change the subject.

"I did," Jack told them as he turned to look around. "He should be here soon."

"Where do bands set up when they play in the restaurant?" asked Cory.

"You can't see it from here, but there's a raised platform in the back of the room. Don't worry, there will be plenty of space for your band."

Marjorie set down her water glass. "Is Zephyr going to play in the Shady Nook? Oh, Cory! That's wonderful!"

"I spoke with your bandleader, Olot, today," Jack told Cory. "You're scheduled for this coming Friday."

"I can't wait!" cried Marjorie.

"Wait for what? Me?" said a thin young man whose blond hair covered his eyes. He shook his head, flicking his hair back for a moment, revealing eyes of an intense blue.

"I'd like to introduce you young ladies to my friend, Tom Tom," said Jack Horner. "He's been away from town for a few years and just returned last week."

Tom Tom, thought Cory. *Where have I heard that name before?* "Oh!" she said as she remembered suddenly. "You're Gladys's son! The one who stole a pig!" As soon as she'd said it, Cory wished she hadn't. Jack Horner glanced at her in surprise while Marjorie's eyes went wide. Tom Tom's reaction was the strongest; his face turned red and he glared at her, saying, "Where did you hear that?"

"From your mother," said Cory. "I babysat your brothers and sisters today."

"That figures!" he said with a forced laugh, making an obvious effort to control his temper. "My mother gets everything wrong."

"You mean you weren't in jail for stealing a pig?" asked Marjorie.

"Not at all. I was in prison for kidnapping a talking pig. I *thought* I was stealing a normal pig until he started screaming and carrying on. I did it on a dare when I was in Junior Fey School. I've spent the last five years in prison, which turned out to be a lot like school. I earned a degree in roadside maintenance, and another in library science."

"That means he worked on the road crew and in the prison library," said Jack.

Tom Tom nodded. "Yes, but they taught us how to do it the correct way and we really did earn certificates.

I was lucky. I found a job when I got out and I really like the work, although it wasn't the kind of work I'd planned to do. To get the best jobs, you need to train for them in Junior Fey School, do an apprenticeship, and stick with it for the rest of your life. Look at Jack here. He always knew he wanted to be a chef and own a restaurant."

"That's true," said Jack. "When I was a little boy, I wanted to make the best pastries in the world. I studied to be a chef in school, did an apprenticeship with the Sprats, and opened Perfect Pastry a year later. Two years after that I opened the Shady Nook."

"What about you, Marjorie?" asked Tom Tom.

"I always wanted to write books. I studied writing in school, worked with Mother Goose for my apprenticeship, then started writing my own books."

"See what I mean!" said Tom Tom. "And you, Cory?"

"I was in the pre–tooth fairy program in school and did my apprenticeship with them when I got out."

"So you're a tooth fairy now?" asked Tom Tom.

"I was . . . until I quit. Now I'm trying to decide what it is I really want to do."

"Why would you quit a great career like that?" asked Tom Tom. "The big guilds have the best jobs."

"I quit because it wasn't right for me," Cory said. "I hated it and couldn't see myself doing it for the rest of my life. I want to help people, but I didn't feel as if I was really helping anyone. I think you should enjoy what you do. Look at Jack and Marjorie. They both love what they're doing."

"We're talking about you, not them," said Tom Tom. "You quit when it got too hard! I don't have any sympathy for someone who throws away a good job when some people have a hard time finding any job at all."

"But if it isn't right for you . . ."

"Yeah, yeah. I hear you. So, Marjorie, what kind of books do you write?"

Cory sat back in her seat, stunned. Not only was Tom Tom exceedingly rude, she was afraid he might be right.

CHAPTER
13

Cory was in a bad mood the next morning, which got even worse when she received a message from Marjorie before breakfast.

Cory,

Thank you for helping me meet Jack Horner, but he really isn't for me. I didn't like the way he sat by while his friend was rude to you. And then all he and Tom Tom did was talk about "the good old days." I was never so bored. Please find me someone else if you can.

Your friend,
Marjorie

"She was bored!" Cory muttered. "I wish I could say the same." Instead she had been angry at Tom Tom for being rude, at Jack for bringing him along, and at herself for wondering if Tom Tom was right, at least in some small part. After sitting there getting madder the more she thought about it, she had finally made her excuses and left. Marjorie had ignored her unspoken invitation to leave with her, so Cory had assumed that her friend was having a good time. Maybe it hadn't been so good after all. And now Marjorie wanted to meet someone else.

Cory sighed. She'd thought she'd seen them in a vision, but apparently her visions weren't any better now than they had been when she was younger.

Ping! Another message appeared in the basket.

"Who could it be this time?" she murmured.

> *I am writing in response to your ad. I need help*
> *canning beans today. My address is 47 Winding Way.*
> *Stella Nimble*

Cory had no idea where Winding Way was located, so she found the basket where her uncle kept his maps and shuffled through them until she found one of the area. It took her a while to find Winding Way, a twisty, turny road a good distance outside of town. After studying the map, Cory decided that it was going to take her at least two hours to get to Stella's home—an hour to get ready and an hour to fly there.

She sent a message to the woman.

I'll be there in two hours.
Corialis Feathering

To her surprise, Noodles was more cooperative than usual and she was able to leave earlier than she'd expected. With the map's directions in mind, Cory flew above the trees, following some easily seen roads. She was partway there when the sky grew dark and it began to rain.

Raindrops that she'd barely notice when human size felt like someone was hitting her with baseballs when she was the size of a flower fairy. Larger raindrops hurt even more. When the first drops fell, Cory darted into the shelter of a maple tree, hiding under one of the leaves. The rain lasted only a few minutes before it stopped and she was able to get on her way again. Three miles down the road, the wind picked up suddenly, blowing her half a mile off course before she was able to take refuge in a flowerpot lying on its side in someone's yard. The wind died down as soon as it could no longer blow her around. Cory started to fly again, but the rain began only a few minutes later.

This time Cory landed, turned back into her human size, and reached into her pocket. She took out her pedal-bus token and rubbed it until it glowed. The bus arrived a few minutes later. When Cory climbed on, everyone was complaining about the sudden rain shower. The rain stayed with them as they pedaled through the countryside. They stopped twice to pick up more passengers. Two fairies got on near a field of sunflowers, already talking about the sudden rainstorm that had started as the bus pulled up. When a gnome who got on near his hollow tree said the same thing, Cory began to wonder if the rain was following her. She was tempted to tell the other passengers what she suspected, but her stop was next and she got off, certain they would figure it out if the rain stayed with her.

The rain grew harder and the wind picked up as Cory headed to Stella Nimble's house. With her head down, Cory plodded through the driving rain, trying to stay on the path to the front steps. She was an hour and twelve minutes late when she finally reached 47 Winding Way.

Cory knocked on the door, feeling as wet as if she'd just taken a bath with her clothes on. A woman with graying hair and a sweet smile opened the door and gasped when she saw her.

"I'm Cory Feathering," Cory said, shivering. "I've come to help with the beans."

"Oh, you poor dear!" said the woman. "You're all wet. Come in and we'll get you dried off. I'm Stella, by the way. You need something to wear while your clothes dry. Go in the bathing room and I'll get you a towel. . . . Here you go. Get out of those wet things and I'll be right back."

Cory had just dried her hair and face with the towel when Stella was back with a soft white shirt and some faded blue pants. "These belonged to my son when he was young. I'm sure he wouldn't mind if you used them. He was such a nice boy. Come join me in the kitchen when you're ready. It's just down the hall."

Cory was relieved to get out of the wet clothes and into warm dry ones. Both the shirt and pants were too big, however, so she rolled the shirtsleeves and pant legs up and hoped the pants wouldn't fall down when she walked.

Following the sound of a chopping knife, Cory found Stella in the kitchen, standing at an old wooden table piled high with green beans at least three feet long and as big around as her wrist. Cory had never seen such huge beans before and was staring at them when Stella noticed her.

"There you are!" said Stella. "Here, take this knife.

We have to cut these up so they'll fit in the jars." She pointed at the end of the table where rows of ordinary glass jars waited to be filled. "I was thinking about that rain," Stella continued. "It was very odd. It started just before you got here and ended as soon as you stepped inside the house."

Cory sighed. "It's the Tooth Fairy Guild. I quit recently and they're punishing me for leaving. This isn't the first time they've used rain."

"The big guilds are all connected and help each other out, not always in nice ways," said Stella. "I know what it's like to have a guild mad at you. I was born a flower fairy, as were my parents and their parents before them. My specialty was pansies and I was quite good at my job. Then I dared to fall in love with a human and married him without the guild's permission. They punished me by taking away my fairy powers, wings and all, leaving me as helpless as a human. The guild used its connections to make sure that my husband couldn't get a job, so we made do with what we could and were happy despite the Flower Fairy Guild's best efforts to destroy our lives. We were even happier after our baby boy was born, but my husband died a few years later, leaving me to raise my son alone in this cottage."

"Did the guild stop punishing you after your husband died?" asked Cory.

"Yes, but by then there wasn't much more they could do to me. I was still happy; I had my wonderful son, who was a good boy and a track star in school, although a little strong willed. Then one day he traded our cow, Pansy, for some magic beans. I was so mad at him that I took the beans from him and threw them out the window," Stella said, pointing at the window above the sink. The view was filled with a few big, green leaves.

"One of the beans grew into an enormous stalk that reached up into the clouds. The day my son climbed it, the sky was a beautiful blue. I remember because I couldn't find him anywhere and I kept expecting to see him on the stalk. Anyway, that foolish boy climbed the stalk with nothing more than a flagon of water and a small ax tied to his waist. When he came back, he was loaded down with a giant's gold. The giant was chasing him and would have caught him if Jack hadn't taken his ax and chopped the stalk in half."

"What happened then?" asked Cory.

"When the top half of the stalk fell, the giant fell with it. He hit the ground with so much force that he made a crater. The hole filled with water and is called Giant Lake now. It lies about a half mile west."

"What happened to Jack?" Cory asked as she reached for another bean.

"He was happy and excited for the first few days,

planning how he was going to spend all the gold, but then the giant's wife and parents came after him."

Cory shuddered, thinking of all the awful things a giant could do to a person.

"Fortunately, Jack left enough of the bean stalk that it still produces beans," said Stella. "I can them when they ripen. They're delicious and I make good money selling them."

Cory and Stella both looked up when there was a knock on the door leading outside. Before they could move to answer it, the door opened and a handsome young man with thick blond hair walked in.

"Hello, Mother!" he said, smiling at Stella. "I see you're canning beans again." He kissed Stella on the cheek, then glanced at Cory. "You have help today."

"This is Cory," Stella told him. "She's a very good worker. We haven't been at this long and we've done a lot already."

Cory glanced at the table and was surprised by how much the pile of whole beans had dwindled while the pile of cut-up beans had grown.

"We were going to take a lunch break soon," said Stella. "Why don't you join us, Jack? I know how much you like beans."

Jack snorted and Stella laughed while Cory glanced from one to the other. "My mother is joking," Jack told her. "I've hated beans ever since I cut down the stalk. I will join you for lunch, though, Mother. In fact, I brought some with me and there's enough to feed a small army."

"He doesn't visit as often as I'd like, but he brings food every time," Stella told Cory. "As if I don't have plenty already! He's such a good boy."

Cory helped Stella and Jack clear the table, then they all sat down to eat the food that Jack had brought in a big wicker basket. There were berry and nut butter sandwiches, fish and herb sandwiches, a delicious cheese with a yellow crust, fresh peaches, and a box of cookies with "Perfect Pastry" written on the outside.

"I just met Jack Horner," Cory said, taking the box of cookies out of the basket. "It's funny. That's two Jacks in three days."

"Names follow trends," said Stella. "Some will be popular for a time, then others will take their place. The name Jack was popular when I had my baby. Mary was, too, back then."

"I know Jack Horner," said Jack Nimble. "I've known him for years. How did you meet him?"

"He's hired my band to play at the Shady Nook," Cory said.

"Really?" said Jack Nimble. "Then your band must be good."

They talked about the band and Jack Horner's

restaurants until the end of lunch. Jack was reaching for one last cookie when he glanced at Cory and said, "Would someone mind telling me why Cory is wearing my old clothes?"

Stella set her cup on the table with a thump. "She quit the TFG and they're harassing her with rain!"

"They made it rain when I was on my way here," Cory explained.

Jack shook his head. "I can't believe the guilds are still able to get away with that kind of thing."

"They'll never change," said his mother.

"And no one will ever do anything about it," Jack added, looking glum.

After they had cleaned up the food, Jack stayed around while Cory and his mother finished cutting up the beans and put them in sterilized jars. When the jars were filled and sealed, he helped put them in a pressure cook-pot on the stove. Once the last jar had been processed and was on the table again, Cory went into the bathing room to change back into her clothes. Jack was waiting for her when she returned to the kitchen.

"Would you like a ride home?" he asked. "The rain could very well happen again, don't you think?"

Cory shrugged. "I suppose it's possible, but since I'm going straight home, I could put on dry clothes when I get there."

"You won't have to if I take you," said Jack. "Have you ever flown in a hot-air balloon?"

Cory's eyes lit up. She had seen the balloons from a distance, but had never actually been in one. "No, I—"

"Then let's go!" said Jack.

Stella held up her hand. "Not until I thank Cory. Here's the money I owe you," she said, giving an envelope to Cory. "Thank you so much for all your help. It would have taken me more than twice as long to can all those beans." When she leaned closer to give Cory a hug, she whispered in her ear, "I think my son likes you. He never stays around this long! Good-bye, my dear. I'm sure you'll be hearing from me again soon."

Even as Cory followed Jack out the door, she planned to fly back to town on her own. Sure, Jack Nimble was handsome and successful, and he might actually like her, but she couldn't shake the feeling that he wasn't right for her. Under the circumstances, riding in a hot-air balloon for who knows how long might be awkward. All of that flew out of her mind, however, as soon as she saw the balloon.

Cory gasped and changed her mind in an instant. A swirl of colors danced around the balloon like a captured rainbow; she couldn't take her eyes away as Jack helped her into the large basket below it and they rose into the air. When she finally looked down, her heart began to race. Although Cory flew all the time, she couldn't help but feel that this was entirely different. Fluttering her wings was work and always left her tired. Flying in a hot-air balloon was a delight that left her feeling excited and invigorated.

"Tell me something," said Jack. "Why did you look so surprised when I walked into the cottage?"

"Your mother had made it sound as if you were dead. I mean, she talked about what a good boy you were, and how the giant's wife and parents came after you. From the way she said it, I thought they had—"

"What? Ripped me limb from limb?" Jack said, and laughed at the expression on Cory's face. "The giants did come after me, but I was long gone by then. I used some of my gold to hire the best lawyer available and the giants weren't able to do a thing to me. I used the rest of the gold to start a business. You might have heard of it—Nimble Sports. We make all sorts of athletic clothes, including running shoes. I just opened an outlet store in town."

"It sounds as if you're doing very well for yourself," said Cory.

"I am indeed," Jack replied. "I learned an important lesson from what happened to my parents. I'm living my life the way I want to live it without any connection or interference from fairy guilds. I know it's hard for you now, what with the guild harassing you and everything, but plan your course and go for it. The guild can do a lot to you, but they can't take away who you really are."

"I'll keep that in mind," said Cory.

Jack smiled. "Good. Now if you tell me where you live, I'll look for a place where I can drop you off."

After a few minutes search, Cory was able to point out her uncle's house. Jack set the balloon down in the park across the street, making all the neighbors come outside to watch. Her uncle Micah was among them, and when he saw her climb down from the balloon, he hurried over to her.

Cory waved as Jack took off again before turning to her uncle. "Is something wrong?" she asked.

"Not wrong, precisely," he told her. "We've been invited to your grandparents' house for supper tonight. We're supposed to be there in half an hour."

"Then I had better hurry and change out of these wrinkled clothes," said Cory. "I don't want to hear Grand-mother's lecture about appearances again."

"Or her lecture about being late," muttered Micah.

Cory gave him a humorless smile. "She is your mother."

"Don't remind me," said Micah. "Deidre is the least motherlike woman I know."

When Cory and Micah walked in the front door, her

grandfather was in the main room working on a scale model of a castle.

"There's my girl!" he said when he saw her. "How are you, darlin'? Where's my hug?"

"I'm fine, Grandfather," Cory said, wrapping her arms around the old man's narrow shoulders. "What castle are you working on now?" She stepped closer to his workbench to get a better look at the little castle and its many turrets that reflected light as if it were covered with hundreds of tiny prisms.

"Ah! This is Rupert's castle in the Blue Forest. He commissioned me to make him the model as a gift for his new bride. I have three more days to finish it. I'd be a lot farther along if the scales weren't so slippery," her grandfather said, picking up a rag to wipe the remnants of the shiny scales from his fingertips.

"Do your joints still ache? The last time I was here you told me that your hands—"

Cory jumped when her grandmother stuck her head out the kitchen door and cried, "What are you two doing out there? Cory, come see me! All the interesting people are in here. Micah, you can stay there and talk to your father."

"Mother is as charming as ever," Micah murmured as Cory walked past him.

"Don't complain," she whispered back. "At least you get to stay out here."

When Cory entered the kitchen, her grandmother was stirring something in a pot. Cory opened her mouth to speak and froze; her mother was seated at the kitchen table shucking peas.

"Don't just stand there gaping like a guppy out of water," said her grandmother. "Come give me a kiss."

Cory kissed her grandmother on her cheek, but made no effort to go any closer to her mother. "Uncle Micah didn't say that Mother would be here."

"That's because I didn't tell him," her grandmother replied. "Your mother is very upset about this rift between you. I want you to sit down and work it out."

"There isn't anything to work out," said Cory. "We'll be fine if she'll stop trying to make me do something that I know is wrong for me."

Her grandmother tapped the spoon on the edge of the pot and turned to face Cory. "Really? Your mother said you quit the Tooth Fairy Guild. It seems to me that you have a great deal to work out."

"I'm fine with what I did. I'm not going back!" Cory cried, glaring at her mother.

"Now, Cory, you're being unreasonable," said Delphinium. "You must realize by now that you're never going to get anywhere doing what you're doing."

"What's she doing?" Grandmother demanded.

"I'm helping people," said Cory.

Delphinium sighed. "She's doing odd jobs, working for anyone who will pay her."

"And what's wrong with that?" asked Cory. "They're respectable people and I'm doing respectable work!"

"What did you do today?" asked her grandmother.

"I helped a woman can beans," said Cory.

Her grandmother raised one thin eyebrow. "And you're making a career out of this?"

"I'm doing it until I find exactly what I want to do with my life."

"And how long will that take?" asked her mother. "You're never going to find a career better than one at the Tooth Fairy Guild!"

Throwing her hands in the air, Cory said, "You really don't listen to me, Mother! I've told you time and again that the TFG is not for me. That's enough. I'm not talking about this anymore. Good-bye, Grandmother. I'm sorry I can't stay for supper."

Cory turned on her heel and left the room, but her mother and grandmother continued talking in voices loud enough that she could still hear them.

"She's just as stubborn and opinionated as her grand-father," her grandmother declared. "The whole time you knew him, he never would back down or change his mind."

"I know," said Delphinium. "I don't think I ever heard him admit that he was wrong. Now you see what I've had to deal with! Cory doesn't seem to understand that she's never going to amount to anything this way. I've tried to appease the TFG, but there won't be any stopping them if she doesn't return to them soon."

"It's your fault, you know. You never should have let it happen," Cory's grandmother declared. "You're her mother and you were her mentor. She lived in your house, yet you let her quit!"

"I didn't *let* her quit, Mother . . ."

"Uncle Micah, I'm going home. You're welcome to stay here if you want," Cory told him.

"I guess I will," said her uncle. "They're only just getting started with this fight. I should probably stick around to patch up the bruised egos when it's over."

CHAPTER
14

Cory didn't have any plans for the next day other than to put her mother's nagging out of her mind. It had preyed on her all the way home and kept her awake long into the night. She knew she shouldn't let it bother her, but it soured her mood and made her snap at Noodles when he nibbled her toes, something that didn't usually bother her.

Cory was pouring milk on her bowl of mixed grain and nuts when her uncle stopped by the kitchen to say good-bye. He had gotten up early and already eaten his breakfast.

"When did Mother and Grandmother stop fighting?" Cory asked him.

"They didn't, as far as I know. They were still at it when I left."

"Poor Grandfather," said Cory. "I'm sure he has to listen to that kind of thing all the time."

Micah shook his head. "Don't feel sorry for him. I think he's gotten good at tuning it out. It just becomes so much background noise after a while. So, what are you doing today?"

"Looking through the paper to see if anyone wants help with a project, I suppose," said Cory. "I am meeting a lot of interesting people this way."

Her uncle leaned down to give her a kiss on her cheek. "In that case, I hope something good turns up."

Cory waved as Micah left the room. She was reaching for the paper he'd left on the table when she heard the front door close and her uncle begin to whistle a tune. "I'm glad someone around here is happy."

Cory frowned when she opened the paper. Another picture of Santa Claus crowned the front page. Underneath it was an editorial saying that Santa Claus had no right to complain about the paparazzi. Public figures as prominent as Santa should expect to be under public scrutiny all the time, even when they were on vacation.

Cory didn't agree. As far as she was concerned, everyone should have some time to relax without anyone pestering them. She was studying the picture when it occurred to her that what Santa needed was something more private, like a vacation home. And she knew precisely which one. It didn't take her long to write a message.

Dear Santa,

    I think you need to take your vacation in a quiet spot where no one will bother you. I know just the place. A friend of mine is selling her house. It has lots of space and is right on the beach. Contact me if you are interested.

Corialis Feathering

To her surprise, Santa Claus sent her a reply only a few minutes later.

Dear Corialis,

    I would like to see the house, but I am very busy today. I will contact you when I have some free time.

Best wishes,
Santa Claus

She was returning to the kitchen when she heard a *ping!* behind her. It was Mrs. Dumpty wanting her to babysit Humpty again. Cory was pleased. She liked Humpty and would enjoy spending the day with him.

Cory had just entered her newest appointment in the notebook when she heard yet another message arrive.

Taking the notebook with her, she went back into the main room to fetch the message.

Cory,

My name is Priscilla Hood and I am a friend of Marjorie Muffet. She's told me that you are fixing her up with dates. Would you be able to do the same for me?

Sincerely,

Priscilla (Little Red Riding) Hood

Cory reread the note. She wasn't sure what to do. Finding the right person for Marjorie hadn't gone very well so far. The poor girl hadn't met anyone she wanted to see more than once, and Cory's visions hadn't been a bit of help. Oh, well. At least Marjorie was meeting eligible young men, which was all she'd really asked for.

Although Cory had never met Priscilla Hood, she didn't know of any reason why she couldn't try to help Marjorie's friend the way she was helping Marjorie. Cory seemed to be meeting more eligible bachelors all the time. Perhaps one of them would be the perfect match for Marjorie or her friend. After a few messages back and forth, Cory and Priscilla agreed to meet the next morning.

❯❯

Mrs. Dumpty met Cory at the door, holding a finger to her plump red lips. "My little angel is taking a nap," she said in a loud whisper. "You can sit in the main room while he sleeps. He'll come find you when he wakes up. Have fun!"

As soon as Cory stepped inside, Humpty's mother scurried out the door, her purse over her arm. Cory shut the door behind her, then went to check on Humpty. He was asleep on his bed clutching a stuffed toy mouse. Reassured that her charge was all right, Cory made her way to the main room.

Although the room was a little too yellow for her taste, it was pleasant enough and the upholstered chairs all looked very comfortable. Taking a seat on an over-stuffed chair in the corner, she spotted a pile of books on the table beside it. The biggest book on the bottom caught her eye, although it wasn't the title as much as the author that she found interesting. *One Hundred and One Unusual Insects and Where to Find Them* had been written by Marjorie Muffet.

The book was filled with brightly colored illustrations and descriptions of how and where Marjorie had found each subject. Some of the descriptions were fascinating and showed that sweet little Marjorie wasn't afraid to travel in very unusual places. One butterfly could be found only on the milkweed plants that grew outside a minotaur's cave. A certain kind of mantis lived in the grasslands where griffins hunted their prey. Mosquitoes as big as her hand swarmed in the forests where the Sasquatch roamed. None of them looked like places that Cory would want to visit.

Cory was leafing through the book when she came across a picture of the spiders that overran Marjorie's house. According to the caption, Marjorie had come across them in the deepest, darkest part of the Enchanted Forest while researching another book she had written titled *Odd and Unusual Creatures I Have Known*. Was it possible that the spiders had hitchhiked back in Marjorie's luggage?

Cory was flipping through the book when she heard a sound in the back of the house. Thinking that Humpty had woken from his nap, she set the book down and hurried to his bedroom. His door was open and his bed was empty. "Humpty!" Cory called. "Where are you?"

Cory searched the house from top to bottom, looking under beds, in closets and cupboards, behind doors, inside a clothes hamper, and on the top shelf of the linen closet without any luck. When she was sure that Humpty wasn't in the house, she went outside to search the yard. She looked in the trees and under the trees, behind the shrubs and in the shrubs, on the wall across the street and behind the wall across the street in case he had climbed up and fallen off the other side. She was look-ing behind the garden shed when she heard giggling and glanced up to find Humpty peeking down at her.

"What are you doing there?" she asked, craning her neck to peer up at him.

"Waiting for you to find me," the little boy replied. "I want you to come up here."

"Not today," Cory told him. "Today I want to play down here."

"I don't wanna," Humpty replied, dragging his stuffed toy mouse off the shed roof and hugging it to his chest.

"That's a very nice mouse," said Cory. "Can I see it?"

"You can if you come up here," said Humpty.

"I have some mice at my house," Cory said. "They live in a cage in my bedroom."

"Really?" said Humpty. "Are they real mice? The kind that squeak and run around?"

Cory nodded. "Yes, they are. I think you would like them very much. There are three of them and they're awfully cute," she told him in a very soft voice. "All three are brown, but one has a white spot on its chest."

"What did you say?" Humpty shouted. "I want to hear about the mice."

"And one has longer whiskers than the others," Cory continued, her voice so soft it was almost a whisper.

"But do you know what makes them different from any other mice I've ever seen?" she asked.

"What is it? What are you saying?" Humpty cried. "Hold on, I want to hear this!"

Cory watched as the little boy scrambled off the roof and down the ladder he had propped against the side. He scurried over to sit beside Cory and poked her in the ribs. "Tell me about the mice. I want to hear everything."

Cory repeated everything she had said, finishing with, "They are different from any other mice I have ever seen, because all three are blind and don't have any tails."

"Wow!" Humpty said. "I'd like to see a mouse like that! Could I see one? Could you bring one here?"

"If you are very good, and listen to me today, and don't try to climb anymore, I'll see if I can bring all three the next time I come. In the meantime, why don't you help me think of names for them?"

"I can do that!" said Humpty. "We can call one Fuzzy, or Tiger or Giggles or . . ."

Cory and Humpty were still sitting in the grass talking about the mice when his mother returned home. She seemed delighted to find them there and handed Cory some money even as she thanked her over and over for keeping Humpty on the ground.

"He was a very good boy today," Cory said as Humpty ran into the house with a small toy flower-fairy cart that his mother had just bought him. "The next time I come, he wants me to—"

Mrs. Dumpty started to back away. "Excuse me, but I've got to run inside. I don't want Humpty to play with that cart on my good furniture. It has water in a little toy barrel and he . . . Never mind! I'll see you next time! I'm sure whatever you want to do will be just fine!"

"—bring some mice," Cory finished, her voice fading away as Mrs. Dumpty dashed into the house.

It was late afternoon when Cory returned home to find another message waiting for her. A woman named Mary Mary needed some help with odd jobs. She wrote that she wanted to come by to discuss the jobs and talk about the fee. Cory felt a sense of satisfaction as she sent her a confirmation for a meeting the next morning. She'd had a good day with more work headed her way. She was making more money than she'd ever made as a tooth fairy while actually helping people. Delphinium might not like what her daughter was doing, but for once Cory could say that she was enjoying her work.

CHAPTER
15

Cory was up early the next day and dressed for her first meeting before her uncle Micah had even left the house. While waiting for Mary Mary to arrive, Cory washed the breakfast dishes, stood outside waiting for Noodles to finish snuffling around the yard, then went inside to tidy the main room.

Noodles was asleep in the kitchen when Mary Mary arrived. Although Cory had no idea what her visitor looked like, she didn't expect the stern-faced woman who knocked on the door. Mary Mary was older than Cory's own mother and looked as if she had never smiled in her whole life. Her eyes were a cold gray and her handshake was just as chilly.

Cory felt uncomfortable when Mary Mary's eyes

swept over her from head to toe. "So you're Cory. There's not much to you. Probably can't manage any heavy work. I don't know how you make a living doing this."

"What kind of jobs did you have in mind?" asked Cory.

"This and that," said Mary Mary. "I wanted to meet you before I invited you into my house. Unlike some of your customers, I won't let just any riffraff in. So tell me, what kind of work do you do exactly? How much experience do you have? I'll need a list of your former employers and references from each of them before I'll even consider hiring you."

Cory decided that she didn't like this woman. She wasn't sure if she wanted to do any work for her. "I'm afraid I don't give out the names of my clients," Cory replied. "And the work I do for them is confidential."

"How do I know you're honest and won't rob me?" said Mary Mary.

"I, uh . . ."

"If I'm not satisfied with your work, I won't pay you," Mary Mary declared.

"That's not how it—"

"It's the only way I'd hire you," the woman announced. She let her gaze wander across the room, examining everything from where she stood. Suddenly, she turned back to Cory, saying, "I need a drink of water. The air in your house is very dry."

"Uh, sure," said Cory. "I'll be right back."

Cory was fuming when she entered the kitchen. Not only was the woman unpleasant, but she was rude and demanding as well. While Cory fetched a glass of fresh spring water, she resolved to ask the woman to leave once she'd had her drink. However, when she returned to the main room, she forgot all about the water. The woman was standing by the message basket, paging through the list of clients in Cory's notebook.

"What are you doing?" Cory demanded.

The woman shut the notebook and set it down. "Don't use that tone with me!" she said as if Cory was the one who was rude.

"I want you to leave this house right now," Cory told her. "Get out and don't come back."

Mary Mary looked down her nose at Cory and said in a haughty voice, "No one has ever spoken to me that way before!"

"Well, someone has now!" Cory said, taking a step toward the woman.

Mary Mary retreated to the door. After casting one last disdainful glance at Cory, she strode from the house, leaving the door standing open behind her. Cory was closing the door when Noodles shambled into the room, sniffing the air as if he smelled something bad. Picking him up, Cory rubbed her cheek against his fur, gaining a small degree of comfort from his warmth.

"I don't know what just happened here," she murmured into his fur. "But I'm glad she's gone."

Cory thought for a moment about contacting Johnny Blue, but what would she tell him? Should she say that a nosy woman snooped through her notebook? Or that someone had come to her house and been very rude? She didn't really think that Mary Mary's visit was enough to report to the FLEA. After all, the woman hadn't taken anything. But even more than that, Cory was afraid that if she contacted Johnny Blue to tell him what had happened, it might look as if she was making up excuses to see him. For all she knew, it might be true.

Cory met with Priscilla Hood at Perfect Pastry for rose-hip tea. Priscilla arrived only a few minutes after Cory, who had already ordered them each a chocolate éclair. The waiter set the éclairs in front of them just as Cory turned to Priscilla and said, "Tell me a little about yourself. What do you do for a living?"

"I model outerwear," said Priscilla. "I just finished a big campaign for Lambkin's newest line of jackets. I started modeling when I was a little girl. That's where I got the name, Little Red Riding Hood."

"Uh-huh," said Cory. She wasn't surprised that Priscilla was a model. The young woman was as beautiful as a flower fairy with her long dark hair and green eyes. Cory had a feeling that men were going to fight over the chance to go out with Priscilla. "You're a beautiful young woman. Why do you want my help?"

"Most men go by first impressions. I want to meet someone who likes me for the person I am, not for the way I look or what I can do for them. Half of the men I meet want to show me off to their friends. The other half want only one thing from me—free outerwear. They dump me as soon as they learn that I don't have anything to do with men's overcoats or parkas. I want to meet ordinary men and I thought an ordinary girl like you could help me."

"Yeah, ordinary," Cory said with a wry twist to her lips. "What do you like to do?"

"I like to hike, swim, go rock climbing, hunt, and fish," said Priscilla. "Outdoors things mostly. I grew up in the forest and that's where I like to spend my free time."

"What kind of person do you want to meet?" asked Cory.

"Oh, gee," said Priscilla. "I guess he has to be intelligent, friendly, and adventuresome. He needs to like the same outdoors things that I do, especially hunting.

That's very important. Now I have a question for you. How much do you charge for helping people?"

Cory wasn't sure what to say. She had never thought about charging Marjorie, the only other person she had tried to help.

"How about fifteen gold crowns to start?" said Priscilla. "That's all I can afford right now, but if you think it should be more I can see about—"

"No, no! Fifteen gold crowns is just fine," Cory said, trying not to show her excitement. That was more than her mother earned in three months as a tooth fairy. To think that someone would be willing to pay that just to meet the right man!

"And in exchange for the fifteen gold crowns, you'll introduce me to eligible men until I meet the one I really like?"

"Uh, yes, that's exactly what I'll do," said Cory. Even if it took her years, she was sure she could find the right person for Priscilla.

Cory had to walk home because of the heavy coins, but that didn't stop her from smiling all the way to her uncle's house, the weight of the coins in her purse a reminder of her new wealth. Even the discovery that Noodles had chewed a hole in her bedroom carpet didn't dampen her spirits.

After cleaning up the bits of carpet fiber, she was walking through the main room when she glanced at the birds' nest on the mantel. The eggs had started hatching and the parents were flying out the window and returning with insects to feed their babies. While Cory watched, an adult bird brought back a large, wiggling spider to drop into a waiting hatchling's open beak. Suddenly, Cory had an idea.

After sending Marjorie a message, Cory gathered what she needed. She carried all of Noodle's toys to her room and closed him in, determined to talk to her uncle about a better way to house the woodchuck. The flight to Marjorie's didn't take long, and she was happy to find her friend waiting for her with a pitcher of tea and two tulip cups.

"I haven't seen you in a few days, so I thought we could talk for a bit before you get started," said Marjorie. "What have you been up to?"

"All sorts of things," Cory said, accepting a cup of tea. "I learned how to can beans, and I babysat again. Oh, a friend of yours contacted me. Priscilla Hood wants me to help her find the right man for her."

"I did mention you to her, but I didn't know she was thinking of contacting you," said Marjorie. "Are you going to do it?"

Cory nodded. "She's paying me to help her. For the amount she offered, I couldn't turn her down."

"She's paying you! Then I suppose I should, too. How much do you charge?"

"I don't intend to charge you anything," said Cory. "I'm doing it as a friend."

"Yes, I know that, but I think it's only right that if Priscilla is paying you, that I pay the same amount. How much is she giving you?"

"Fifteen gold crowns, but that's—"

"Then fifteen it is! I'll have to get my purse, though. It's in the house. So, now that that's settled, do you have anyone else for me to meet?"

"I do, actually," said Cory. She had given it a lot of thought and decided that Marjorie and Perky might get along very well. Marjorie wanted to meet someone with a good sense of humor and Perky had made everyone laugh at the last band rehearsal. Perky was a lot taller than Marjorie, but some girls preferred taller men. "His name is Perky and he's one of Santa's elves. He's living here in town now and has already joined Zephyr. I think you'll like him. He has a great sense of humor."

"I'd love to meet him!" Marjorie cried. "When can you arrange it?"

"Zephyr is playing at the Shady Nook tomorrow

night. Come see the show and I'll introduce you to Perky between sets."

When both of the girls had finished their drinks, Cory took the small bag of birdseed out of her purse. "I don't see how you can get rid of spiders with that," said Marjorie.

"Open the door to your house and watch," Cory told her.

Marjorie looked skeptical when she opened the back door, but she stepped aside and watched as Cory scattered birdseed across the yard and through the open door. A few minutes later, a sparrow spotted the seed and landed on the ground close enough to inspect it. As the little bird hopped closer, other birds came to investigate the bounty and soon a flock had gathered to peck at the seed. When one adventurous bird hopped across the threshold, following the trail of seed into the house, others soon joined him.

Cory and Marjorie peeked through the opening, trying not to startle the birds. A crow was pecking at the seeds on the kitchen floor when a spider the length of Cory's thumb emerged from under a cupboard. The bird cocked its head to the side, eyeing the spider. An instant later it jumped on the spider and swallowed it in one gulp. As other spiders emerged from the cracks in the floorboards and cupboards, birds flocked to snatch up the tasty treats.

Cory was beginning to think that her plan had been a success when a spider as big as her head scurried in from another room. The moment the enormous spider showed itself, the birds scattered, squawking and flying every which way until they found their way out the door. The spider froze at the sound of their cries and seemed to shrink in on itself, not moving until the birds were gone.

"Well, it got rid of some of the spiders," Marjorie said when she saw the disappointed look on Cory's face.

"I know, which is better than nothing, but I was hoping it would get rid of them all," said Cory. "I'll find something that will eventually, I'm sure of it."

"I'm sure you will, too," Marjorie told her. "It's just a matter of time."

"Speaking of time," said Cory. "What day is today?"

"Thursday. Why?"

"Because I have somewhere that I have to be on Thursday and I forgot all about it! I have three lawns to mow, and if I hurry I might have time before the sun sets."

"Bye, Cory!" Marjorie said as Cory shrank and spread her wings. "Thanks for trying!"

⇛➤

When Cory arrived at Cozynest Lane, she wasn't sure at first that she had reached the right place. Only one cottage stood at the end of the street—the brick house where Alphonse Porcine lived. The other two cottages were gone, their yards filled with debris. Straw, twigs, and pieces of broken furniture littered the ground where the houses had stood.

Cory was horrified. Had a tornado come through the town and touched down only on this street? Had something exploded, knocking these two cottages down? She hoped the two pigs who had lived in them were all right!

Cory glanced at the still-standing brick cottage and saw one of the curtains twitch back in place. Hurrying to the front door, she knocked and called out, "It's me, Cory. What happened here?"

"Is he gone?" called a frightened voice.

"Is who gone?" Cory asked. "There's no one out here but me."

"Go look around the house. We're not opening this door until we know for sure he's not there."

"I'll go look," said Cory. "But it would help to know who I'm looking for."

Cory walked around the house, looking for someone hiding in the bushes or behind the trees. She didn't see anything suspicious until she spotted large paw prints that showed some animal approached the house, and walked away again. She found the same thing in three other spots, but no sign that the animal was still there. After searching the area thoroughly, she returned to the front door and knocked again. "I looked all over. No one is out here."

"Are you sure?" a pig asked, opening the door a crack so she could see only part of its face.

"Yes, I'm sure. Tell me, what happened?" Cory said.

"It was the wolf," Alphonse told her as he nudged his brother aside and opened the door all the way. "I don't know how he found us, but he came by just a little while ago."

"He threatened Roger first," said Bertie. "When Roger wouldn't come out of his house of straw, the wolf blew it down."

Roger stepped into the doorway. "I ran out the back door to Bertie's house."

"So then he threatened us both. When he started huffing and puffing, we ran out the back door of my house and came here, to Alphonse's. The stupid wolf blew down my lovely house of twigs!" said Bertie.

"He tried to blow my house down, too," said Alphonse, "but even a wolf as big and bad as Lewis can't blow down bricks."

"You know his name?" said Cory.

Bertie nodded. "He's the reason we went into hiding."

"Let me tell her," said Roger. "It's my story. One day when I was just a piglet, I was on my way home from school when I saw the wolf blow down a flower fairy's shop."

"It was Goldenrod, a friend of ours, who had given up taking care of goldenrod flowers so she could sell lots of different kinds. The Flower Fairy Guild got mad and sent Lewis after her. No one would have known that if Roger hadn't seen Lewis blow down the shop," said Bertie.

"My story, remember!" Roger told him. "Anyway, when I told Alphonse and Bertie what I'd seen, they had me go to the Fey Law Enforcement Agency. The FLEA went after Lewis, and he was locked away for a year. Before he went to jail, he sent one of his men to kidnap me."

"Tom Tom had Roger for less than an hour before the police caught him," said Alphonse. "It scared us all, so we went into hiding. I wish I knew how they found us today."

"I think I might know," said Cory. "A woman came by my home this morning. She looked through my notebook when I left the room and may have seen your address there. I suppose it's possible that she told the wolf."

"So it's your fault!" Bertie exclaimed.

"Now we're going to have to move again!" cried Roger. "Where are we going to go?"

Alphonse sighed. "We'll have to start looking. And I did so like this neighborhood."

"Did you call the FLEA today?" asked Cory.

"Why? I would just make Lewis madder and then he'd come back for sure. We want him to go away and stay away."

"But the FLEA could protect you," said Cory.

Alphonse shook his head. "What are they going to do—camp out in front of our house? They won't do anything until something dire happens first. No, the only thing that can protect us is a house with stout walls and we're going to have to find that ourselves!"

When Cory returned to her uncle's house, she sent a message to Johnny Blue as soon as she walked in the door. All she did was ask him to come see her, because she wasn't sure what else to say. The pigs weren't going to contact the FLEA, but at least she could report her side of what had happened. She felt terrible about what the wolf had done and was convinced that it *was* all her fault. If only she hadn't written their names and addresses in her notebook. If only she hadn't let Mary Mary in the house, or left her alone in the room. If only . . . Cory sat on the edge of a chair and stared blindly out the window. She could "if only" from here to tomorrow, but that wasn't going to change the real reason this had happened: she had left the Tooth Fairy Guild and tried to make a living without it.

Cory glanced down when Noodles made a chirring sound and shoved his head into the palm of her hand. His big, dark eyes looked sympathetic, almost as if he understood what she was thinking. "It's my fault, Noodles. I feel just awful! It was one thing to mess up my own life, but I never meant to mess up anyone else's! I was trying to help people; instead I'm making some of their lives more difficult. And look at poor Uncle Micah. He was kind enough to let me stay with him, and what has he gotten for it? His house vandalized, his rug torn up . . . Well, that part was your fault, Noodles, but it still happened because I'm here. What should I do, Noodles? I can't keep going like this!"

The woodchuck chirred again and Cory reached down to pet him. *At least he's all right*, she thought.

There was a knock on the door a few minutes later. When Johnny Blue saw her face, he took her hands in his as if to console her. It was the first time he had touched her and it made her stomach queasier than ever. She pulled away and tried to make it look natural by bending down to pick up Noodles. The feeling eased but didn't go away.

"What's wrong?" he asked.

Cory glanced at him, wondering if he had noticed her reaction for what it was, but decided that he was talking about the message. "I wanted to tell you about something that happened to some friends of mine. They're pigs, and I mean that literally. Three brothers, actually, who had a run-in with a wolf a few years ago. The FLEA locked the wolf away, but not before he told one of his henchmen to kidnap the youngest pig. The young man was found and sent to jail, too. The pigs moved away and were safe for a time, until they met me. After I went to their house to mow their lawns, I put their names in my notebook. A woman named Mary Mary came by and looked through my notebook when I was out of the room. Before you know it, the wolf had found the pigs and threatened to blow down their houses. He actually blew down two of them and they all took refuge in the third."

Noodles squirmed in Cory's arms, so she set him on the floor again. He ambled over to Johnny and bumped his head against the young man, asking to be picked up.

"And you feel responsible for the wolf finding the pigs," said Johnny.

When Noodles became more insistent, Johnny bent down to scratch the woodchuck's head.

Cory shrugged and said, "If I hadn't written their

addresses in my notebook, that woman wouldn't have read them and the pigs would still be safe in their homes. But that isn't why I asked you to come see me. I knew something wasn't right about that woman, Mary Mary, when she was here. I should have told you then. I have a feeling that she might have something to do with the TFG, and I was hoping you could find out if it's true. Are they trying to get at me through my friends now? It was bad enough when they made it rain or sent plagues of seagulls, but it's so much worse if they are actually taking it out on people I'm trying to help."

"I'll see what I can find out," Johnny told her. When he said good-bye, Cory thought his eyes looked sad, and she hoped it wasn't because of her.

CHAPTER
16

*W*hen Cory stumbled out of her room the next morning, knuckling the sleep from her eyes, she noticed that the front door was standing open. "Uncle Micah?" she called.

"I'm out here," her uncle replied from the front porch. "We've had another visitor."

Cory's heart sank as she headed for the porch. What awful thing had the TFG done this time? Expecting to find splattered mud or squirming worms, she was surprised to see that the vandalism was actually pretty. Someone had planted bright red poppies in the front lawn, spelling out *Corialis Feathering Is a Traitor!*

"The flowers are so beautiful that I almost hate to dig them up," her uncle told her.

"If only it said something nice," said Cory.

Micah turned to face her. "Are you too busy to deal with this today? You could dig them up or mow them down. Mowing would be faster if you're pinched for time."

"I think I'll transplant them," Cory told him. "I don't have any plans until tonight. Zephyr is playing at the Shady Nook, but I'm free until then. The way things are going, I think I'd rather stay home today anyway."

"In that case," said Micah, "you can plant them wherever you'd like."

"I know just where to put them," said Cory. "But first I should send a message to Johnny."

This time she kept the message very short.

More vandalism.
Cory

Cory was outside waiting for Johnny when he rode up on a solar cycle. The cycle reminded her of the noisy motorcycles she'd seen in the human world, only these were solar powered and nearly silent. A rider started the cycle by pedaling for a minute or two. After that, the solar power kicked in and he wouldn't need to pedal again unless the day became overcast. The more expensive cycles were spell powered and never needed pedaling, but Johnny's was the less-expensive kind.

After propping his cycle against a tree, Johnny came to the porch to see her.

"It was like this when my uncle got up this morning," Cory told him as she gestured to the flowers. "I love the poppies and would leave them there if they didn't call me a traitor."

Johnny nodded and went right to work examining the flowers and writing things down on a fresh leaf while she stood on the porch and watched him.

"Someone took a lot of care in planting these flowers," Johnny said a few minutes later. "Whoever did it planted them at just the right depth. If we were to dig them up now, I bet we'd find that they had been fertilized, too. It looks like flower-fairy work. If the Tooth Fairy Guild is behind this, they must have enlisted the Flower Fairy Guild to help them."

"I met a woman recently who told me that she used to be a flower fairy, but after she married a human the guild kicked her out and tried to ruin her life."

"I had no idea that the guilds did this kind of thing," said Johnny. "I don't know if anyone in the squad does either. To be honest, the officers act like I'm wasting my time here. I tried to find out if that woman, Mary Mary, is a member of the TFG, but the guild is very secretive. When I asked the members of the squad, they were less than helpful. I'll keep digging and see what I can find.

Speaking of digging, would you like some help with the flowers? Do you want to dig them up or mow them down or what?"

"Actually, I thought I'd transplant them and—"

A faint chime rang nearby. Johnny patted his pocket and pulled out a rigid, flat leaf. After studying it for a moment, he put it back in his pocket and said, "I have to go. Send me another message if anything else happens. I'll try to see what I can learn about the guilds."

Cory watched Johnny ride off, wishing he could have stayed a little longer. He was nearly out of sight when she went back inside to feed Noodles and eat her own breakfast. When they were finished, she lugged him outside and kept an eye on him while she dug up the plants at the end of the sentence. She was placing the plants in a basket to carry to another part of the yard when a little woman walking her boar stopped by.

"'Corialis Feathering is a trai' . . . ," the woman read. "At first I thought you were planting the flowers, but now I see you're digging them up. What's wrong with them? Did you misspell something?"

Cory sighed. It was bad enough explaining to people she knew that she'd quit the guild. It was worse if the people asking questions were strangers. Who in their right mind leaves a prestigious career without knowing what she's going to do next? Even so, Cory hated lying even more than she hated explaining herself.

"I quit the Tooth Fairy Guild recently," she finally said. "They're showing how mad they are by doing things like this. Before I started digging the flowers up, it said, 'Corialis Feathering Is a Traitor.'"

"A guild did that? Pay them no mind. The guilds think they can run our lives. They don't own us, and it's about time they learned it."

"You sound as if you were in a guild," Cory said.

"No, but two different witches' guilds have tried to make me join. The OWOW, or Organized Witches of the World, and the WU, Witches United. I'm an independent and always have been. Theodore! Stop rooting around those flowers! This isn't your yard."

The boar snorted and turned to look at the witch. Taking a beet out of her purse, she waved it in the air until the boar came waddling over. "I'd better go," said the witch. "Theo gets ornery if he's not fed right after his walk. We're neighbors, by the way. I live two doors down in the house with the miniature mangrove swamp in the back."

"Nice to meet you!" said Cory.

"You, too!" said the witch. "I'm Wanita, by the way. Too bad about the flowers. They are pretty!"

"Would you like some?" Cory asked, gesturing to the rest of the poppy sentence. "I really don't need so many."

"I *could* use some in my window box . . ."

"Help yourself!" Cory told her.

Promising to return with a basket for the plants, Wanita left, taking her boar home. Minutes later, Salazar and his iguana, Boris, passed by. The genie wouldn't have stopped if the iguana hadn't seen the flowers and tried to drag his owner halfway across the yard.

"Sorry about this," Salazar said as he pulled the iguana off the lawn. The lizard had a mouthful of blossoms and kept turning its head to eye the rest.

"It's all right," said Cory. "It just means there are fewer to transplant."

"'Corialis Featheri,'" read the genie.

Wanita arrived in a puff of smoke with a large, flat-bottomed basket. ". . . 'Is a Traitor!' I don't mean she is, but that's what the sign said. The Tooth Fairy Guild is persecuting her because she quit the guild."

"Really?" said Salazar, his wispy blue eyebrows shooting up. "Good for you! I wish I'd quit the Genie Guild when I was young enough to do something else. I retired last year after a thousand years of the same old drudgery. Oh, sure, I enjoyed the job for a century or two, but after that it was the same thing, year after year. If I could have found another way to make a living, I would have done it a dozen times over. So, what is it you do now?"

"I'm sort of between careers," said Cory. "Right now, I'm taking jobs here and there until I find what I really want to do."

"That's a good idea!" said the witch. "A lot of people would be happier if they turned their favorite pursuit into a career. I know that I've been happier since I started creating mayhem."

Wanita was still talking when the brown-haired, cat-eyed girl who lived down the street strolled to the edge of the yard. The black leopard she was walking sat down beside her to stare at Cory. "What's going on?" the girl asked. "Are you planning some sort of party? Because if you are, I want in. What's that you wrote? 'Corialis Featheri' . . . Is having a birthday party? Is that what it's going to say?"

"I didn't actually write this," Cory said as she glanced at the poppies. When she turned back to the girl, she blinked and stared openmouthed. A spotted leopard now sat where the girl had stood, and a girl with long black hair stood where the black leopard had been sitting.

"The Tooth Fairy Guild did it," announced Wanita. "Don't mind Felice and Selene," she told Cory. "They're shape-shifters and love to play that trick on people. They live in the house just past mine."

The girl with the long dark hair laughed. "Sorry, we can't resist. I'm Selene and my sister is Felice."

The air shimmered around the spotted leopard and it disappeared, leaving the girl with brown hair in its place. "Whoever planted the flowers did a beautiful job. I didn't know the members of the Tooth Fairy Guild were so good with plants," she said. "If you ask me, they had a flower fairy do it."

"I think you're right," Cory said. "I met a former flower fairy recently who said that her guild hounded her, too. She told me that the guilds all stick together."

"Well, I've never been a guild member and I never want to be!" said Selene. "It sounds as if they can be really nasty if you cross them."

"Which flowers can I take?" Wanita asked, holding up her basket.

"Whichever ones you want," said Cory.

"Can I have some, too?" asked Felice. "I'd like to put them by the entrance to our den."

Cory laughed, happy to have fewer plants to move. "Be my guest. Would you like some as well?" she asked the genie.

"I'm tempted, but I really shouldn't," he replied, tugging the iguana back with its leash. "Boris would eat them and get sick to his stomach."

"This is very kind of you," Wanita said as she filled

her basket. "And I've made a habit of rewarding kindness. Is there anything I can do for you in return?"

"Not really," said Cory. "But I'll let you know if I think of something."

After her neighbors had taken some of the plants, Cory transplanted the rest to the sunny side of the house. It took her most of the day, with only a short break for lunch. Noodles waddled around the yard, nibbling grass and starting a hole by the garden shed. He seemed to enjoy spending the day outdoors, but Cory's knees and back hurt by the time she was finished.

That night Cory left early for the Shady Nook with her uncle Micah, who wanted to hear the band play. Cheeble, Olot, and Chancy were there when they arrived and had already unloaded Cory's drums from Olot's cart. She was checking her drums, making sure everything was the way she wanted it, when she saw Marjorie come in and take a seat by the stage. A few minutes later Olot introduced the band and Cory became lost in the music.

They started with "Morning Mist," earning even bigger applause than when they'd played it at Sprats'. The clapping had scarcely died down when they began to play "Rebirth," a song that carried the audience from autumn through spring. "Owl Goes A-Hunting" brought the night sounds of the forest into the restaurant, ending with the squeak of a captured mouse. More than one person jumped in his seat, as startled as the mouse, then laughed at his own reaction. "Storm-Chased Maid" brought the audience to their feet and some of them began dancing. After playing "Shooting Stars," the band finally took a break.

"Perky, come with me," Cory said, gesturing to the elf before he could leave the stage. "There's someone I want you to meet."

Perky's eyes lit up when he saw Marjorie. She welcomed him to her table, and Cory excused herself, thinking that she might find Johnny Blue. He wasn't there, however, and she was surprised by how disappointed she felt. She'd been so certain he'd come to hear Zephyr as he had when they'd played at Sprats'.

Cory was headed into the back room to get a drink of juice when she bumped into Daisy. They went in together and got their juice before taking seats in an out-of-the-way corner. "How are things with you and Peterby?" Cory asked before taking a sip. "Has he freed any unicorns lately?"

Daisy shrugged. "Probably. He's in the Blue Forest now. Yesterday he heard that Prince Rupert had a unicorn in his menagerie, so he went to free it. When we started dating, I didn't know he was going to be gone most of the time."

"If he's freeing unicorns . . . ," said Cory.

"I know, I know. He has to go where the unicorns are held, but that doesn't mean I have to like it. That's all right. I already have a new boyfriend. He works for one of the guilds, so he spends most of his time in town."

"What does he do?" Cory asked.

"Security," said Daisy.

Olot appeared in the doorway and waved to them. "Come along, ladies. Our break is over."

Cory and Daisy drained their drinks and hurried after him. "We'll talk later," Daisy said as they approached the bandstand.

When everyone had returned to the stage, they played more of their older songs, starting with "The Last Flight of Silver Streak." Cory had a long solo in "Thunder's Clap" with Cheeble stepping in now and then to wave a big sheet of metal, creating the rumble of thunder. People got up and danced during most of the last set, so the band ended with a slow song, "Dusk in the Meadow," inviting more couples to dance.

Cory felt exhilarated when they finished playing. The audience had loved their music, Zephyr had played their very best, and she had enjoyed herself tremendously. She was so excited that she wanted to talk to someone about it, and noticed that Perky was talking to Marjorie, and Daisy was talking to Micah, Olot, and Chancy. Before she could join them, however, she had to take care of her drums.

She had just finished covering her drums when a waitress who had been talking to someone near the stage turned suddenly and bumped into her. A glass of raspberry juice fell over on her tray, dumping its contents on Cory.

"I'm so sorry!" the waitress cried.

"It's all right," said Cory, examining the damp spot on her shirt. "Just tell me how to get to the washing up room so I can clean this off." Cory left and was back only a few minutes later, but when she looked for her friends, the only ones left were Olot and Chancy.

"Where did everyone go?" she asked Chancy.

"They left just a minute ago," said Chancy. "We thought you'd already gone."

Feeling let down, Cory left the Shady Nook and turned toward home. She was too excited to fly straight there, so she decided to walk, hoping she might run into her friends on the way. Although it was after midnight, the streets were still bustling with people enjoying the cool night air. Cory was passing Sprats' restaurant when she noticed a sign on the door announcing that Johnny Blue was appearing there solo that night.

That's why he didn't come to hear us, she thought, feeling oddly relieved. There was no one at the door to seat her, so she slipped inside and stood near the back of the room. Johnny was perched on a stool in the middle of the stage, playing a song that was so beautiful she was entranced within moments. When he finished playing, the restaurant was completely silent until suddenly the applause began and everyone was on their feet. Johnny looked up and grinned. "Thank you," was all he said before leaving the stage.

Johnny was on his way to the office in the back of the restaurant when Cory started toward him. When he stopped to speak with someone, she hurried to get closer and was at arm's length when he finally noticed her.

"Cory! What are you doing here? I thought Zephyr was playing at the Shady Nook tonight."

"We were, I mean, we did," she told him. "We finished just a little while ago."

"In that case, why don't you join me for a late supper? Unless you aren't hungry."

"I'm hungry, all right," said Cory. "I haven't had much to eat today."

Many of the restaurants' patrons had left when Johnny finished playing, so they didn't have any trouble finding a table. Cory was delighted when he pulled a chair out for her, something Walker had never done. "How did it go?" he asked as he sat down. "Did you like playing at the Shady Nook?"

"It was fantastic!" said Cory. "I think it was the best we've ever played, and the audience loved us and my solo went off perfectly and . . . Wait! Here I am talking about my playing when I really wanted to tell you how much I loved yours. I heard only the last song, but it was so beautiful!"

"Thank you!" he said, giving her a warm smile. "I wrote it myself. I'm sorry I missed hearing you play tonight. Maybe next time . . ."

A waiter appeared at the table and they sat back in their seats while he placed menus in front of them. He was just walking away when a beautiful blond-haired girl only a little older than Cory appeared.

"Johnny? Johnny Blue? Is that really you? I'm sure you don't remember me, but my family used to live just down the lane from yours. I'm Mary Lambkin. When I was a young girl, you had a black sheep and one summer you got three bags of wool from it. You gave one to the man you were working for, one to your mother, and one to me. That wool changed my life."

"I remember that!" said Johnny. "What did you do with the wool?'

"I washed it and carded it and spun it into yarn. That wool is what started my interest in fashion. I have my own company and . . . oh, do you mind if I sit down?" she said, turning to Cory.

"Not at all," Cory said, although she really didn't like the way the girl had intruded and wished she would go away.

The girl gave her a bright smile and took a seat between Cory and Johnny. Turning her back to Cory, she continued to tell Johnny Blue about how much the gift of wool had meant to her.

"We were about to order supper," Johnny said when the waiter stopped to see if they were ready. "Would you like to join us?"

"I'd love to!" she replied. "I just need a moment to look at the menu."

Cory's heart sank as the waiter walked away. Up until then, she had assumed the girl would leave at any moment, but now she knew that wasn't going to happen. The more Mary Lambkin talked about old times, the more left out Cory felt. When the waiter came back again, Cory set her menu on the table and pushed back her chair. "I'm sorry, it's getting late and I'm going to have a busy day tomorrow. Thank you for inviting me to stay," she told Johnny. "Enjoy your supper," she told them both.

Cory walked away, thinking that Johnny and Mary Lambkin were really hitting it off, but when she glanced back and saw the way he was watching her instead of the girl sitting beside him, Cory wasn't so sure.

CHAPTER
17

Once in a while Cory's visions came in her sleep. The only reason she knew they were visions and not dreams was that she was able to remember them so well the next day. That night she had a vision of a girl she thought might be Red Riding Hood and a boy who could perhaps be Jack Nimble, although their faces were so blurry that she couldn't be sure. Even so, she was already planning to send messages to both Priscilla Hood and Jack Nimble when she left her bedroom that morning. It took her only a few minutes to write them. When she went to send the messages, she found that one had arrived the night before while she was out. Doris Dumpty wanted Cory to babysit from eleven to five.

"I can babysit today," Cory told Noodles, "but I'm going to have to decide if I really want to be a babysitter or what." Zephyr had played even better than they'd hoped at the Shady Nook, and were actually starting to make money. There was a chance that she could quit doing her odd jobs altogether and concentrate on her music. In a way the thought delighted her, but in another way it didn't feel quite right. She loved playing with the band, certainly more than she'd liked collecting teeth, but was it really helping anyone? Cory hadn't left the TFG because of money, although that had been part of it.

Cory sent a message back to Mrs. Dumpty, saying that she would be there at eleven. Two other messages arrived as Cory was turning away. The first was from Priscilla, thanking her for finding someone so quickly, and saying that she wondered if Cory could meet her at the park at five thirty. The other message was from Marjorie. Cory was certain that her friend was going to have only good things to say about Perky, but she was wrong again.

> *Cory,*
>
> *I'm sorry to have to tell you this, but Perky is not the right one for me. All he talks about is Christmas and Santa Claus. He wasn't at all interested in hearing about me or what I like to do. Do you know of anyone else I could meet?*
>
> *Marjorie*

Cory sighed. It sounded as if Marjorie wasn't planning to give Perky a chance. But then, maybe they really *weren't* right for each other. She sent a message to Marjorie saying that she would keep looking.

The finch on the mantel sang the half hour, reminding Cory that it was almost time to leave. In order to show the mice to Humpty, she'd have to take the pedal-bus instead of flying. If Mrs. Dumpty was back by five o'clock, Cory could take the bus to the park and still get there with time to spare.

Cory arrived at the Dumptys' house precisely at eleven, but Mrs. Dumpty was already in a hurry to leave. Holding up the shoe box, Cory said, "Before I see Humpty, I want to ask you if it's all right if I—"

"I'm sure it's fine, whatever it is," Doris Dumpty said, checking her reflection in the mirror on the wall as she pinned a tiny saucer-shaped hat to her hair. "I'm having lunch in town with RJ, then going shopping with some friends. Humpty has been waiting for you all morning. You two have fun today! Bye!"

Mrs. Dumpty was gone before Cory could say anything more. "I tried!" she told herself as she started toward Humpty's room.

The little boy was sitting on his bed with a book

open in front of him. "Did you bring the mice?" he asked. "I found a story you could read to them. It's about a mouse that pulls a thorn out of a big cat's paw and they become friends. I have some other books they might like, too."

"I have the mice right here," Cory said, sitting down beside him. "We have to be careful when we open the box. You don't want them to get loose."

"Ooh!" Humpty said as Cory lifted the lid. The little mice were nibbling some cereal she'd given them and they turned toward Humpty when he cooed. "Can I hold one?" he asked, his hand hovering above the box.

"I don't know why not," said Cory. "I've been handling them ever since I brought them home, and they've never tried to bite me. Just be gentle."

Humpty reached into the box and lifted out one of the mice, holding it ever so carefully. Cory smiled when she saw the look of delight on his face and decided that taking the pedal-bus just so the little boy could see the mice had been worth it.

While Humpty held each of the mice, one at a time, Cory read his books out loud. Everything was fine until Cory said that he had to put the mice back in the box.

"Can I show them my room before I put them back?"

he asked, and gave her such a plaintive look that she couldn't say no.

"They're blind, remember? They can't see it."

"Then I'll tell them about it!" said Humpty. Still holding one of the mice, Humpty picked up the other two before squirming off the bed. Starting with the table by the wall, he carried the mice from place to place, describing everything in detail. "And this is the floor," he finally said, getting down on his knees and elbows. "It's flat and you could run all over it if I put you down. There's a rug on it that would feel good under your paws. Here, I'll let you feel it for yourselves."

"Humpty, no!" Cory cried, but the little boy had already set the mice on the floor. An instant later, the three blind mice had run under the bed.

"Uh-oh!" Humpty exclaimed, sitting back on his heels. "They got away."

"There has to be a way to get them to come out," said Cory. "Maybe if you make noise at that end, they'll come down here and I can catch them."

"Okay!" said Humpty. He tapped on the floor, but the mice didn't appear.

"Do you have any crackers or cereal?" Cory finally asked. "They might come out for food."

"I'll be right back," Humpty said, and took off down the hall. When he returned, he had a handful of cookies.

Giving one to Cory, he climbed onto his bed and began to eat the others.

Cory broke off a piece of cookie and set it on the floor. She sat back to wait, but no mice appeared.

"Read me another book!" said Humpty.

"I will after we've caught the mice."

Humpty scowled, but his face lit up again when he said, "I'll watch for the mice while you read the book! I'll tell you when I see them."

"All right," said Cory. "But we have to catch them before your mother comes home."

"I know," he said, and got down on the floor so he could see under the bed.

For the next fifteen minutes, Cory read stories to Humpty while he lay beside her with his head pillowed on his arm, watching for the mice. She was reaching for another book when she realized that the little boy had fallen asleep. Not wanting to wake him, she took a folded blanket from the end of his bed and covered him with it.

None of the mice appeared for the next hour and a half. When Humpty woke, Cory made his lunch while he watched for the mice. After he ate, they played board games on the floor next to his bed until they heard his mother at the front door. Humpty went with Cory to see her.

"How was your day?" Mrs. Humpty asked as she took off her hat.

"The mice got away, and we couldn't catch them!" Humpty announced. "I took my nap on the floor and ate cookies before lunch!"

"What?" Mrs. Dumpty said, turning a horrified look on Cory. "Did he say *mice*?"

Cory nodded. "I told him about my pet mice the last time I was here and he wanted to see them. I tried to ask you if it was all right, but you were so busy. I brought them today and—"

"You brought mice into my *house* and let them *loose*?" Mrs. Dumpty shrieked. "What were you thinking?"

"Humpty was being very careful with them until—"

"That's enough!" the woman shouted. "Get out of my house! You are never coming back here again! And I thought you were such a good babysitter!"

Cory started toward the door, then hesitated, wondering if she should apologize or say anything at all.

The woman took a step closer. "I am not going to pay you, either, if that's what you're waiting for. Go on. Leave!" She started making shooing motions with her hands, chasing Cory out the door. "In fact, I'm going to send you a bill for the exterminator."

Mrs. Humpty was closing the door when Cory heard Humpty ask, "What's an exterminator, Mama?"

Without the box and the mice to weigh her down, Cory was able to fly to the park across the street from Sprats', so she arrived there earlier than she'd expected. She was sitting on a bench, feeling bad about the mice, when she saw Priscilla Hood get off the pedal-bus with Mary Lambkin.

"Cory!" Priscilla called. Grinning, she hurried over to the bench where Cory was seated, while Mary followed behind "This is Mary Lambkin, my friend that I wanted you to meet," said Priscilla. "Mary, this is Cory."

"Mary and I have met," said Cory, nodding to Priscilla's friend. After what had happened at the Dumpty's house, she wasn't feeling very sociable.

"Right!" said Mary. "Last night. You were sitting with Johnny Blue. You left so suddenly that I didn't really get to talk to you. Last night was such a disappointment! Johnny was an old friend of mine," she told Priscilla. "He was very shy when he was young and I see he hasn't changed. I'd hoped I might be able to fan some flames, but there wasn't even a spark. I was so disappointed!"

"I bet Cory could help you, too," said Priscilla.

"I hope so!" Mary said. "I really want to meet someone special, but I'm way too busy to meet someone on my own. How much do you charge?"

"I'm not sure I'm taking on any more clients right now," said Cory.

"Don't be silly. I'll pay whatever Priscilla is paying you. Twice if necessary. Here's my leaf. Call me when you're ready to talk."

While the two girls walked away, Cory glanced down at the leaf Mary had left in her hand. Written on the leaf were Mary's name and messaging address. "I don't know about this," Cory said with a sigh. She had yet to help anyone find a match they really liked. Should she really take on more people?

When Cory returned home that evening, she found a message from Gladys waiting for her.

Cory,

The strangest thing just happened. I was coming home from work when a woman followed me to my front door like she'd been waiting for me. She wouldn't give me her name, but she insisted on telling me what a bad businessperson you are, and that you do terrible work. She told me that you neglect the children you babysit, you let them eat whatever they want, make them sleep on the floor, and play with vermin that you bring to the house. I wish you could have heard the way I told her off! I said that none of that was true and that you had helped me out when I really needed it. I

*told her that you were great with children and that my
brood, who hate most babysitters, can't wait to have
you back. I don't want to upset you, but I thought you
should know about this crazy woman.*

> *Best wishes,
> Gladys*

"I bet it was that woman, Mary Mary," Cory said to
Noodles, except the woodchuck wasn't there. "Noodles!"
she called, peeking in the kitchen. He wasn't there
either, nor was he in her bedroom, or her uncle's room,
or anywhere else in the house. "Did I take him out this
morning and forget to bring him back in?" she wondered, although she was sure she'd put him in her room.
After checking the house one last time, Cory stepped
out the back door, locking it behind her.

"Noodles!" she called as she checked the yard, looking
behind every shrub and around the far side of the garden
shed where he'd been digging a hole.

When Cory couldn't find Noodles in the yard, she
began to search the neighborhood. She met Wanita
walking her boar and Felice with her sister, Selene,
and told them that her woodchuck was missing. They
offered to watch for him on their walks. Cory scoured
the three blocks around her uncle's house, including the
park across the street. She did spot a woodchuck in a

small meadow, but it was much bigger than Noodles and didn't look anything like him. The sun was starting to set when the rain began, but Cory didn't give up until it was almost too dark to see.

When Cory returned home, she noticed that the porch light was on; her uncle was home. Worried about Noodles, she was anxious to talk to Micah and might not have noticed the parchment half hidden under the sea-grass mat if the breeze hadn't made the end flutter. Cory picked it up and discovered that it was a note written in the same sprawling script as the previous notes.

This kind of thing doesn't happen to tooth faiRies!

Cory sucked in her breath as she finally understood what had really happened. Noodles hadn't wandered off. The Tooth Fairy Guild had taken him!

CHAPTER
18

*B*efore she got dressed the next morning, Cory sent a message to Johnny Blue.

The Tooth Fairy Guild kidnapped Noodles.
Cory

When she shuffled into the kitchen, her uncle said, "Here's something I never thought I'd see."

"What?" Cory asked, glancing down at her robe and slippers. "I look like this every morning."

"Not you," said Micah. He held up a message he'd plucked from the basket. "This! It's a message for you from Santa Claus."

Cory snatched the message from his hand and read it out loud.

Corialis Feathering,

If you have the time today, I'd be interested in seeing that house you mentioned.

Ho, Ho, Ho,
Santa Claus

Cory was still half asleep after staying up most of the night, worrying about Noodles. "Of course he would pick today," she said, yawning.

Micah reread the note over her shoulder. "What house is he talking about?"

"Suzy's. I guess I should ask her if we can come by."

"Good idea," said her uncle. "Although I can't imagine that anyone would mind a visit from Santa."

It took Cory just a minute to write the note.

Suzy,

If it is convenient for you, I would like to bring Santa Claus around to see your house this morning. He needs a vacation property and I think yours would be perfect for him.

Cory

She was surprised by how quickly Suzy wrote back.

Cory,

Santa Claus! Of course you can come over!

Suzy

"I'll be right back," she told her uncle, yawning again. "I'm going to get dressed before I eat. Johnny should be stopping by soon."

"Is he the only one the FLEA sends?" her uncle asked.

Cory nodded. "They don't think it's very important, so they send an officer-in-training. I'm glad, though. At least I feel as if he believes me."

She was still in her room getting dressed when Johnny knocked on the door. Cory threw on the rest of her clothes and hurried to answer it. Her uncle was there before her and had already invited Johnny inside. Although Johnny was at least two feet taller, Micah seemed to be the one in charge.

"Yes, sir," Johnny said, looking slightly nervous. "I did keep up with my music lessons. I even play in public now sometimes."

"And your parents? How are they?" asked Micah.

"Just fine, sir. Thanks for asking." When Johnny glanced up and saw Cory, his expression softened.

Micah turned and saw his niece standing there. His

mouth quirked in an almost smile as he stepped out of the way. "I'll let Cory tell you what happened," he said. "Keep up the good work, Officer."

"You know my uncle?" Cory asked once they were alone.

Johnny nodded. "I had him for some classes in school. He was my favorite teacher. In fact, if it weren't for him, I would have given up playing the trumpet in my second year. Money was tight in my house, but he talked to my parents and told them how important music was to me. Practicing my music was the only thing that kept me from spending all my time with a pretty rough crowd. It was the only thing I'd ever found that let me express how I really felt. Your uncle talked to my music teacher and we worked it out so I could get a part-time job and still take lessons. So he's your uncle, huh? I didn't know that. You don't have the same last name."

"He's my mother's brother," said Cory. "Fleuren is a flower-fairy name, although neither my mother nor my uncle became flower fairies."

"You said that the TFG took Noodles?" Johnny said, referring to a leaf. "That was the woodchuck, right?"

"I've had him for about five years," said Cory. "I came home yesterday and he wasn't here. I thought he might have wandered off, so I looked all over the neighborhood for him. When I got home last night, this note was left on the front porch." Cory handed him the note and watched while he read it.

"It's escalating," he said finally. "Whoever is behind this is going beyond damaging property. I'll talk to the captain and see what he says."

"Do you think the person who kidnapped Noodles is going to hurt him?" Cory asked, her fear showing in her eyes.

"He'd better not," said Johnny. "I like that little woodchuck."

Cory left the house soon after Johnny did. She arrived at Suzy's only minutes before Santa's sleigh appeared in the sky. Santa and Mrs. Claus had seven elves crammed in with them when they landed. As soon as the reindeer touched down, Santa stepped out of the sleigh and turned to help his wife. Dressed in a flowered orange and yellow shirt and bright green shorts, he stood over six feet tall; the top of his wife's head came only to his chest. The elves were quarreling when they piled out of the sleigh, while Mr. and Mrs. Claus both looked tired and annoyed. It made Cory think of a large family going on vacation, especially when she saw that the elves ranged from two feet tall to nearly as tall as Mrs. Claus.

As Cory and Suzy hurried down the steps to greet the Clauses, the elves were rolling up the legs of their pants and running down to the water's edge. Santa and Mrs. Claus laughed when they saw them and were still chuckling as they started toward the house.

"Which one of you lovely ladies is Cory?" Santa asked in his big, booming voice.

Cory took a step forward and extended her hand. "I am, and this is Suzy, the owner of the house."

Santa enveloped Cory's hand in his and gave it a gentle squeeze. "If this works out, you are a lifesaver! Mama and I need to take a break now and then, and we can't seem to find any place quiet."

"Well, it's quiet here!" said Suzy as Santa shook her hand. "Let me show you around."

Santa's eyes lit up when he glanced back at the ocean, where the elves were chasing each other in and out of the water. "My elves seem to like it already."

"Come on, Papa," said Mrs. Claus. "I want to see inside."

The porch had been cleared of all the tables and merchandise and filled with comfortable-looking wicker furniture lined with bright, colorful cushions. With all the shutters open, the ocean breeze kept the porch cool and Cory was tempted to sit and wait for Suzy to finish her tour. Instead, she trailed Suzy and the Clauses from room to room, smiling when the couple exclaimed about how lovely it looked. The sun was shining, so the interior of the shell house was even brighter than it had been when Cory saw it on a rainy day. Mrs. Claus exclaimed how much she loved the translucent, pink-tinted walls and how it made everything seem so warm and cheerful. She liked the big kitchen, too, and even Santa declared that he liked the seashell decorations.

They were on the porch again, admiring the view of the ocean and watching the elves wading in the shallower water, when the one of the elves shouted at another, "Ouch! What did you do that for?"

"What are you talking about?" asked the second elf. "I didn't do anything."

"That thing just stung me!" another elf cried, pointing at something in the water.

Cory gave Suzy a questioning look, and together they ran to the water's edge as the elves splashed to dry ground. "What are those things?" Cory asked, spotting clear, floating blobs.

"Jellyfish," said Suzy. "But I've never seen so many at once."

The water was filled with them, washing back and forth across the beach with the movement of the waves.

"Does this happen often?" Santa asked. He and Mrs. Claus had stopped where the sand was still dry.

"Jellyfish show up once in a while, but nothing like this," said Suzy.

Cory sighed. "It's probably because I'm here." Turning to the Clauses, she told them about quitting the Tooth Fairy Guild. "And ever since I refused to go back, they've been plaguing me with birds and crabs and worms and rain and all sorts of things."

"That's outrageous!" declared Santa. "I've never heard of such a thing."

"Do you still want to see the other cottages?" asked Suzy.

"Of course," Mrs. Claus replied. "We'd love to."

Cory glanced back at the elves. They were sitting on the sand now; some were building sand castles just past the water's edge while the rest were covering one of their friends in sand from his waist to his feet.

Suzy led the way to the first driftwood cottage, a small building with a cozy covered porch and colored sea glass in every window. Like the shell house, most of the decor was done in seashells with seashell-decorated headboards on the beds, lamps on tables, and waste-baskets in the corners. The other cottages were much the same, although no two were exactly alike. Some had one tiny bedroom, some had two, but they all had excellent views of the ocean.

When they'd toured the last cottage, they started back toward the shell house. The tide was coming in now, the waves washing farther up the shore.

"It's perfect for us!" said Santa. "Mama and I can stay in the house with a few of the elves and the rest can stay in the cottages."

"I love it!" cried his wife. "I can already imagine our vacations here!"

Suddenly, the elf who was half buried in the sand started shouting and thrashing around. He erupted out of the sand, slapping at himself as he brushed the sand off. Hopping from one foot to the other, the elf began to scratch furiously at his legs where red welts were already forming.

"It looks like sand fleas bit him," Suzy said even as the elves who had been building sand castles cried out. The waves that were advancing up the shore carried great ropes of seaweed, depositing them on the castles and wrapping them around the elves' feet.

Cory's hair blew into her eyes and sand stung her bare arms and legs. The wind had sprung up, carrying grains of sand with it.

"Ow!" cried an elf running past her. A moment later all the elves were running to the sled, where they pulled blankets from the back and hid under them.

Santa Claus stood with his back to the wind, sheltering Mrs. Claus. "We like the house and the cottages," he said, "but the beach might be too much. We want a restful, quiet place."

"But it is, when I'm not here!" Cory shouted over the rising wind.

"We'll have to think about it," Santa told her as he shuffled through the sand toward his sled. "Thanks for showing the house to us!"

Cory followed Suzy onto the porch to help her close the shutters. They were struggling against the wind when Santa's sleigh rose into the air. Bucking and swerving, the sleigh fought the buffeting wind. When it was finally out of sight, Suzy turned to Cory. "I might have been able to sell this place if you hadn't been here! I know these things aren't your fault, but even so . . . You know, if you hadn't called me, I would have gone to Greener Pastures to look at houses with my sister. I had a ride all set up, but I'm sure it's gone by now. I'd been so looking forward to it, too! You're a nice girl, Cory, but please don't bring anyone else by to see my house."

"I'm so sorry, Suzy," Cory began.

"I know it's not your fault," Suzy interrupted, "but these things don't happen when you're not here."

"Then I guess I'd better go," said Cory. She sighed when Suzy nodded and went inside.

Cory felt terrible as she headed toward town. She still thought Suzy's house would be perfect for the Clauses, but there was no way they'd want it now. All she'd really done that day was get the elves stung and bitten, and wasted everyone's time.

She was mentally kicking herself when she realized that she was flying over the brick house where the three pigs lived. Spotting movement by the back door, she flew closer to see who was there. It was Roger, the pig who had lived in the straw house.

Cory turned back to her human size, startling the little pig so much that he jumped and squealed.

"It's me, Cory!" she exclaimed when she saw how frightened he looked. "I just stopped by to see how you were doing."

"We're doing rotten, and it's all your fault," Bertie said from the doorway. "Get back inside, Roger. You don't know who else is out there."

Roger scowled at Cory before hurrying into the house.

"Don't be rude, Bertie," Alphonse said as he joined his brother. Turning to Cory, he added, "The house is crowded and certain pigs are getting a bit testy, but we're okay."

"Any luck finding a new house?" asked Cory.

Alphonse shook his head. "Not so far. None of the houses we've seen have felt safe enough. They either have too many windows or too many doors."

"If I can help in any way—" Cory began.

"You've already done enough!" cried Bertie. "Just leave us alone!"

Cory cringed when the pig slammed the door in her face. She had meant it when she said she wanted to help, but maybe the best thing she could do for the pigs was to leave them alone. A headache was forming behind her eyes, and the only thing she wanted to do now was take a nap until it went away.

Cory was unlocking the door, thinking that she'd have to take Noodles out before she could lie down, when she remembered that the woodchuck was missing. She felt the same empty ache in her stomach that she'd felt when she woke that morning and saw his empty bed. The woodchuck might be obnoxious at times, but he was hers and she loved him just the same.

The key was still in the lock when she turned to look behind her. She had the strongest feeling that someone was watching her, but the yard was empty and there was no one on the street. Even so, she couldn't shake the feeling, so she opened the door and hurried inside, locking it behind her. Although she knew she had locked all the doors before she left that morning, she went around the house, checking them once again. When she peeked out the front window for the third time, she decided that she had to get busy or she would drive herself crazy. As nervous as she felt, taking a nap was no longer an option.

Cory hadn't cleaned her room since the last time Noodles chewed her shoes, so she straightened it and collected all her dirty clothes, dumping them in the basket her uncle kept beside the big stone basin where they washed the laundry. Her stomach rumbled while she collected the soiled towels from the bathing room, reminding her that she had left the house before breakfast. After dropping the laundry in the basin, she started the water and added the soapstone washing pebbles. The pebbles had their own magic, but it was slow and wouldn't be finished for nearly an hour, so she went to the kitchen to find something to eat.

Cory ate a lunch of bread slathered with nut butter. When she finished the sandwich, she was going to hand her crust to Noodles until she remembered that he was missing. It made her depressed all over again. She was thinking about the woodchuck when she carried her plate and cup to the sink. If only she could find out who had taken him.

Something blocked the sunlight streaming through the window above the sink. Cory glanced up and gasped. An enormous wolf was standing on its hind paws, watching her through the window. When it saw that she was looking directly at it, the wolf growled, "Little girl, little girl, let me come in!"

"You have got to be kidding!" Cory exclaimed. "I wouldn't let you in for all the fairy dust in the world!"

"Then I'll huff and I'll puff and I'll blow your house in!"

"Go away!" Cory shouted. She set the bowl in the sink and reached into the closest drawer. Grabbing a long-handled pancake flipper, she held it in front of her, waving it in the air as if she was about to bop the wolf with it.

"Foolish girl, I warned you!" growled the wolf. "Now you're asking for it!" Taking a deep breath, he blew at the window, steaming up the glass and rattling it in its frame. The stems of the begonias in the window box snapped and petals fell off a daisy.

The wolf turned and dropped to all fours. It walked into the yard before facing the house again. Taking a very deep breath, it huffed and puffed until its eyes bugged out. A loose piece of trim banged against the wall and the red poppies planted next to the house bent flat.

"This is ridiculous," Cory muttered. She hurried into the main room and scribbled a quick message to Johnny Blue.

A wolf is trying to blow down my uncle's house. Please come quickly!

Cory

The wolf was circling the house, blowing at it from different angles, when a return message arrived.

I'm on my way. Do not go outside!

Johnny

The more Cory worried about what the wolf was doing, the more her head ached, but that didn't stop her from running from room to room, peering out the windows. When she spotted the wolf again, it was still circling the house as if looking for its weakest point. Cory watched as the wolf found a half-filled watering can and stopped to drink from it. His muzzle was dripping as he turned to study the house. Licking his lips, he took three steps closer and opened his mouth.

This time when the wolf huffed and puffed, Cory could feel the entire structure shake. The wolf's breath whistled around the house, sounding like the wind during a bad storm. There was a tearing sound overhead and two loud bangs on the porch. Cory's hand covered her mouth as she backed away from the window, certain

that the wolf's next breath would bring the walls crash-
ing down.

The wolf was taking another deep breath when
it suddenly stopped and turned toward the street. A
moment later, it tore off through the yard in the opposite direction, disappearing through the trees behind
the house.

Cory ran to the front window to see what had scared
off the wolf. Johnny Blue was there along with Wanita
and Salazar. Johnny was hurrying up the walk to the
house while the other two stayed by the street, talking.
In a flash, Cory was out the door, running down the
porch steps in her bare feet.

"Are you all right?" Johnny asked.

Before Cory knew what was happening, he had
scooped her up in his arms and was holding her so tightly
she could scarcely breathe. "I'm fine," she panted. For the
first few seconds, his arms felt wonderful around her.
She felt warm and safe and happy and as if she could stay
there forever. But then the nausea began; a feeling so
sudden and intense that it was almost overwhelming.

"I was so worried!" Johnny said, his breath ruffling
her hair. "I've wanted to tell you how I feel about you
for a long time now. I care about you, Cory. More than
I've ever cared for anyone. I think I might even—"

Cory gasped when her stomach roiled again. "Don't!"

she cried, squirming out of Johnny's arms even as she pushed him away. Her face twisted in a look of revulsion as her stomach continued to churn.

"What's wrong?" Johnny asked.

"I can't . . . I just . . . ," Cory said, but she really couldn't talk. As she stepped back, her stomach grew calmer, although the feeling didn't disappear completely.

Johnny reached for her and she shook her head. "Don't touch me!" she said, then regretted her words the moment she saw his expression change.

"Do I disgust you that much?" he asked.

"No, that's not it at all!" said Cory, although she couldn't help but take another step back.

"It seems that I do," Johnny Blue said, his eyes showing how hurt he felt. "In that case, I won't overstay my welcome. Before I go, I wanted to tell you that I spoke with the captain. He said that I'm not supposed to investigate this anymore. If the Tooth Fairy Guild is involved, it's guild business and we aren't allowed to interfere. Judge Randal Jehosephat Dumpty backs the guild in all of these cases, which is why we've never won a case against them."

"I know the wife of an RJ Dumpty," said Cory. "It's possible that he's the judge. But I couldn't ask for any help from her. She hates me."

"Then don't even mention it to her," Johnny told her.

"So you're not going to look into it anymore?" asked Cory. She couldn't blame him. Not after she'd hurt him so badly.

"Officially, no. But I'm not giving up. Contact me if you need me."

"There's something I don't understand," said Cory. "The captain didn't know that you were helping me until you told him, right? But you said you'd talked to the other officers in the FLEA, so they had to know."

"They knew all right. They just thought it was a big joke. Most of them thought I was using the investigation as an excuse to see my girlfriend."

"Why would they think I was your girlfriend?"

Johnny Blue looked away, unable to meet her eyes. "I might have said how much I like you. And I might have told them how much I enjoyed seeing you play with your band. They thought I was dating you, and I suppose I let them."

"Oh," Cory said, and suddenly she felt even worse than before, although this time it wasn't her stomach that hurt. It was somewhere in her chest.

Johnny Blue left then, his back rigid, his eyes straight ahead as he strode to his cycle. Wanita and Salazar were still standing by the street, talking while the boar and the iguana eyed each other warily. When Cory saw them, she slipped on her shoes and went outside.

"Did you see the wolf?" she asked them.

"Why do you think we're here?" said Wanita. "Salazar and I heard all the ruckus and saw that nice young man tear past on his cycle. We followed him and got here just as he started waving his arms at the wolf. It looked as if he needed some help, so we did our best to scare the wolf away."

"Whatever you did, thank you!" Cory cried. "How *did* you chase the wolf off?"

Wanita laughed. "We can both be scary when we want to be. Watch this." Holding her arms straight out to her sides, the witch began waving them while shouting a spell. As the last word of the spell left her lips, sparks started shooting from her fingertips.

At the same time that the witch was casting her spell, the genie began to grow and didn't stop until he was twelve feet tall. His eyes turned red with a flash and he was engulfed in a ball of flame.

"That would do it," said Cory. "You're both terrifying."

"Sorry we didn't get here before the wolf damaged your house," Salazar told her as he returned to his normal size.

Cory turned around to look the house over. Twigs and broken branches were scattered across the yard, and great sections of thatching were missing from the roof. The two chairs had fallen over on the porch; one of them was broken. Many of the poppies she had planted only days before lay flattened on the ground.

"It's not nearly as bad as it could have been," she told her neighbors. "I guess you've paid me back for the flowers."

"What? This?" said Wanita. "No, this was fun! I still owe you for the flowers. I'm sure I'll think of something!"

Cory wasn't sure what the witch might do to pay her back, but she appreciated what Wanita and Salazar had done. She waited until they started down the street before cleaning up the yard. After putting the broken poppies in the composter behind the garden shed, she collected the twigs and branches, making a pile next to the composter. She would ask her uncle later if he wanted her to carry them into the woods or keep them for firewood. A lot of the thatch had blown away, but she picked up what she could find, not sure if the roofer could use any of it.

As soon as she went back in the house, Cory sent a message to someone who could fix the roof, adding the cost to all the other things she'd have to pay for. While waiting for a reply, she washed the plate and cup she'd left in the sink, and made herself a cup of herbal tea to get rid of her headache. She sat at the table, sipping the tea, until a *ping!* in the main room announced the arrival of a message. The roofer would be out the next day.

It was past the time she should have left for band rehearsal when Cory stepped onto the porch and locked the door behind her. Knowing her uncle should be home soon, she'd left him a note on the table telling him what had happened and that she had scheduled a repairman. Her head still ached, and she had considered skipping rehearsal, but the way her day had gone she thought it would be nice to see people who actually liked her.

Cory's head wasn't getting any better by the time she reached Olot's cave and she was almost sorry she'd gone. She tried to smile at her friends, but she wasn't feeling very friendly. When they began to play their instruments, the music seemed so much louder than usual, and her headache only grew worse. After they had finished practicing and were putting their instruments away, Olot came to see her.

"Is something wrong?" he asked. "You don't seem like your usual self."

Cory shrugged. "I've had a truly rotten day."

Olot pulled a stool over and sat down. "I'm ready to listen if you want to tell me about it. I know it helps me to talk about things sometimes."

"Are you sure?" Cory asked him. "Chancy might need you to—"

"Chancy will be fine," said Olot. "What happened?"

It didn't take long for Cory to tell him about the wolf

trying to blow down the house, and all the things that had gone wrong when the Clauses were looking at Suzy's house. Olot was so understanding that she told him about Humpty and the mice, how the pigs were afraid in their own home, how the matches she set up hadn't been working, and how Noodles had gone missing. Olot's frown was so deep by the time she finished that it looked as if someone had used a chisel to carve the creases in his forehead. When she told him that everything that had gone wrong had been her fault and that she felt terrible about it, he patted her shoulder as gently as an ogre could.

"I'm sorry to hear that things have been so rough lately, but maybe I can help solve one of your problems," he told her. "I own another cave not far from here. It's smaller than this one, and I've been using it for storage, but I've been thinking about selling it. I put a nice stout door on it last year, so no one could break into it. We could take your pig friends to see it if you think they might be interested."

"I don't know," Cory said. "How would they get to town to work or do their shopping?"

"They could take the pedal-bus, like Chancy and I do," said Olot. "It goes right past here."

"In that case I'll tell the pigs about your cave tomorrow and let you know if they're interested."

"Good," said Olot. "Chancy would like to have neighbors."

Cory's headache wasn't as bad when she flew home and she was definitely in a better mood. It was dark out when she reached her uncle's house, but the lights were on inside, making it look warm and welcoming. Landing at the bottom of the stairs, she stepped onto the porch in her human size and almost tripped over the furry creature chewing the sea-grass mat.

"Noodles!" she cried. The woodchuck glanced at her and grunted when she picked him up.

Struggling to open the door while supporting Noodle's weight, she called to her uncle, "Look who I found! Do we have any salad for a hungry woodchuck?"

CHAPTER
19

Cory had a terrible time going to sleep that night. Although Noodles was back, Cory was still worried about who had taken him and where he had been. She was also afraid that the wolf might come back to try again. But it wasn't thinking about Noodle's kidnappers or the nasty wolf that kept her awake, it was the thought of how she had upset Johnny Blue when he came to help her. She liked Johnny, and when they were apart she knew that she liked him a lot. Otherwise, she wouldn't think about him all the time, would she? But even thinking about him made her feel a little queasy. Being with him made her stomach hurt. It was worse when they actually touched. The whole thing was very confusing and she didn't know what to do.

Cory wasn't sure Johnny Blue wanted to hear from

her, but she thought she should send him a message anyway. She had already reported that the woodchuck was missing, and thought it was only right to report that he had returned. As soon as she got out of bed the next morning, she hurried to send a short message.

Noodles is back.
Cory

She joined her uncle for breakfast a few minutes later. He tried to start a conversation more than once, but she didn't feel like talking.

Only minutes after Micah left for work, there was a knock at the door. Cory opened it, expecting to see either the repairman or Johnny, and nearly shut it again when she saw that her mother was standing on the porch.

"May I come in?" her mother asked, giving Cory a tentative smile.

Cory shrugged. "I suppose." She knew that she wasn't being very gracious, but after all the things that the Tooth Fairy Guild had done to her, she felt as if her mother was working for her enemy.

Her mother took a seat in the main room, setting her rose petal–covered purse by her feet. "I know you don't really want to talk to me, but I had to come see you. I'm worried about you, Cory. The Tooth Fairy

Guild will be patient for only so long before they take stronger measures."

"You mean they'll do something worse than plaguing me with worms and crabs and seagulls?" Cory asked, feeling her temper rise. "Or tormenting me with bad weather, or the long-winded wolf and oversize teeth and mud? What about the—"

"Yes," her mother interrupted. "They are quite capable of doing things that are much worse than any of those. I begged them to give you one more chance to return to the guild, but if you don't do it now, well, I really can't say what they might do."

"I'm not rejoining the guild, Mother," Cory said. "Especially after what they've already done."

"Are you sure? Please reconsider, for your own sake!"

Cory shook her head. "I'm never going to change my mind."

Her mother picked up her purse and tucked it under her arm as she got to her feet. "Then I'm wasting my breath. I really shouldn't have bothered arguing with the guild on your behalf. I knew you had a lot of your father's father in you, but I hoped there was still a chance that you would listen to reason. You're just as stubborn as he ever was. He's always been certain that he was right, too. Well, when it's all over, don't say I didn't warn you."

"Did you say he *is* certain, Mother? You've always led me to believe that he's dead," Cory said, following her mother to the door.

Delphinium looked alarmed when she turned back to Cory. "No! No! It was just a slip of the tongue. You don't have to pick apart every little thing I say! Now, be careful, Cory. And please remember that I'll always be there when you need me."

Cory let her mother leave without saying any more, but she was sure that Delphinium hadn't been completely truthful.

After cleaning up the breakfast dishes, Cory sent a message to the three little pigs, telling them about the cave. When they said that they were interested and able to look at it that morning, she suggested that they take the pedal-bus and gave them the address that Olot had mentioned, promising to meet them there.

Noodles started whining while she was changing her clothes, so she took him outside and let him wander around the yard for a few minutes while she kept a close watch. He walked in circles, making little moaning sounds, so she wasn't surprised when he threw up everything he'd eaten for breakfast. As soon as he looked a little better, she took him to her room and sat down for a minute to pet him. She thought she still had some time before she had to leave to meet the pigs, so she collected all his toys, setting them beside his bed, then went into the bathing room to finish getting ready. When she came back, Noodles had thrown up again.

Cory sighed and went to fetch the cleaning supplies, annoyed because she'd already used up most of her extra time and really needed to go. She was on her hands and knees, cleaning up the mess, when she found a hard object about the size of a gold coin. *That's odd*, she thought, wiping it off with a rag. It was an onyx buckle, the kind you might find on expensive clothes. Apparently, Noodles had eaten something he shouldn't have, as he so often did. Because no one in the house had a buckle like it, Cory wondered if it had belonged to his kidnapper. She wrapped the buckle in a clean rag and set it aside to look at later. Once she had put the cleaning supplies away and said good-bye to Noodles, she locked the house and was on her way.

Olot had given her good directions to the cave, so she was there before the pedal-bus. She always liked watching the pedal-bus, even more when people she knew were riding it. Finding a large rock by the side of the dirt path that wound around the mountain, she sat down to wait. She heard the bus long before she saw it; the jingling of the bells was distinctive in the clear mountain air. Olot must have heard it, too, because he came strolling down the path before the pigs slid off their seats.

Eight of the ten seats on the bus were occupied. A satyr and a goblin girl were in charge of the bus and they both looked expectantly at the pigs, who were struggling to dismount. Once the pigs had gotten off, the only riders left were three flower fairies and a brownie with a large sack propped in his basket. The bus had just started to head back down the mountain when the bells sounded a different note. The goblin girl, who was in the front, consulted a disk affixed to the bar in front of her. A moment later they were headed up the mountainside. Apparently, someone else wanted a ride.

When Cory turned to the pigs to begin introductions, she was afraid that they might be leery of the ogre. Olot was big and could look frightening when he wanted to, but he was actually a gentle being who loved animals of all species. Animals seemed to know this and the pigs were no exception. They looked less afraid of him than they had of Cory when she'd visited their house the first time.

Olot smiled when Cory introduced him to the pigs. He crouched down so he was talking to them at their eye level. "Cory told me about the trouble you've been having, and I thought this cave would be ideal for you. I know this is a bit out of the way, but there are actually more beings living on the mountain than you might guess. I would be your next-door neighbor and if you ever needed anything, my wife and I would be happy to help. Now, you can't see the cave from the path, which is one of its security features. Come with me and I'll show you."

Cory trailed behind as the pigs trotted after Olot. Although she was unable to hear what they were saying, Olot soon had the little pigs talking and laughing. She had come to make sure that everything went well, but she'd already begun to feel as if they didn't really need her there.

After rounding a group of tall saplings and a patch of thick underbrush that grew at the edge of the path, they followed another, narrower path that angled back and forth until they reached a massive door set in the side of the mountain. Olot opened the door with a key and the pigs followed him inside. They had taken only a few steps into the pitch-black space when Olot flipped a switch on the wall, turning on fairy light.

"I had the fairy lights installed last year when I began to think about selling the place. Some friends helped me install the plumbing," Olot said as he led the way down a wide tunnel. "The cave has its own spring and the water is always fresh and clean. This is the main room."

The pigs gasped when they stepped into the cavern.

Cory could understand why. Smaller than the cavern in Olot's cave, it was prettier with layers of different kinds of rock creating multicolored stripes in the walls. The ceiling was lower, too, at only a few feet above Olot's head. Cory thought that made it cozier, although the pigs exclaimed over how high it was.

"What's behind all the doors?" asked Alphonse.

"That one leads to the kitchen," said Olot, "and those five are bedrooms."

"Five bedrooms!" Bertie said, quivering with excitement.

"The bathing room is back there," Olot said, pointing to the back of the cavern. "There's a shallow pool that you could swim in if you chose."

The three little pigs squealed and started running toward the back.

"It looks as if you have everything under control here," Cory told Olot before he could follow the pigs. "I don't think you need me anymore, so I'm going now."

"That's fine," said Olot. "I'll make sure they get on the pedal-bus safe and sound. See you later at Sprats'."

Cory nodded. With all that had happened that day, she'd forgotten that the band was scheduled to play at the restaurant. When they heard the sound of splashing coming from the bathing room, Olot excused himself and hurried after the pigs.

"I'll just let myself out," Cory called after him. She started to the front door, happy that at least this time the Tooth Fairy Guild hadn't tried to interfere. The door swung open silently and she was making sure that it had closed behind her when a swarm of gnats descended on her, getting in her eyes, her nose, and her mouth.

"Bleh!" she said, spitting out some gnats. Batting at the tiny insects with her hands, she hurried down the path. She was certain that the gnats would disperse as soon as she left, so she couldn't help laughing to herself. This time the Tooth Fairy Guild had been too late to do any damage.

When Cory returned home, the thatched roof was repaired and her uncle was kneeling in the garden, weeding. She landed on the grass and resumed her human size before sitting cross-legged beside him. "You're home early," said Cory.

Micah set down the trowel and wiped the perspiration from his forehead. "A novice water nymph blew out all the pipes in the school. Everyone was sent home until the pipes are fixed. They say we should be able to go back in by tomorrow. The roofer was here when I got home." Micah sat back on his heels and turned to look at the roof. "I think he did a good job. He left just a few minutes ago. Oh, Johnny Blue stopped by as well.

He was sorry he missed you and said he'd see you at Sprats' tonight. How was your day?"

"Mother came to see me this morning," said Cory. "She tried to talk me into rejoining the Tooth Fairy Guild again. Then she said something that I thought was curious. She compared me to my father's father, but she talked about him as if he was still alive."

Micah picked up the trowel and began jabbing at the roots of a stubborn weed. "Really? That's interesting."

"Well?" Cory said. "Is he?"

"I don't know," Micah told her as he jabbed the weed again.

"Oh, come on! You have to be able to tell me something about him. Mother certainly hasn't. She used to get mad at me if I mentioned him, so I stopped asking questions about my father's side of the family when I was a little girl. Now the only time she refers to my father's father is to say something unkind or that I'm as stubborn as he was. You met him, didn't you? Can't you tell me anything?"

Micah turned to face her. "Yes, I suppose I can. I think your mother has taken things too far. I understood her justification for cutting off ties with him, but I never approved. I liked your grandfather; most people did. He was strong-willed and very self-assured, but he did know his job."

"Why did Mother dislike him so much?" asked Cory.

"Because your grandfather didn't think your parents should marry. He told them that they weren't right for each other, and that the right people for each of them would come along if they waited. Your parents were young and thought they were in love, so they refused to listen to him and ran off to get married. When they came back, they were already expecting you, so your grandfather didn't say anything more. The damage had already been done, however, and when your father left, your mother refused to see your grandfather or even hear his name mentioned. I've always thought it was because she didn't want to admit that he had been right. You know, I might have something for you. Come inside while I look for it."

"What is it?" Cory asked as they walked toward the porch.

"You'll see in just a minute," her uncle replied.

Cory made them each a cup of tea while her uncle rummaged through the desk in his bedroom. When he came out he was carrying an envelope made from papyrus. "Here, you can have this," he said, handing the envelope to Cory. "You and your mother were staying with me when your grandfather sent it. Delphinium threw it in the trash without opening it, but I fished it out and kept it for you."

Cory Feathering, it said on the outside of the envelope. Ripping it open, she pulled out a pretty card decorated with flowers and baby bunnies. *Happy Vernal Equinox*, it said inside, along with the signature, *Lionel Feathering*.

"That's my grandfather's name, Lionel Feathering?" said Cory. "I never even knew that much. Mother refused to tell me his name."

After examining the card, she returned to the envelope. Along with her name and her uncle's address, there was a return address. "Do you think he still lives there?" Cory asked her uncle.

"As far as I know he does," said Micah. "It's the only address I have for him."

Cory glanced out the window at the sundial. She'd have to get ready to go to Sprats' soon. "Then I guess I'll find out tomorrow."

Sprats' was packed when Cory arrived, and people she didn't know greeted her as she made her way to the stage in the back of the room. Olot and Chancy were there and Cory's drums were already set up. Cheeble was there as well, and he gave her a quick wave and a grin before returning to his conversation with a cute, young brownie woman who was sitting by the side of the stage.

"He's in a good mood," Cory said when Olot came to see her.

"Our success is going to his head. He's gotten a following already. I heard him telling Skippy that he might quit his day job soon." The ogre gestured to the satyr, who had taken a seat in the audience to talk to a table full of beautiful nymphs. "Skippy said he might quit as well."

"Are we making enough money that they could do that?"

"If things go the way they have been, we will be soon," said Olot. "By the way, the pigs are buying the cave. They take possession next Thursday."

"I'm not surprised. They seemed to love it."

Olot laughed, a great booming sound that had people turning to glance at the stage. "Love it! I had a terrible time getting them out of the pool. I bet they'll spend most of their time there once they move in. They were talking about adding mud to make it a mud bath."

Olot had gone to talk to Chancy when Priscilla Hood approached Cory. "I know you're busy," said Priscilla, "but I just wanted to tell you that I went on that date with Jack Nimble. He's very nice, but he isn't right for me. He likes the outdoors like I do, but he isn't at all interested in hunting. At dinner last night, he said he'd rather climb mountains to catch a glimpse of rare creatures than take a nice leisurely walk through the forest to shoot them. I ask you, what's the point of looking for animals if you aren't going to get a trophy? Anyway, do you have anyone else for me to meet now?"

"I'll have to think about that," said Cory. "I'm sure we'll find the right person for you, but it may take some time."

Priscilla returned to her seat with Marjorie, who smiled when Cory looked her way. Johnny Blue was seated by himself at a table not far from theirs; he waved when he saw Cory glance in that direction. She grinned and waved back, but her smile disappeared when she saw Daisy enter the restaurant with Tom Tom.

He had his arm around Daisy and they were talking with their heads together. When they reached the edge of the stage, he kissed her and left to find a seat, striding across the dance floor in front of Cory. She watched him for a moment, noticing the arrogant way he moved, his new-looking leather pants and shirt, and . . . Cory gasped when she saw Tom Tom's scuffed boots. If the band hadn't been about to start playing, she would have gone to talk to Daisy, but Olot was giving them the signal to warm up. The conversation would have to wait.

The audience talked and moved around while the band warmed up, but the moment Olot struck the first chord on his lute, everyone grew silent and all eyes turned to the stage. A new song, "Drifting Snow," was the first piece they played. After that they turned to some of their favorites, including "Morning Mist." Whistling and applauding, the audience showed how much they loved Zephyr's music.

The band members basked in their praise, but the moment the break started, Cory headed straight to Daisy and practically dragged her to the back room, where the Sprats were offering cool fruit drinks and dried figs for snacks. Cory glanced at Tom Tom as she hustled Daisy between the tables and saw him scowl and get to his feet.

"You didn't tell me you were dating Tom Tom!" Cory said as soon as they were in the room.

Daisy shrugged. "I didn't know I needed to."

Cory sighed, exasperated. "Listen, you've never asked me for advice about choosing a boyfriend, and I can respect that. I've never tried to tell you who to date either, although I have thought you've made some questionable choices. However, I have to say that I think you're making a mistake with Tom Tom. He's not a good person, Daisy. He kidnapped a pig once, he doesn't help his own family, and he was very rude to me the day I met him."

"Really?" said Daisy. "He's always been nice to me. I didn't even know you knew him. I met him when he came by to ask questions about you. I probably should have told you that, but I've been so busy and—"

"What's going on?" Tom Tom asked, pushing past Skippy to get in the room.

"You're not supposed to be in here!" Skippy told him.

"Stuff it, goat boy!" snarled Tom Tom. He turned to Cory even as he put his arm around Daisy.

"What have you been telling her?" he said. "You should learn to mind your own business. My relationship with Daisy has nothing to do with you."

"Yes, it does," said Cory. "A good person doesn't stand by and let her friend get hurt. Daisy has been my friend for most of my life, and I'm not going to let her date a bully without knowing the truth. I think you were the one who kidnapped Noodles. I bet the guild you work for is the Tooth Fairy Guild!"

"Somebody kidnapped Noodles?" said Daisy, her gaze flicking from Cory to Tom Tom.

Cory nodded. "Yes, but he's back now. And the day after he came back he threw up something he'd taken from his kidnapper. Look at Tom Tom's boots, Daisy. Do you see how the left one is missing a buckle? I found one just like those when I cleaned up Noodle's mess."

"Don't listen to her. She doesn't know what she's talking about," Tom Tom told Daisy.

"I still have the buckle," Cory told her friend. "The next time you come to my house, Daisy, I'll show it to you."

Olot came through the door then, his size making the room look small. When he saw Tom Tom scowling at Cory, he pointed at the door and said, "You have to leave. Only band members or restaurant employees are allowed in here."

Tom Tom turned to Olot, a sharp retort on his lips. It died as his gaze traveled up and up to the ogre's face. "I was having a pleasant conversation with my friends," he finally said.

"I don't think so," Johnny Blue said from the open door. "I heard an angry voice in here, and I think it was yours." He gave Tom Tom such a pointed look that the young man licked his lips and took his arm off Daisy's shoulder.

"I was just leaving," Tom Tom said, glancing from Olot to Johnny Blue.

No one spoke until he left the room, then Johnny turned to Cory and said, "What was that all about?"

"That was Tom Tom," said Cory. "I think he's the one who took Noodles." Johnny's eyes narrowed as she told him about the buckle that Noodles had brought home.

"Uh-huh," said Johnny Blue. "Don't worry about Tom Tom. I'll keep an eye on him."

When the band returned to the stage, the audience clapped and stomped their feet. Everyone in the band was grinning when they started to play. They played their new version of "Silver Moon" first, followed by "Owl Goes A-Hunting." After that they played old favorites until they were too tired to play anymore. Cory wasn't the only one to get blisters on her fingers that night.

She was covering up her drums when Tom Tom hopped onto the stage. Cory watched him sidle past her bandmates to join her in the back. "I'm sorry I was so rude earlier. I'd like to take you and Daisy out to eat to make up for it."

"Actually, I've had a very long day and I'm tired," said Cory. "I really just want to go home and get some sleep. Thanks for asking, though."

"You can sleep later," he replied, and was reaching for her arm when Johnny Blue stepped onto the stage.

"If she's going out to eat, it will be with me," Johnny Blue said.

He had approached so quietly that Cory hadn't known he was there. Apparently, neither had Tom Tom. He scowled when he saw Johnny Blue, but he let go of Cory and stepped back.

"*And* I'll see that she gets home safely," said Johnny. He glared at Tom Tom, who looked defiant for a moment, then smirked and sauntered off to join Daisy.

CHAPTER
20

The first important thing Cory did the next morning was to send messages to Marjorie and Jack Nimble to set up a date for that very day. The second was to head to the address on the envelope that her grandfather had sent her years before. Cory had never visited the part of town where her grandfather lived. It was in an older, well-established neighborhood where big lawns led up to houses that could almost be called mansions. When Cory found the address on the post by the street, she fluttered in place, wondering if she'd ever been inside the house when she was a baby.

The stone house was three floors tall with a wide covered porch at its center. Tall trees dotted the property, shading the lush lawn that surrounded the nearly circular driveway. A flower garden filled the circle, and in the center of the garden, water splashed from one stone lily to another in a white marble fountain.

Cory returned to her human size after landing in the street in front of the house. She walked slowly up the cobblestone driveway, studying the flowers, the lawn, and the fountain. When she stepped onto the porch, she glanced back and noticed that the driveway wasn't as circular as she'd thought, but instead was shaped like a heart with the rounded top of the heart by her feet and the pointed end touching the road. Now that she was close to the house, she could see that the heart motif seemed to be everywhere. Tall urns flanking the door were filled with bleeding hearts, their heart-shaped red blossoms trailing down the sides to partially cover the hearts etched into the ceramic. Hearts were carved into the wide front door and a heart made of mother-of-pearl that was no bigger than her thumbnail was mounted on the door frame. "Press me" was written on the center of the heart.

"Huh," Cory murmured. "There's no accounting for taste."

She pressed the mother-of-pearl heart and heard bells chiming nearby. After waiting for what she thought was a reasonable amount of time, she was reaching for the heart again when the door opened and the scent of flowers wafted out of the house.

At first Cory thought the person standing with his hand on the door was a brownie or some other kind of sprite. He was about two feet tall and was wearing tan slacks, a light blue shirt, and yellow and blue shoes like she'd seen humans wear for running. At second glance, she saw that his bald head, unlined face, pudgy hands and arms made him look more like a six-month-old human baby. His expression, however, was not at all babylike. He was scowling at her, looking irritated and bored at the same time.

"Whatever you're selling, we're not buying any," he said in a surprisingly deep voice, and started to shut the door.

Cory grabbed hold of the door to stop it from closing. "I'm not selling anything."

"We don't do questionnaires or petitions either," he said, tugging on the door.

"I'm here to see Mr. Feathering," said Cory. She shoved the door open wider and stepped into the large foyer, brushing past the baby-man who was spluttering and making faces at her. Her shoulder bumped a set of bells that were hanging just inside the door, making them sway and ring. They were the bells that had chimed when she'd pushed the button. Cory glanced from the bells to the little man. "You can tell him that Cory Feathering is here to see him."

He shut one eye to peer at her with the other. "Stay right here," he finally ordered, and closed the door with a bang. Turning his back on her, he disappeared into another room.

While Cory waited for him to return, she studied the foyer, noting the wide set of stairs that swept up one side to a landing on the second floor, and curved again until it reached the third floor. She thought the stairs would have been lovely if the banisters hadn't been overdone with carvings of hearts and flowers. Set into the center of the marble floor of the foyer was a huge red garnet heart, and above the heart there was a round table supporting a vase filled with roses, lilies, carnations, baby's breath, hydrangeas, and daisies. The flowers reminded Cory of a wedding bouquet. She had walked over to look at the flowers when she heard someone giggle. Glancing up, she saw two more babylike people peeking at her from the second-floor landing. They both wore plain blue dresses and had miniature mops in their hands. When they saw that Cory was looking at them, they moved out of sight.

A moment later, the little man was back. "Come along," he said. "We don't have all day."

Cory followed her escort, walking slowly behind him as he toddled through the house. At times he seemed so unsure of his footing that she was tempted to scoop him up and carry him, but she was afraid he'd consider it insulting. When she wasn't watching him, she looked around, curious about the house. The heart motif was everywhere—carved on the legs of tables and chairs, embroidered on cushions and in framed pictures on the walls. Some of the pictures included more baby-like people, only these were dressed in diapers and had small feathered wings. There were vases of flowers everywhere.

They were in a hallway when Cory heard a sound behind her. She glanced back and saw faces watching her from the doorways she'd already passed. Every one of them looked like a human baby; some were more feminine than others. A few of the little people waved at her shyly.

A moment later, Cory's escort opened a glass door leading outside to a stone terrace that ran the width of the house. An elderly man was seated at a table, reading *The Fey Express* with a half-filled mug in front of him. When the little man cleared his throat and said, "Here she is," the elderly man put down the paper and turned to look at them.

"Thank you, Orville," said the man, but his eyes were already on Cory's face.

"She says she's Cory Feathering," said Orville.

"You already told me that."

"Well, is she?"

The man studied Cory's face a moment longer and nodded. "I do believe she is."

Wearing a satisfied look, Orville turned and tottered back through the door.

"Please, sit down," the man said, gesturing to a chair across from him. "Would you like some mulled cider?"

Cory took a deep breath. She could smell the tart scent of apple and spices of the man's drink. "Yes, please."

The old man picked up a small bell and rang it. In less than a minute a little woman who resembled a bald baby girl opened a door and stepped onto the porch, looking at him expectantly. "Another mulled cider and some breakfast, please, Margory. I've found I have an appetite after all."

The little woman smiled as if he'd said something wonderful, and scurried back through the door.

There were so many things Cory wanted to ask him, but the first one that crossed her lips was, "If it isn't rude, may I ask what kind of beings Margory and Orville are?" asked Cory.

"They are putti," said the old man. "Putti are much like cherubs, but without wings. The putti you see here worked for me for many years. I'm semiretired now, but I kept them on however I could."

They sat for a moment, inspecting each other in

silence. Cory could see some resemblance between them. His eyes were the same shade of blue as hers. His mouth was the same shape as hers, with a thinner upper lip and a plump bottom lip concealing even, white teeth. His hair was white, but it was as thick as hers, curling across his forehead and down the back of his neck. Although Cory'd never thought much about her own appearance, she thought he was a very handsome man. "You *are* Lionel Feathering, aren't you?" Cory said after a while. "I mean, no one has introduced us."

"I am indeed," he said, looking very serious. "And you are my granddaughter. I'm glad you found me. I wasn't sure you ever would. Your mother was so vehement I stay away that I didn't dare come see you. What made her change her mind?"

"She hasn't," said Cory. "Uncle Micah gave me a card you'd sent. Your address is on the back."

"So your mother doesn't know that you're here?"

Cory shook her head. "I left the Tooth Fairy Guild and Mother didn't approve. We had a big fight, so I couldn't stay there any longer. Uncle Micah has let me live with him."

"I'd heard your mother made you join her guild," said Lionel. "I wondered how long it would last. You have to have a certain temperament to be a tooth fairy and I never saw that in you when you were a little girl. You were too independent and stubborn, just like me."

Cory smiled. "That's what Mother always said—that I was as stubborn as you are. She didn't talk about you much, but what she did say wasn't very nice. From the way she talked about you, I thought you were dead."

When her grandfather laughed, he tilted his head back and opened his mouth wide. It was an infectious laugh and Cory's grin grew broader. "Not dead," said her grandfather, "semiretired. I'd hoped to have a successor by now, but it didn't work that way."

A door opened as Orville and Margory came out bringing two large trays. Cory and her grandfather sat back while Orville unloaded his tray of plates and cutlery, pastries, a mug for Cory, and a pitcher full of mulled cider. When he stepped aside, Margory set down platters of eggs coddled in milk, stacks of hot nut bread, a small plate holding butter shaped like a rose in full bloom, and a large green bowl of fresh sliced fruit.

"Thank you," Cory said. The two putti grinned at her before going back inside.

Cory had eaten a slice of toast for breakfast and normally that was enough, but now her mouth watered and she gazed at the food longingly.

"Please help yourself," her grandfather said, his eyes twinkling.

Not wanting to look greedy, Cory helped herself to a pastry. She took a bite and savored the taste of cinnamon and butter before turning to her grandfather and saying, "If you're semiretired, what did you do exactly?"

"Your mother didn't tell you anything about me, did she?" her grandfather asked as he helped himself to fruit.

"She wouldn't even tell me your name."

"Most people don't know me by my name. It's my title that interests them. For eight hundred and fifty-three years I was Cupid, just as my father was before me. I had hoped my son would follow in my footsteps, but he shunned the job and joined the military instead. Then he married your mother and our relationship was a bit strained. His platoon was sent to fight in the Fairy War and I never heard from him again. Your mother hadn't liked me from the beginning, so I wasn't surprised when she told me that she wanted nothing more to do with me. Losing my son and then my only grandchild nearly broke my heart. You were the only family I had."

"I'm sorry," Cory said, not sure what to say.

"Don't be. It wasn't your fault," her grandfather said, patting her hand.

Looking at her grandfather, a man she was coming to like, Cory grew even angrier at her mother than she had been before. Her mother had kept her from her grandfather for a reason Cory still didn't really understand. He seemed like a very good person, yet she had grown up thinking that something had to be wrong with him for her mother to hate him so much. And then she remembered something her grandfather had said. "Did you say that you're Cupid? I thought that was a little guy who shot arrows at people to make them fall in love."

Her grandfather smiled, which made him seem much younger. "I'm not so little, as you can see. I just liked to work behind the scenes. It would have made my job harder if people recognized me before I shot them with my arrows, and yes, I did use a bow and arrow. My putti represented me when I needed to make public appearances, which is why so many people think that Cupid is a small, mostly naked babylike being. Enough about me. Tell me, if you quit the Tooth Fairy Guild, what are you doing now?"

"I'm in a band," said Cory, "but I'm also taking on odd jobs. I didn't like the guild because I wanted to help people and didn't feel as if I was really helping anyone. I've been trying to find a way to help people, but I haven't been doing very well so far."

"What kind of odd jobs?" her grandfather asked.

Cory shrugged. She was embarrassed that she hadn't

found anything substantial that she could claim as her future career. "Nothing big or important," she said, running her finger around the top of her mug while avoiding her grandfather's eyes. "I've babysat for a few people, helped can beans, mowed lawns; whatever someone says they need help doing. Oh, and you might find this interesting: some people have asked me to help them find their love match, although I haven't had much success."

When Cory raised her eyes, her grandfather was looking at her more intently. "That is interesting! They must sense that you have the ability somewhere inside you. I suggest that you keep on trying. You might surprise yourself someday."

Cory ate two more pastries and let her grandfather talk her into eating eggs and fruit as well. When she said good-bye, it was with the promise that she would keep in touch. Orville reappeared to lead her out. He seemed friendlier now. More putti came to peek at her on her way to the door, and every one of them smiled at her.

Cory was excited when she returned home and was glad that her uncle was there. The pipe in the school hadn't been fixed yet, so the school was still closed. Her uncle was seated on the porch drinking lemonade while Noodles gnawed on a toy at his feet. The squirrel was perched on the railing, and he chattered at Cory as she climbed the steps and sat down on the chair that Micah had already fixed. She had so much to tell her uncle! He listened to her, nodding and smiling as she told him about her morning.

"You knew that he was Cupid, didn't you?" she said when her uncle didn't ask any questions.

"I did," he replied, "but it was up to him to tell you."

"I really liked my grandfather and we had a very nice visit. Mother should never have kept him away! Oh, and he said one thing that I bet you don't know. He said that I might have the ability to help people find their matches. He told me not to give up and . . ."

Cory noticed that her uncle was no longer looking at her, but instead was staring at the street. Micah got to his feet even as she turned her head. A magic carpet had landed on the lawn, and three men wearing black masks and hoods had jumped off and were running up the walk. Cory stood as the men bounded onto the porch. One tackled her uncle and held him down, although he fought to resist. Another grabbed hold of Cory, holding her still while the third tied her hands behind her and fastened something cold around her wrist. Suddenly her arm ached, and she felt heavy all over.

"I know you're from the Tooth Fairy Guild!" Micah cried. "You can't get away with this!"

"And who's going to stop us?" said one of the masked men. "Nobody can go against the guilds!"

The air around her uncle shimmered as he became small and flitted out of the men's reach. Cory tried to change, too, but nothing happened. "Let me go!" she cried, struggling as the two men carried her down from the porch and plunked her onto the magic carpet. When she started to scream, the third man stuffed a handkerchief in her mouth and pulled a pillowcase over her head before sitting down beside her.

Cory swayed as the carpet rose into the air. She tried to steady herself with her hands, but with them tied behind her, she could only just touch the knotted fiber with her fingertips. Rough hands shoved her up when she nearly fell over. A moment later, they were racing through the air, the wind pushing against her so that she had to lean forward to stay upright.

They were in the air only a few minutes before Cory felt the carpet begin to descend. Sounds changed around her, becoming closer and more intimate, and she knew that they had entered a building. The instant the carpet settled onto the floor, the two men hustled her off, shoving her down a smooth-floored hallway and turning her to stumble through a doorway. She took a few steps before they made her stop. When they ripped the pillowcase off her head, she stood, blinking at the light streaming through the window behind a silhouetted figure. She blinked again and the figure came into focus. It was Mary Mary.

"And so it's come to this," Mary Mary said, shaking her head. "We gave you every opportunity to return to us, but you refused again and again. Even after we tried to direct you back on the right path, it was to no avail. Do you know how much time and energy we spent on you, young lady? It's your own fault that we're going to have to take such extreme measures, so you don't have anyone else to blame."

"What are you going to do?" Cory asked.

Something moved behind Mary Mary. It was Micah, still tiny, fluttering outside the window as he waved his arms to get Cory's attention. When she looked his way, he waved once more and took off. Cory was relieved to know that her uncle had followed to see where the men had taken her, but she didn't know what he could do about it. If they were in the Tooth Fairy Guild head-quarters, as Cory suspected, she doubted he'd even be able to get into the building.

"What we should have done before this if only your mother hadn't been such a thorn in my side," Mary Mary was saying when Cory started listening to her again. "You have spurned the guild and now the guild is going to repudiate you. Oh, and don't think you can get out of this. That bracelet on your wrist is a thin band of iron encased in porcelain so the metal doesn't burn you. We're not heartless, despite what you might think."

Cory shivered. Iron was known to negate fairy magic and burn fairy skin. Fortunately, there was little iron in the fairy world, although humans sometimes brought it with them. Fairies did their best to keep their distance from it, and one of the hardest parts about visiting the human world was the presence of so much iron. It had taken her weeks of near misses to learn what she could and couldn't approach when she performed her tooth fairy rounds. If the bracelet on her arm had iron in it, it was no wonder her arm felt heavy and her whole body felt awful!

"You wanted a life outside the guild, and that's exactly what you're going to get," Mary Mary told her. She glanced at the two men and pointed at Cory. "Gentlemen, take her away!"

Turning toward the men, Cory saw them without their masks for the first time. One was a thin fairy with red hair and a scraggly mustache. The other was Tom Tom, who sneered and started toward her. Cory wanted to fend off the men, but the longer she wore the iron-filled bracelet, the heavier and more drained she felt. Tom Tom and the fairy practically had to carry her out of the office and down the corridor to a door at the end of the hall.

"So you do work for the Tooth Fairy Guild," Cory said to Tom Tom.

He sneered and dragged her along, his grip so tight it was painful. "I have been for a while," he told her. "I saw that you cleaned up the broken glass and the mud. I liked what you did with the plants. Too bad so many were destroyed when the wolf tried to blow down your house."

"You were the one who threw the tooth and the mud?" Cory said, horrified. "Those were awful things to do! You should be ashamed of yourself."

Tom Tom laughed. "Are you joking? That was the most fun I'd had in ages. Here we are. Hold still while we open the door."

Cory tried to stand her ground, but they shoved her into a windowless room with a clear cylinder in the center. Cory let herself go limp when they tried to make her walk into the cylinder, so they picked her up and set her in it. The redheaded fairy removed the bracelet and untied her wrists before closing the door. Tom Tom hurried out of the room without looking back, but his companion paused and gave Cory a look filled with pity before he left, closing the outer door behind him.

Once the iron-filled bracelet was gone, Cory thought she would feel better, but she still felt heavy and drained of energy. If she could become small, she could whisper the secret fairy words and pass through the wall itself, but when she tried to shrink, nothing happened. When she examined the column, she couldn't find any way out except the door, and that opened only from the outside. The column was narrow, perhaps twice the width of her shoulders, and the transparent walls were tinged with green and as smooth as glass. Examining the wall more closely, she found thin lines of gray running through it from floor to ceiling. She set her hand on the surface and immediately jerked it away as pain flared in her palm. The gray lines were iron, making the walls as effective as the bracelet. Cory was trapped with no way out.

She was still studying the walls, hoping she had missed something, when a soft hum filled the column. The sound grew progressively louder until her whole body seemed to vibrate with it. Suddenly, the lights flickered and went out. Cory's skin prickled; she felt as if ants were crawling all over her. When the hum continued to grow louder, she stuck her fingers in her ears, although it didn't seem to do much good. The light flickered on again, but it was blue now, and went off and on repeatedly until Cory's head hurt and she felt sick to her stomach. She squeezed her eyes shut, blocking out some of the light. By the time the light became painfully bright, then dimmed to normal, Cory felt terrible. Opening her eyes, she saw the light turn white even as the hum faded away.

There was a soft click and the column door opened. Cory felt weak, but she no longer felt heavy. When she stumbled and caught herself by placing her hand against the wall, the metal in the column didn't hurt her like it had when she'd touched it before.

The door into the hallway was unlocked when she tried it. Tom Tom and the redhead were waiting outside and they gestured for her to precede them down the hall toward Mary Mary's office. A group of people were gathered outside the room, some with their ears pressed to the door. They hurried away when they saw Cory and the men approaching. By then Cory could hear raised voices coming from inside the office. As she drew closer she recognized both speakers. One was Mary Mary, the other was Lionel Feathering, her grandfather.

When they reached the door, the men glanced at each other as if they weren't sure what to do. Cory didn't wait, but stepped forward and opened the door herself. Micah was there, standing with her grandfather across the desk from Mary Mary. He glanced at Cory when she entered the room and motioned for her to join them.

"You foolish woman," her grandfather was saying to

Mary Mary. "That girl is my granddaughter. If you have hurt one hair on her head, you will rue the day you ever heard of the Tooth Fairy Guild."

Mary Mary's face was turning red when she said, "Who are you, old man? What right do you have to come in here and talk to me like that? I'm the head of the Tooth Fairy Guild and there is no fairy with standing high enough to speak to me this way!"

"You're right, of course," said Lionel Feathering. "But then, I'm not a fairy." The air shimmered around him and he stood there draped in a white robe with one shoulder bare and beautiful feathered wings sprouting from his back.

Mary Mary gasped. "You're a demigod! I didn't know. No one ever told me. Delphinium should have . . ."

"A good leader does not try to pass the blame to others. Cory is my granddaughter and should never have been treated in such a high-handed manner, nor should anyone. I understand that your organization has been harassing her. I'll be launching an investigation into your actions today."

Lionel turned to Cory and held out his hand. "Cory! Are you all right, my dear?" he asked as she slipped her hand into his. "What did they do to you?"

"I don't know," Cory replied. "They put me in a

cylinder with iron in its walls. There were lights and a loud sound. I feel very odd."

Cupid turned to stare at Mary Mary. The woman spluttered, her hands fluttering as she said, "We didn't hurt her! We just took her fairy powers away."

"What do you mean?" Cory asked. She had tried to turn small while in the cylinder, but the walls had kept her from changing. Letting go of her grandfather's hand, she tried again now. Nothing happened. Cory glanced from her grandfather to her uncle, horrified. "If I can't become small, I won't have wings. I'll never be able to fly again!"

"What gives you the right to do this?" Micah demanded of Mary Mary. "She was born able to change her size and fly. The Tooth Fairy Guild didn't give her those abilities! I can understand if you want to take back what you've given her, but you've gone too far!"

Mary Mary shrugged. "We couldn't take part of her fairy talents without taking them all."

"You've made me no better than a human!" Cory cried as despair filled her heart.

CHAPTER
21

Cory didn't stir until Noodles nipped her toe. She was still half asleep when she pulled her feet away, wondering why he was on her bed. As the woodchuck tugged the blanket, she woke enough to remember what had happened the night before—the kidnapping, losing her fairy abilities, the look on Mary Mary's face when Cory's grandfather scooped her up and made the glass in the window disappear with a glance. He'd flown her back to Micah's house then, tucking her into bed and kissing her cheek. The last thing she remembered was Noodles whimpering when he couldn't get close to her, and her grandfather placing him on the bed.

A sharp pain in her foot made Cory sit up and frown at the woodchuck who had nipped her again while gnawing on her blanket. "Cut that out! This is exactly why you shouldn't be up here! You smell, too. I have to give you another bath."

Picking up the woodchuck, she climbed out of bed and set him on the floor. When she straightened, she caught a glimpse of herself in her mirror. Although the night before she'd felt like she'd been chewed up, spit out, and stomped on, she felt wonderful now. She looked wonderful, too. The dark shadows she'd had under her eyes from lack of sleep were gone. Her skin was flawless and had a glow that she'd never noticed before. Even her hair looked thicker and shinier. Cory touched it, wondering how she could look and feel so good after everything that had happened. Her abilities had been wrenched from her, she couldn't get smaller when she tried, and her wings . . . Cory gasped when she remembered that her wings were gone. She would never fly again, or do any of the fairy things she'd always taken for granted.

Noodles was scratching at the door when Cory turned away from the mirror. After slipping on her robe, she opened the door and let him scamper out. She could hear her uncle talking in the kitchen.

"I tell you, there have been others. Cory isn't the first one to be treated this way by a guild."

"I've already started an inquiry. I don't think anyone on the council knew about this," said a voice.

Cory followed Noodles into the kitchen and found her grandfather seated at the table while her uncle poured him a cup of herb tea. They both looked up when Cory entered the room.

"How are you feeling this morning, my dear?" asked her grandfather.

"If you mean physically, I've never felt better," Cory said, taking a seat at the table. "Is this how humans usually feel?"

Her grandfather smiled and shook his head. "Not at all. But then, you aren't human."

"But I'm not a fairy either, am I?" said Cory. "Not if they took away my abilities. You seem awfully cheerful about this. Am I missing something?"

Her grandfather took a sip of tea, then set his cup down. "It's time that I explain what I think has happened. I am a demigod, as was your father. You would have been as well, but your father married a full fairy woman. I tried to stop their marriage, but they refused to listen to me. Fairies are magical beings. Demigods are beings with powers. When the two have children, the fairy magic obscures the demigod powers."

"Does that mean that fairies are more powerful than demigods?" asked Cory.

"Not at all. Think of it this way—if you have a

beautiful gem and it gets covered with paint, what do you see?"

"The shape of the gem with the color of the paint?"

"Exactly!" said her grandfather. "But if you remove the paint, you see the gem. That Tooth Fairy Guild woman removed the paint, something I didn't know was possible. And now, I'm hoping that what is left behind is what you always were underneath—a demigod. It's possible you have the talent to be the next Cupid. From what you've told me, you already lean in that direction. Let's try a little experiment. Close your eyes and think about one of your friends. Now ask yourself—who is that person's soul mate?"

Cory closed her eyes, thought about Marjorie, and said to herself, *Her soul mate is . . .* A clear image of Jack Nimble's face popped into her head. Cory gasped and her eyes flew open. "I thought about my friend Marjorie. I've been trying to match her up, but I didn't have her meet Jack Nimble until yesterday. That's who I see her with when I think about her."

"Wonderful!" said her grandfather. "And who do you see when you think of your uncle?"

"Say now!" said Micah. "That isn't necessary. I'm fine the way I am and don't need any love match, thank you very much!"

Cory laughed even as she closed her eyes. She didn't think she would see anyone for her uncle, and was surprised when the image of a fairy woman with curly pink hair took shape. "I see someone, but she isn't anyone I know," Cory said, looking from her grandfather to her uncle.

Her uncle looked intrigued when he said, "Really?"

"That happens quite often," said her grandfather. "Now that you know what she looks like, your abilities should help you find her."

"What does being one's soul mate mean?" asked Cory.

"It means that your friend Marjorie is meant to be with Jack and will not be completely happy with anyone else."

Cory clapped her hands in delight. "Uncle Micah! You have a soul mate!"

"Well!" he said, and sank onto his mushroom stool as if his legs could no longer support him.

"Does this mean that I'm the next Cupid?" Cory asked her grandfather.

"It might!" he said with a smile.

"Can I fly like you? Will I get wings that are like yours?"

"Let's see," he replied. "Think 'wings!' and see what happens."

Cory was nervous. The last few times she had tried to get small so she could fly had been failures. After that she hadn't thought she'd have another chance, but if this worked and she really could get wings again . . .

Wings! Cory thought, and held her breath. Nothing happened. She turned to her grandfather, her eyes clouded with disappointment.

"You have to believe it's going to happen," said her grandfather. "Try again and *know* that you can do it. Even a little doubt can be enough to prevent it. Picture what your wings will look like. They'll be feathered and larger than a fairy's. More streamlined, too."

Cory nodded and took a deep breath. "I can do this," she told herself. She imagined her wings. Feathered. White like her grandfather's. Reaching from behind her head to her calves. Sturdy enough to support her weight and carry her for hours. She felt a tingling between her shoulder blades and took it as an encouraging sign. Suddenly it was easier to believe in her wings. "I have wings," she told herself. "I have wings," she repeated over and over, and then, between one moment and the next, she did.

"They're beautiful!" she whispered, turning her head to look over her shoulder. Unlike her grandfather's white wings, her feathers were the color of fresh cream with a pale rainbow of colors shimmering over them when she turned them a certain way. She could move them just as she had her fairy wings, but she could already tell that they were stronger.

"Wow!" her uncle said. "Very nice!"

"Is there anything else I should know?" Cory asked her grandfather.

He laughed and shook his head. "I think that's enough for today. Why don't you get used to what you can do now? Come see me when you have questions or just need to talk."

The old man stood and gave Cory a kiss on her cheek. Then he was gone in a pale blue haze that left the odor of eucalyptus leaves behind. "I'm going outside to test my wings," Cory told her uncle.

"I think you should eat something first," he said, and got up to fill her plate with scrambled eggs with cheese and fried potatoes with herbs.

"I'm not very hungry," Cory told him, then surprised herself by eating it all.

Her uncle volunteered to take Noodles out while Cory got dressed. She'd never had wings when she was big before, so she found them a bit awkward at first. When she walked through the main room, her wings nearly knocked the nest off the mantel, upsetting the finch and her babies. Her wings got in the way when she tried to go into her bedroom, getting jammed in the doorway so that she was stuck until she closed them. Changing her clothes proved to be even harder. Somehow, the power that created them let the wings go through the clothes she was wearing without damaging them. Unfortunately, they also kept her from taking them off. After struggling to remove her robe, she finally thought to make her wings disappear. *No wings*, she thought, and they were gone.

Cory dressed quickly, and was soon out the front door. She was so used to her wings by then that all she had to do was think *wings!* and they were back. Flying wasn't much different from when she was a fairy, except she was bigger and people could actually see her from the ground. Having people notice her was novel at first, but she soon grew tired of the staring and pointing, so she rose into the air so she was less obvious. She found that she could actually go higher than she'd been able to with fairy wings, and that she could soar, something the delicate butterfly-like wings had never allowed. The clouds looked enticing when she drew close enough, but when she flew into one, it was cold and wet and not nearly as much fun as she'd thought it would be. It was too much like flying through a very thick fog, one where you couldn't see where you were going. Although there wasn't anything to trip over, there were birds and larger creatures like the occasional griffin or dragon that she was sure she'd run into if she wasn't careful.

Cory was shivering when she decided to leave the cloud, but by then she was disoriented and not sure which way to turn; the cloud seemed to go on forever in every direction. It occurred to her that the only way out of it was to head down, a direction that she could actually find. All she had to do was tuck her wings to her sides and let herself start to fall. When she came out of the cloud, she saw that she wasn't far from Marjorie's house, so she flew down to pay her a visit, landing in her friend's yard. Cory could tell by the angle of the sun that it was late afternoon. She'd been having so much fun that she hadn't noticed how much time was passing.

Cory looked around the yard before she landed, but didn't see anyone. From the delicious smells coming from the house, she knew that her friend was already cooking dinner. She didn't like visiting at mealtimes unless she'd been invited, and thought about leaving, but she was already there and the news she had to share was too exciting to keep. When she started to the door, her wings snagged on the rose-covered arbor in front of the house. Impatient, Cory thought, *No wings*, and the weight on her back disappeared. After knocking on the door, she ran her fingers through her windblown hair while she waited.

Marjorie looked surprised when she opened the door.

"I'm sorry I didn't send a message first, but I was out this way and thought I'd stop by," said Cory. "A lot has happened and there's so much I want to tell you."

"I wanted to talk to you, too," said Marjorie. "Jack Nimble and I went on our date yesterday. At first I thought we were really hitting it off. He took me on a picnic in his hot-air balloon to see the dragon-hatching grounds by Shell Lake. We had a wonderful time, but on the way back he started talking about his mother and I knew what was wrong with him—he's a mama's boy!"

"It's not like he lives with her or anything," said Cory.

"No, but he visits her all the time."

"Not according to her."

Marjorie looked puzzled. "You've met his mother?"

"Before I met him," said Cory. "She's actually very nice."

"That's what people said about my mother and we never got along," Marjorie replied.

Cory laughed. "I know what that's like! But you have to give him another chance! I *know* he's the one for you. He's your soul mate—the one you're meant to be with for the rest of your life."

"Why are you suddenly so sure?" Marjorie said, sounding skeptical.

"Because I *saw* you together. That's what I had to tell you. I met my grandfather and you'll never guess who he is."

"I don't know. Santa Claus?"

"No, of course not! Although Santa is a very nice man, we're not at all related. My grandfather is Cupid!"

"Your grandfather is a pudgy little baby?"

"That's who I thought Cupid was, too! But he's actually a very distinguished gentleman. I may be the next one! Cupid, I mean. After the TFG kidnapped me and stripped away my fairy abilities, I learned all sorts of things about myself."

"The TFG did what? When did this happen? Did you report it to the Fey Law Enforcement Agency? You really should you know."

"My grandfather is on the council's supervisory board. He's already started an investigation. Anyway, what I was trying to tell you was my visions work now. You're *supposed* to be with Jack Nimble."

"Cory, I believe you think that's true, but he had his chance and he *isn't* the one for me. Listen, I don't know about this whole Cupid thing, but if the TFG really did take away your fairy abilities, they probably left you a little, well, messed up. I'm sure it's just a temporary thing and you'll feel better after you've had some rest."

"That isn't it at all!" said Cory. "My visions are real now! They are so clear and I *saw* you with Jack."

"That's nice, but it isn't going to happen. Listen, I'm about to eat dinner. Would you like to join me?"

Cory shook her head. She finally really knew what she was doing, and Marjorie didn't want to believe her! Frustrated and annoyed that her friend had brushed her off like that, Cory made her excuses and left. If a good friend like Marjorie didn't believe her, the other people she'd been trying to find matches for probably wouldn't either. She'd been so excited when she arrived, only to feel disappointed and discouraged now.

Cory went to bed early that night. Her dreams were filled with matches for the people she knew, but when she tried to tell them what she'd seen, not one person believed her.

CHAPTER
22

*E*arly the next morning, Cory sent a message to Olot, asking if they could rehearse in a new location. She told him why it was necessary, and was sure he'd understand. When she left the house, he hadn't replied yet, but she couldn't imagine that he wouldn't agree.

Dew was still glistening on the grass when she reached her grandfather's house. She left footprints behind when she landed on the lawn and started toward the front door. After shaking her wings to realign her feathers, she closed them and wished them away before stepping onto the porch. The bell jingled on the other side of the wall loud enough for Cory to hear. Although Orville was wearing a sour look when he opened the door a crack, the moment he saw her standing there, he grinned and opened it all the way.

"Welcome!" he said. "We were wondering when you'd come back. We heard the good news. Congratulations! I must say, we're all very excited. A new Cupid! Imagine that! I'll show you to your grandfather, then get you a bite to eat. He'll be so happy to see you!"

The putti who had barely talked to her during her earlier visit couldn't seem to contain his excitement now. He chattered the entire way to the terrace where her grandfather was seated, then toddled off to get the food.

"I wondered when you'd come see me again," Lionel said, echoing the putti. "How are you doing?"

Cory kissed him on the cheek and took the seat across from him. "The flying is wonderful and my visions are crystal clear, yet when I tried to tell a friend of mine what I'd seen she didn't believe me. I want to help people, but how can I help them if they don't believe what I tell them?"

"They usually don't," her grandfather replied. "A cupid has to be extra convincing to get the idea across."

"Here we are!" Orville sang out as he swung the door open. A procession of putti poured through the door, carrying trays of pastries, steaming dishes of eggs and fish, four different kinds of bread, bowls of fruit cut up and whole, jugs of fruit juice, milk and tea, and another table to put it all on. After they had arranged everything to their satisfaction, the putti gathered around Cory and Lionel, smiling as if they couldn't stop.

"Everyone wanted to see you to say how happy we are that you've inherited your grandfather's gifts," said Orville.

"You're going to make a wonderful Cupid," Margory blurted, blushing when Cory turned her way.

A putti wearing an apron said, "Just let us know what you need and we'll be ready to do it!"

"Thank you very much!" Cory said, glancing from one to the next. "You're all very kind."

"Ask her," a putti said, poking the one standing beside him.

"No, you ask her!" the other said, poking him back.

"What is it?" Cory asked.

"They were just wondering if they could see your wings," said Orville.

"Of course you can," Cory said. She pushed her chair back and stepped to the edge of the patio. Although she felt self-conscious for a moment, she saw the expectant faces and didn't hesitate. *Wings!* she thought, and they appeared, the colors shimmering across the creamy feathers as she twitched her shoulder blades.

"Ooh!" the putti all cried, their eyes enormous.

Lionel waited until they'd had a good long look before clearing his throat and saying, "I believe that's enough for now. You'll be seeing my granddaughter and her wings quite often, I'm sure, so please get on with whatever you were doing." When they didn't move, he added, "Her breakfast is getting cold."

"Sorry!" a few putti said, bobbing their heads and backing away. Others continued to stare at her wings in awe and didn't move until their friends pushed and tugged them toward the door.

When the last dawdling putti had peeked at Cory once more and shut the door behind him, Lionel smiled and said, "You can't really blame them. They've been so afraid that after I'm gone there wouldn't be a Cupid and no work for them to do. After spending their entire lives in my employ, they can't imagine doing anything else."

"Are you offering me the job?"

"Do you want to be the next Cupid?" he asked, watching her face.

"I don't know if I can. I mean, I know I have some of the abilities now, but what if I can't do it all?"

Her grandfather shook his head. "If you have the wings and the visions, you're more than halfway there. The rest will come with time and it will all seem very natural. I was two years older than you are now when I started seeing people's matches in my mind. My father had told me what to expect, but it still came as a surprise."

"What would happen if I didn't accept?"

"Then the world would have to get along without a Cupid. Fewer people would find their soul mates. There would be less love in the world. You can see some of it already. I told you that I'm semiretired. I cut back on my hours because my health demanded it, but I wanted to do more. I've noticed that since I cut back, more couples have gotten divorced, and more people are unhappy in their marriages. I'm not saying you *have* to be Cupid, but the world would be a better place if you accept the position. You said that you wanted to help others. What better way to help than to bring together soul mates who might not ever meet without your intervention?"

"I understand what you're saying. But if I do make this my career, can I stay in my band and live my life the way I want to? I don't want to walk away from my friends."

"No one is asking you to walk away from anything," said Lionel. "As Cupid, you'll get to set your own schedule. You'll be able to do what you want when you want to do it."

"You're very convincing," said Cory. "I don't think this is going to be a hard decision to make."

"Good!" her grandfather replied. "Now what would you like to eat? It would be a shame if they went to all this trouble and this delicious food went to waste."

Cory's appetite had grown along with the strength of her wings and she ate more than she would have even a few days before. She nibbled the first bite of pastry, then devoured the rest and helped herself to fried eggs and smoked fish, slices of melon; and a casserole of spiced potatoes, cheese, and onions.

She had just served herself another piece of fish when she thought of a question for her grandfather. "You said that you were trying to remain anonymous and let the putti represent you. Did you tell anyone that you were Cupid? Did your friends know, or your relatives?"

"I let the fewest people possible know. Your grandmother knew, of course. And so did your father. He was the one who told your mother. A few of my more discreet friends knew, but most of my friends and relatives thought I was just a successful businessman. If you don't believe people can keep a secret, don't tell them. People think and act differently toward you if they know that you're Cupid."

"Good idea," said Cory. "My best friend, Daisy,

couldn't keep a secret for five minutes, but I bet Marjorie could keep one forever, which is a good thing, because I already told her. And Uncle Micah is very good at keeping secrets. He knew about you and didn't tell me."

"I always liked Micah. I'm sure you could tell him anything and he would never betray the confidence."

Cory nodded and thought about the other people she knew. She wouldn't tell her mother, but Delphinium might figure it out for herself if she already knew about Lionel. Cory wouldn't tell her grandmother, although her mother's father would be okay. The only other person she could think of who could be trusted with the news was Johnny Blue, except she wasn't sure he wanted to talk to her anymore.

Cory ate one more piece of melon, then sat back and glanced at her grandfather. He was watching her with a smile on his face. "I used to be able to eat like that," he said, nodding toward her plate. "Now, if you're finished, there's something I'd like to show you. It's how I convince people to accept what I've seen in my visions."

Lionel stood and reached for her hand. Together they walked down the steps onto the lawn that stretched from the terrace to the river at the bottom of the hill. They hadn't gone far before he stopped and let go of her, only to hold his hands in front of him, palms up. A moment later the air shimmered and a bow appeared in one hand, a quiver of arrows in the other. After shouldering the quiver, he set an arrow in the bow. Cory watched as he pulled the bow string back and let the arrow loose, aiming at a target that hadn't been there when they walked across the lawn.

"Let me get this straight. You convince people by shooting at them if they don't listen to you?" asked Cory.

Lionel laughed. "You aren't far off. I don't use an ordinary bow or ordinary arrows when I'm working. I use these for practice, but when I am on the job as Cupid, I use magic arrows that will penetrate the heart, but not the flesh. The arrows don't hurt them; they just change what their hearts tell them." When he saw the confused look on Cory's face, he added, "Let me explain. The arrows come in pairs. The person I shoot with the first arrow and the one I shoot with the second will fall in love with each other. It's a process that would have happened eventually, under the right circumstances. I just make sure it happens."

"But I don't know how to use a bow and arrow," said Cory.

"Then that's what we're going to work on today. Hold out your hands the way I did," Lionel told her. "And think 'bow.'"

When she did, a bow and a quiver of arrows appeared

in her hands so quickly that their weight surprised her and she almost dropped them.

"Those are yours and will appear whenever you want them," said her grandfather.

He taught her how to stand to shoot, how to notch the arrow and pull it back so that her thumb nearly touched the corner of her mouth, and how to hold the bow steady and keep her aim true.

Cory was hitting the target nearly every time when she turned to her grandfather and said, "Learning how to shoot an arrow is all well and good, but how do I do it in public? Someone is bound to try to stop me if I pull out weapons like this."

"When the time comes, no one will see your bow and arrow."

"I don't understand," said Cory.

"It's another ability of Cupid's. You'll understand soon enough. Look, Orville is bringing us something to drink. I suppose it is time for a break."

The putti brought out water, tea, and fruit juices so cold that the pitchers holding them were frosted. Cory's arms were getting tired and she was happy to stop for a few minutes.

"Tell me," said Lionel. "Is there a young man in your life? Have you met someone special yet?"

Cory shook her head and swallowed her juice. "No,

there isn't. Even when I was dating someone, I knew he wasn't really the one for me. I haven't looked yet to see my true love's face."

"It wouldn't do any good if you had," said her grandfather. "Cupid can never see the face of his or her true love before they meet, and the arrows don't work on members of our family. Believe me, if they did I would have used one on your father. In fact, true love doesn't present itself the same way to us as it does to other people. When I met your grandmother, my stomach bothered me every time she was close. I couldn't stop thinking about her, or I would have stayed away. It wasn't until I'd kissed her for the first time that we both knew we were meant to be together. From what I've heard, the same thing happened to my father when he met my mother. I told your father this, but he didn't believe me at first."

"So my mother wasn't his true love," Cory said as she handed her cup to Orville.

"Yes, and I was foolish enough to tell him that when he was infatuated with her. They resented me for it, your mother more than your father. I think he eventually understood, but by then they were married and you were on the way."

"When I do meet someone . . . Will it matter if my true love isn't a demigod?" Cory asked, examining her bow.

"Not unless he has some sort of magic that can obscure your powers the way a fairy's can. My mother was a human. I inherited my father's abilities the same as if she had been a demigod like him."

"That's good to know," Cory said, smiling to herself.

They practiced more then, until Cory was hitting the bull's-eye nearly every time. When Orville and Margory brought sandwiches and more cold drinks, Cory and her grandfather took another break.

"I was wondering," Cory said when they had finished eating. "Will I shoot only at people who are standing still?"

"You'll find that time stands still when you call for your bow and quiver. You'll be able to move, but your targets won't," Lionel told her.

Cory picked up her bow and quiver. The heft of the bow had felt right in her hand from the first time she held it. It was the arrows that were unusual, although they looked fairly normal—white with bright blue fletching. When she'd first started shooting, not all the arrows had hit their mark. Those that missed had returned to the quiver on their own. Later, when her aim was better, other arrows appeared in the quiver to replace the ones still vibrating in the target. Curious, Cory pulled the arrows out to peer inside the quiver, but it looked quite ordinary.

"Maybe I should practice shooting at moving targets just in case," Cory said as she studied one of the arrows more closely.

Her grandfather scratched his chin. "I suppose we could have the putti run back and forth in front of you carrying the targets."

Orville made a choking noise as he refilled Lionel's glass, but he managed to smile at Cory when she looked his way.

Cory laughed and shook her head. "Never mind. It was just a thought."

"Tell me," said Lionel, "are you going to talk to your mother again anytime soon? She may not be my favorite person, but I'd hate to think that you were going to remain estranged."

"I'll see her, but it won't be soon," said Cory. "I have a lot to think through before I talk to her again."

"When do you plan to start using your skills?" her grandfather asked.

"In a few days," said Cory. "I'm thinking about having a party."

CHAPTER
23

Cory was cleaning the kitchen the next morning when someone knocked on the front door. After all the things that had happened over the last few days, she was reluctant to answer it, especially when she peeked out the window and saw Doris Dumpty standing there looking furious. Certain that she was going to get another blistering rebuke, she was surprised when she opened the door and Mrs. Dumpty's expression softened.

"I've come to apologize," said Doris. "I was just so angry, but then I learned the truth and I, well, I had something else to deal with before I came to see you. Humpty, tell Miss Cory what you told me."

The little boy had been hiding behind his mother. He peeked out now, his cheeks pink and his expression grave. "I told a fib," he said, his lips quivering. "I let the mice go on purpose, and then I pretended that I didn't see them, but I really did."

Mrs. Dumpty's lips were pressed into thin lines when she nodded. "He told me only after I had sent a message to an exterminator. It seems he wanted to keep the mice and was afraid you wouldn't let him if he asked. I certainly wouldn't have, but I have to say, since he started taking care of them, he has been very good and has not tried to climb anything higher than his seat at the kitchen table. He's very good with the mice and he's begged his father and me to let them stay. I told him he had to apologize to you and ask for your permission. He understands that they are really your mice and that you might say no, especially considering the misunderstanding. Isn't that right, Humpty?"

The little boy wrapped his arms around his middle and looked so sad when he nodded that Cory didn't have the heart to say no. "Yes, you may keep them, Humpty," she said, "provided you promise not to lie anymore and you will take very good care of the mice."

Humpty's face lit up like the sun breaking through on a cloudy day. "I promise! I named them already. Their names are Squeaks, Fuzzy, and Cheese. I named him Cheese 'cause he likes to eat it as much as I do."

"I think those are very good names," said Cory.

"I must apologize for something else," Mrs. Dumpty said. "Before Humpty told me what he had done, a woman came by. She wasn't very pleasant and was actually quite nosy, asking questions about you and your work habits. I'm sorry to say that I was still angry and told her some things that I later regretted. I have no problem with your work, and I . . . Let me see, yes, here it is. This is for you." She took a small bag jingling with coins from her purse and handed it to Cory. "That's your pay for the last day you babysat Humpty, plus a little extra for putting up with all of this nonsense."

"Uh, thank you," Cory told her.

"If there is ever anything I can do for you, just let me know," Mrs. Humpty added.

The woman was about to turn away when Cory spoke up. "Actually, there is something you could do for me, provided your husband is Randal Jehosephat Dumpty, the judge."

"He is," Mrs. Dumpty said slowly. "What did you need?"

"I've been having a problem with the Tooth Fairy Guild," said Cory. "I quit recently and they've been hounding me ever since."

Doris Dumpty listened with increasing interest while Cory told her about all the trouble the guild had inflicted on her after she quit. "So, would you be able to talk to your husband? Apparently, he has let the guilds do whatever they want, but if you let him know what they were really up to, he might change his mind."

"I'll talk to him, all right," said Mrs. Dumpty. "That's outrageous! No one should be able to get away with such nastiness." Turning to her son, she reached for his hand. "Now come along, Humpty. We have a lot to do before we go home. Your father's office will be our first stop."

Cory was glad that Mrs. Dumpty had come by, especially when she saw how much the woman had given her. It was more than twice as many coins as she owed Cory. Even the payment for babysitting was money Cory had never thought she'd see.

Singing to herself, Cory went back to work cleaning. She was throwing a party in two days and had lots to do to get ready. After finishing in the kitchen, she started on the main room. Armed with a soapstone, water, and a scrub brush, she was cleaning the mantel around the bird nest when her mother burst into the house. Delphinium froze when she saw Cory and said, "What are you doing? Shouldn't you be resting in bed after your ordeal?"

"I guess I don't have to ask if you know what happened to me, do I, Mother?" Cory said, setting down the scrub brush. "But then you did warn me. You knew the TFG was going to kidnap me and shut me in a box and rip my fairy abilities from me. They even took my wings!"

"Really, Cory, don't be so dramatic. I'm sure the guild didn't—"

"That's *exactly* what they did! I can't believe my own mother let them."

"I warned you that you couldn't just walk away!"

"You warned me, but you never tried to help me. Grandfather said that—"

"Your grandfather!" Delphinium said, practically spitting the words. "Mary Mary told me that Lionel had come to see her. She was taken completely unaware and is furious that I didn't tell her that he's a demigod. How was I to know that you would drag him into this, after I tried so hard to shield you from him?"

"You weren't shielding me! You were protecting your pride. He told you something you didn't want to hear and he was right. You were the one at fault, not Grandfather!"

"How dare you!"

"I dare a lot after what I've been through, and I don't think you have any right to barge into my home and . . . Why did you come here, anyway?"

"For the same reason I came by yesterday and the day before, knocking on your door until your neighbors came to see what was wrong. I thought you were in bed, hiding from the world. I was worried about you. Most fairies would be traumatized if they were stripped of their abilities, but you seem to be fine. I thought you needed me. I see that I was wrong."

"How can you let the TFG try to ruin my life, and think I want your help afterward?"

"You're my daughter! I came to take you home where you belong. This isn't your house; it's your uncle's and you've imposed on him long enough."

"That's just it. He doesn't think I'm imposing. We're family and we act like it. Please leave now, Mother. I don't live with you anymore and I'm never coming back."

Delphinium stared at her, her mouth opening and closing like a fish's. Finally, she turned on her heel, stomped from the house, and slammed the door behind her.

"Well, that was unpleasant," Cory told Noodles, who was sniffing at the door. "I can only imagine what she would have done if I'd told her I was the new Cupid. To be honest, I hope she never finds out. There are very few people who I want to tell, and she's not one of them!"

Cory left for Marjorie's house a short time later. She had contacted her to say that she and some friends were stopping by, but hadn't said what they planned to do.

After two failed attempts to get rid of the spiders, she didn't want to get Marjorie's hopes up again.

Only a few minutes after she arrived, Olot and Chancy showed up with the cart full of instruments. Cory had told Olot about the spiders and he wanted to see them. Chancy didn't like spiders and wasn't sure she wanted to go inside, but finally did when Marjorie assured her that they didn't bite people.

"I don't see any webs," Chancy said, hesitating at the door.

"They aren't web-building spiders," said Marjorie. "This kind of spider goes looking for its prey."

Chancy shuddered. "I'm not sure, but I think that might be worse."

She carried Olot's lute in while Cory and Olot managed the drums. Fortunately, they didn't see any spiders then. It wasn't until Cory was setting up her drums that the first spider emerged. It was a smaller one, only as long as Cory's little finger. Chancy didn't notice it as she went outside to get something Olot had left on the cart. The next time Cory looked up, a dozen spiders were crawling over her drums and most of them were bigger than her fist.

"You might want to tell Chancy to stay outside," Cory told Olot.

"Good idea," he said as a spider climbed onto his shoe. He had to shake his foot to get the spider off and he didn't look as intrigued by the creatures when he left the room.

Olot was still outside when Skippy arrived. Perky came next, then Daisy and Cheeble showed up. Cory opened all the doors before they began to practice and noticed that Chancy had stayed outside. Soon after they started their first song, Marjorie went out as well. The music had been loud in Olot's cave and in the restaurants. In Marjorie's little house, it was almost deafening.

At first the noise made the spiders agitated. They skittered off Cory's drums and out from under the chairs, fell from the fairy lights on the walls, and tumbled off the table. Some collapsed onto the floor, drawing their legs close to their bodies as if they were in pain. Others ran in circles making a high-pitched noise that sounded like "Ick! Ick! Ick!"

"Play louder," Cory shouted to her bandmates.

They did, playing as loudly as they could. The spiders started to run out the doors, just a few at first, then more and more until a steady stream fled the house. Cory thought she heard Chancy scream once, but when Olot looked out the window and continued to play, Cory didn't even pause. Before the first song was done, she was fairly sure all the spiders were gone, but they kept playing until they had rehearsed as long as usual.

Cory was packing up her drums when Marjorie came to see her. "I've looked everywhere, but I can't find a single spider. I think they're all gone! I don't know if you could see out the window; a flock of crows got a lot of them. The rest ran to the forest down the street. Thank you so much! I thought I'd never get rid of them. How did you ever think of this?"

"I remembered how they hadn't liked the birds' screeching when I tried to get rid of the spiders last time. Then at our last rehearsal, our playing was so loud it made my headache worse. I could imagine what it would do to the spiders."

"I'm glad you did!" said Marjorie. "I love my little house and I didn't really want to sell it."

Daisy joined them then, saying, "I don't know how you could stand living with those spiders! They were huge and scary and they watched you wherever you went."

"At least they didn't bite me," said Marjorie. "I would have left then and never come back if they had. Excuse me. I have to thank your friends."

"Well, that was an experience I never hope to repeat, but at least we were able to help Marjorie," Daisy told Cory.

"Finally!" Cory exclaimed. "I've tried and tried to get rid of those spiders. I'm glad *something* worked."

"You really do want to help people, don't you?" said Daisy. "You're not just saying it without meaning it, like some people do. I know you were trying to help me when you told me about Tom Tom, and I appreciate it. I thought about what you said, and broke up with Tom Tom the next day."

"How did he take it?" Cory asked.

"He was mad, but he'll get over it," said Daisy. "They all do."

That afternoon, Cory sat at the kitchen table with an ink stick and a fresh leaf to think about the love matches for her friends and clients. She could see the images of Marjorie and Jack Nimble as clearly as if they were standing in front of her. She recognized Priscilla Hood's match, but the matches for the others were strangers to her. Even so, she knew she would recognize them if she saw them. After making a list of who she wanted to invite, she made lists of what she wanted to cook, and what she needed to buy at the market. She sent a message to Olot and all the members of the band, inviting them to the dinner and asking them to play that night. Her uncle had already said that he'd help her cook, but she wanted him to enjoy the party, too, so she arranged to have Josef, the young man at Perfect Pastry, come help. The rest of the afternoon flew by as she wrote and sent out her invitations.

Cory spent the next two days getting ready. By the night of the party, she was so excited that she couldn't sit still. It was light out when Josef arrived. Then her neighbors showed up and Cory was glad to see that neither Wanita nor Salazar had brought their pets and that the twins were both in their human forms. Only minutes after she greeted the first arrivals, Marjorie was there along with Daisy and Priscilla. Mary Lambkin walked in the door just as Lionel Feathering stepped onto the porch. Cory introduced the other guests to her grandfather, omitting his title, then returned to the door to greet the next arrivals.

Nearly everyone was there when Lionel took Cory aside. "How is everything going? You look a little nervous."

"Everything's fine," said Cory. "It's just that, well, someone isn't here yet, and I really had hoped that he'd come."

"If you're talking about Johnny Blue, I'm sure he'll be here soon."

"How did you know about Johnny?" she asked.

"I have my sources," he said with a mischievous grin.

"Uncle Micah?" she said, glancing toward the kitchen, where her uncle was checking on the cooking food.

"He may have told me a few things," her grandfather replied. "When I realized that this Johnny Blue might be the one you were *not* telling me about at breakfast the other day, it occurred to me that it was important he attend your party. I spoke with Johnny Blue's captain. The man agreed to send Johnny to your party to watch for suspicious characters."

"How did you get him to do that?" asked Cory.

"I am on the FLEA board, remember? I haven't been very active lately, but I've decided to change that. The board is looking into the guilds' activities against their members now."

"Do you know Judge Randal Jehosephat Dumpty? Johnny told me that he's been keeping the guilds from being prosecuted. I spoke with his wife and she is going to ask him to stop. I don't know if that will do any good, but it might if you used your influence, too."

"I'll take care of it," he said. "Between your friends and my work on the board, the guilds are going to have to answer for what they do very soon." He glanced at the doorway when someone else walked in. "Say, is that the young man?"

Cory turned and saw Johnny. Her face lit up even as she felt her grandfather give her a small push and said, "Go see your young man while I ask if your uncle needs any help."

Cory nodded and swallowed hard. She was partway across the room when Mary Lambkin waylaid her to talk about another date. When Cory looked up, Johnny was deep in conversation with Cheeble, who was gesturing and talking in an excited voice. She was going over to join them when she saw the three pigs standing in a corner looking forlorn.

"Come with me," she told them, and led the pigs to her neighbor. "Wanita, I'd like you to meet some friends of mine, Alphonse, Bertie, and Roger. Gentlepigs, Wanita is one of my neighbors. She has a wild boar living at her house."

The pigs ears perked with interest. Wanita looked intrigued to meet pigs who stood on their hind legs and could actually talk to her. The witch told them about her boar, then asked if they liked living in town. When Cory left them, they were telling Wanita about the wolf and the boy named Tom Tom who had kidnapped Roger.

Cory found Johnny Blue standing beside the mantel eyeing the bird in its nest. He looked pleased when she first walked up, then his eyes became wary as if remembering their last meeting.

"I'm happy to see that you look well," Johnny said. "I heard about the kidnapping from the guys on the squad the day after it happened. You didn't tell me—"

"I couldn't tell you," Cory said, her words tumbling over his. "It happened so fast and then my grandfather was there and I had so much to think about and I thought you—"

"I came to see you as soon as I heard, but you weren't here. Then I came by the next day and you were out again. And then when you didn't send me a message, I thought that maybe . . ." Johnny's voice trailed off and he looked away.

"Maybe what?" asked Cory.

"Maybe you didn't want to see me because I'd let you down. I'd said that I would keep an eye on Tom Tom, but then he was one of the people who kidnapped you, wasn't he? I don't blame you for being angry with me. I failed you when all I wanted to do was protect you."

"You couldn't have stopped him. He came with two other men on a flying carpet! I don't blame you for anything. I was gone because I was working out some things and I didn't send you a message because I thought you didn't want to see me. After I said what I did, I thought I'd hurt your feelings so badly that you didn't want to have anything more to do with me."

"That wasn't it at all!" Johnny told her, taking Cory's hand in his.

Her stomach lurched and her head felt woozy, like when you stand up too suddenly, but she squeezed his hand and felt unreasonably pleased when he squeezed back.

"Sure, I felt awful when you told me not to touch you. Then I thought about it and I knew that there had to be more to it," said Johnny. "I care about you too much to just walk away. You aren't going to get rid of me that easily!"

"I don't ever want to get rid of you!" Cory said.

People began to form a line by the table set up at one end of the room; Josef and Micah had brought out the food and everyone seemed eager to serve themselves.

"I should go see what else there is to do," Cory said, giving Johnny's hand one last squeeze before she let go. "I want to talk to you again later."

"I'll be here," he said with a grin.

Cory was busy for a while then, making sure that there were enough serving spoons and napkins, cleaning up juice that Skippy spilled and finding salt for Olot and water for Salazar. She was refilling platters when the band began to play old songs that didn't need a drummer. When Micah took a platter from her and sent her out to join the band, she wiped her hands on a napkin and hurried to her drums. They played newer songs then, most of which the band had written. Everyone loved "Morning Mist" and swore that it made them feel as if they were really there.

When her grandfather heard this, he smiled and nodded. The moment they stopped to take a break, he gestured to her, pointing to the door and the front porch. "Do you get that reaction to your music often?" he asked once they were alone.

"To our new songs," said Cory. "The ones we wrote together."

"Have you had a hand in writing these particular songs?" he asked.

Cory nodded. "Every one. I wrote most of 'Morning Mist' and 'Thunder's Clap.' Why do you ask?"

"I thought I detected a hint of power!" said her grandfather. "Apparently, some of your demigod abilities were coming through even when you had your fairy traits. When you wrote your music, you poured your heart and your emotions into each piece. Your demigod side evoked those same emotions in the audience. That's why everyone says they feel as if they're there."

"Really!" said Cory. "I just thought our playing had gotten better."

"You do play very well," her grandfather said with a grin. "I'm sure that's part of it, too! Have you tried your bow yet? You said you were going to use it at your party."

"And I will," said Cory. She peeked through the doorway into the house and spotted Marjorie talking to

Daisy. "I suppose that now would be as good a time as any. If you'll excuse me . . ."

The other members of the band were still playing when Cory invited Marjorie to join her on the porch. On their way out, she stopped and spoke to Jack Nimble. Marjorie gave Cory a questioning glance with a raised eyebrow when Jack began to follow them.

"You'll understand in a minute," said Cory.

Once they'd stepped onto the porch, Cory closed the door behind them. "I know you two went out on a date together and it didn't work out, but you really are meant for each other," Cory told them.

Jack looked surprised and shook his head; Marjorie looked exasperated. "I told you it wouldn't work," she said to Cory.

"Oh, but it will!" said Cory. *Bow*, Cory thought, holding out her hands. Suddenly, time seemed to stand still. Her bow appeared in one hand, her quiver in the other. They weren't the same as those she'd used for practice. Instead, this bow was silver with a golden string, the quiver was made of soft white leather, and the arrows were silver with gold fletching and fine writing on the shaft. Moving with the ease of practice, Cory drew out the arrow with "Marjorie Theresa Muffet" written on the shaft and placed it in her bow. Imagining a target over her friend's heart, she took aim and . . . hesitated.

This was a lot different from shooting at targets. She'd never actually shot a person before! What if these really weren't magical arrows, but regular arrows that could hurt her friend. A shot like this could kill her, especially at such close range. Cory bit her lip and lowered the arrow. Then, as if he were standing beside her, she could hear her grandfather's voice in her head. "Without a Cupid there will be less love in the world." Although Marjorie had never actually said it, Cory knew that the one thing that her friend wanted most was love and this might be the only way she would ever find it.

Taking a deep breath, Cory pulled back the bow-string, aimed the arrow at Marjorie, and let the arrow fly. A shimmer of gold puffed from Marjorie's chest, but she didn't move or even blink. Satisfied that the arrow was doing what it was supposed to do, Cory drew the second arrow from the quiver. "Jack Benjamin Nimble" was written on the arrow. Taking careful aim, she shot Jack in the heart without a moment's hesitation. Once again there was a puff of gold, only this time Marjorie and Jack began to glow until a bright light suffused them both.

From the time Cory had thought *bow* to the time the light faded from around Jack and Marjorie, nothing had moved except Cory—not Jack or Marjorie, the leaves on the trees, or the squirrel watching from the railing. The noise of the party inside the house had grown silent as had the normal sounds of the night outside. Now, however, as bow and quiver disappeared, the light around the couple faded away, and sound and movement returned.

Both Marjorie and Jack stood stunned for a moment, then, as if a puppeteer had pulled their strings, they turned to face each other. "I think I was wrong about you," Marjorie whispered, looking into Jack's eyes.

"We were meant to be together!" he said, reaching for her hand.

Cory smiled to herself as she went back inside the house, leaving Jack and Marjorie alone on the porch. She slipped through the crowded room to the kitchen to bring out more food, stopping to talk to Josef on the way. When she returned to the main room a few minutes later, she saw that Marjorie and Jack were huddled in a corner, gazing into each other's eyes, so she began looking for Priscilla Hood. She found Priscilla talking to Selene and Felice about their favorite kinds of fur.

"Pardon me for interrupting," she told the girls, "but I need to talk to Priscilla."

"That's all right," said Felice. "Selene and I are going to get more of that lovely smoked fish."

"What did you want to talk about?" Priscilla asked as Cory led her to the porch.

"Your love life," said Cory. "Oh, good. Here he is."

Josef had followed them out the door just as Cory had told him to. He was offering a tray of fruit juice to Priscilla when Cory thought *bow*. It took her less than a minute to shoot them both. This time the couple wandered off the porch and into the yard, leaving Cory behind.

Too excited by what she had done, Cory couldn't bring herself to go back in the house. She took a seat on one of the chairs, wishing there was someone else she could help fall in love that very night, and knowing that the two couples she had just helped were the only ones she'd "seen" together. True, she had "seen" her other friends with the loves they were meant to find, but the people they were with were strangers to her and she would have to locate them first before she could bring the couples together.

Cory was sitting by herself, enjoying the night air and thinking about what she should do over the next few days, when the door opened and Johnny Blue came out.

"There you are!" he said, crossing the porch. "I was talking to your uncle when it occurred to me that the only person I really wanted to be talking to was you, and I couldn't find you anywhere. Then one of those girls with the cat eyes told me you were out here. You're probably going to have to put out more of that fish, by the way. The girl and her sister ate it all."

Cory laughed and got to her feet. "I'm not surprised. I should have set out more. When I invited them they told me that the only things they eat are fish and vegetables. Listen, I know I said I wanted to talk to you later, but I think we've talked enough. My grandfather told me something that I think I should check out for myself." Walking up to Johnny, she took his head between her hands and pulled him closer. Then, standing on tiptoe, she tilted her head and pressed her lips to his.

The moment their lips met, Cory knew that everything was going to change. Instead of feeling ill, she felt warm and wonderful inside. Her heart began beating faster, matching the beat of his heart as he took her in his arms and pulled her close. He picked her up to hold her even closer as the kiss grew longer and deeper. As her world filled with thoughts of Johnny Blue and nothing else, Cory would have been happy if the kiss had never ended. This was her true love, the person she was meant to be with for the rest of her life.

Then, suddenly, someone else was on the porch and an angry voice was grating at her. "Well, isn't this a pretty sight! Little Miss Busybody has a boyfriend! And it's the Boogie Man! Why am I not surprised? I know she told my girlfriend to dump me, but were you in on it, too?"

Johnny Blue set Cory down and stepped in front of her in a protective gesture that she thought was very sweet. Peeking from behind Johnny, she caught a glimpse of Tom Tom and the angry look on his face. She was very glad that Johnny was there.

"I was looking for you," Johnny Blue snarled at Tom Tom, who backed up half a step.

A low-throated growl made Cory peek again. Tom Tom had brought a wolf with him and it looked like the same animal that had tried to blow down the house.

"You can't kidnap someone and get away with it," Johnny said, taking a step toward Tom Tom.

"I was doing what I was ordered to do!" Tom Tom shouted.

The door opened and people from the party spilled onto the porch. Although Olot and Lionel were the first, Selene and Felice pushed their way to the front to eye Tom Tom and the wolf. Wanita followed them, a look of anticipation on her face.

Although Cory couldn't see him in the crowd, Roger must have been there as well because he suddenly squealed, "That's them! That's Tom Tom, who kidnapped me, and the wolf that blew down my house!" The sound of pig's trotters scrabbling on the porch floor told Cory that Roger had run back inside.

Wanita's mouth spread into a creepy smile that Cory hoped was never aimed at her. "So you're the ones who like to harass the small and defenseless?" Wanita said to Tom Tom and the wolf. "I know the cure for that!"

With a wave of her arm and a few muttered words, Wanita turned the young man and the wolf into cute little pigs, smaller than Alphonse and his brothers.

"We haven't chased anyone in a long time, sister," Felice said to Selene.

The air shimmered around the girls. In an instant, two leopards stood in their place, one black and the other spotted. The spotted leopard screamed, a chilling sound that made the creatures in the nearby forest grow silent. Squealing, the two little pigs tumbled off the porch and darted across the lawn. The leopards turned to look at each other before taking off after the pigs.

"Are those girls going to eat them?" asked Johnny. "I planned to arrest Tom Tom for vandalism, if nothing else."

"The twins told me that they don't eat meat, remember?" Cory told him. "And I have a feeling that the Fey Law Enforcement Agency is about to ensure that Tom Tom will answer for all the things he's done."

"Pardon me for interrupting," said Wanita. "But I

just wanted to tell you that *that* bit of magic takes care of the favor I owed you. I have to say, this has been the best party ever!" Turning around, the witch headed back inside with the rest of Cory's guests trailing behind her.

"Yes, it has," Johnny Blue said to Cory as he gathered her into his arms again.

ACKNOWLEDGMENTS

I would like to thank Victoria Wells Arms, whose advice I will always value; Brett Wright, who knows how to get things done; Kim, my research assistant and sounding board; Ellie, who is smarter than I am; and Kevin, my tech wizard who knows a lot about lawn mowers.

Don't miss the second book in the Fairy-Tale Matchmaker series!

Can Cory help the very picky Goldilocks
find her perfect match?
Only if Cory acts fast enough!

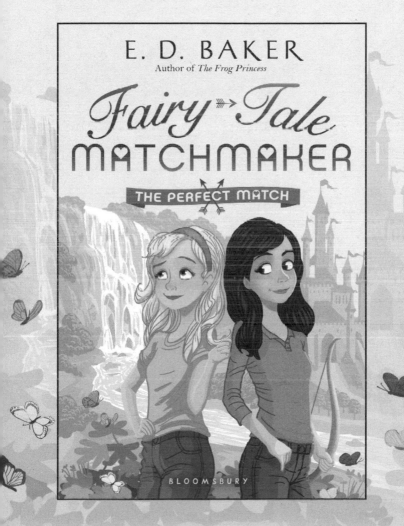

E. D. BAKER

Author of *The Frog Princess*

Fairy → Tale
MATCHMAKER

THE PERFECT MATCH

BLOOMSBURY

Read on for a selection from E. D. BAKER's newest book.

Cory crossed the street, thinking about how good it would feel to take a long, hot bath. She opened the front door and was on her way to the bathing room when she heard someone banging around in the kitchen. Wondering why her uncle was home early, she stepped into the kitchen and stopped. It wasn't Micah; it was that awful girl Goldilocks, poking around in the kitchen cabinets!

"What are you doing here?" demanded Cory. "How did you get in?"

Goldilocks glanced over her shoulder at Cory. "Waiting for you and through the back door. The lock on your back door is lousy. I'd change it if I were you, especially considering how many people you've managed to infuriate. Where do you keep your tea bags? Surely you have tea?"

Water was already boiling in the teapot on the stove, and Cory's favorite mug was waiting on the table. Cory was tired and hurt all over. Her mind was muzzy, but it was working well enough for her to wonder how long Goldilocks had been there.

"Next cupboard over, bottom shelf," said Cory. "Why do you want to see me?"

"I give as much money to someone as I gave to you, I expect personal attention. Ah, here it is. Chamomile? Is that all you have?"

Cory shrugged. "It's my uncle's. I'm not a big tea drinker."

"I suppose it will do," Goldilocks said, carrying the jar of tea to the table. Anyway, I ..." She stopped halfway across the room, having gotten a good look at Cory. "Say, what happened to you? You look like something the cat dragged in after she chewed it up and spit it out."

"Blue took me to the matinee performance of the water nymphs' ballet. There was an accident."

"I heard about that!" Goldilocks said, looking concerned. "Were you hurt?"

Cory shook her head. "Just cuts and bruises. And my throat hurts from swallowing that nasty water."

Goldilocks turned off the stove and started for the door. "What you need is to get out of those filthy clothes and take a hot bath. Come on, I'll get the water started."

"I don't really think …," Cory began, but Goldilocks had already left the kitchen.

"Where's your bathing room?" Goldilocks called as she went down the short hallway. "Never mind. I found it."

The hot water was running in the tub when Cory reached the bathing room. She paused in the doorway and watched as Goldilocks rummaged through the cupboard. None of this seemed real, but Cory was too tired and sore to care.

Goldilocks took a big, fluffy towel off the shelf and kept looking. "Wait right there and I'll have a hot bath ready for you in a New York minute."

"What's a New York minute?" asked Cory.

"I have no idea," Goldilocks told her. "It's just something my father used to say. My real father, not the man who kidnapped me."

Cory peered at her through the steam rising from the tub. "Your last name doesn't happen to be Piper, does it?"

"That's my adopted name. My last name used to be Sanders. I was Megan Sanders before I came here. The Pied Piper called me Goldilocks because of my hair and the name stuck. You don't happen to have any bubble bath, do you?"

Cory shook her head. "I don't know what that is. So, you're one of the children Gladys Piper raised."

Goldilocks expression softened. "You know my mother? Isn't she great? I remember the day we all showed up on her doorstep. I could tell she was overwhelmed, but she welcomed us and loved us and raised us all by herself. We haven't seen the Pied Piper since the day he brought us here and the FLEA took him away for kidnapping. Mama had to do everything. It wasn't easy and we never had enough money, but she loved us and that's what mattered."

"She told me that her oldest children had moved out," said Cory.

"I moved out three years ago. I send money back whenever I can. That's part of the reason I visit people's houses when they aren't home. I'm an artist and I make decent money with my artwork, but my family needs the money more than I do. Even I have to eat, though.

There, that should be enough," Goldilocks said, turning off the hot water. She stuck her finger in the bath and jerked it out again. "That's too hot. Why don't you get undressed while I add a little cold water. Don't worry, I won't look!"

Cory slipped off her clothes and dropped them on the floor. When the water was the right temperature, she stepped into the tub. The cuts stung as she lowered herself in the hot water, but she knew she had to clean them out before she put anything on them. Reaching for the soap, she washed herself as gently as she could. "What is bubble bath?" she asked Goldilocks, who was leaning against the sink with her back turned.

"Stuff you add to the water that fills the tub with bubbles. It's fun, that's all. I miss it, just like I miss cotton candy, soda, pizza, TV ... Anyway, I came to see you because I wanted to find out who you're going to fix me up with next. Jack Horner didn't work out. We didn't have anything in common. He barely spoke a hundred words to me the entire evening. Who else do you have in mind?"

Cory set the soap down and leaned back in the tub. She was drowsy from the hot water and her mind still wasn't very clear. She thought about the eligible young men she knew. None of them were Goldilocks's Mr. Right, of course, but until Cory found the man she'd *seen* in her vision, she could still set Goldilocks up on a date. Jonas MacDonald's face was the first one to come to mind.

"I know a young man named Jonas McDonald. He has a big farm and is a hard worker," Cory said.

"He'll do. Listen, I've got to go. Will you be all right by yourself? You're not going to fall asleep in the tub and drown or something, are you?"

"I'll be fine," Cory told her. "I'll get out in a few minutes and go lie down for a little while. Thanks for doing this. You've been a big help."

"Hey, I ran baths for my little brothers and sisters for years. I'm a real pro at bath time! Let me know what you set up with the farmer."

"I will," Cory said, but Goldilocks was already gone. A few seconds later, Cory heard the front door close. *That was a surprise*, she thought. *I guess she's not nearly as bad as I thought she was.*

After a good long soak, Cory rinsed herself off and climbed out of the tub. Finding some salve in the cupboard, she smeared some on her cuts. It was sticky, but it made her cuts hurt less.

Cory had just put on clean clothes when there was a knock on the door. When she peeked out of the window and saw that it was her neighbor Wanita, she opened the door and stepped outside.

"I hate to bother you," said the witch, "but I've had a little magical mishap and I need your help."

"Was someone hurt?" Cory asked, locking the door behind her.

She followed Wanita down the steps and across the lawn as the witch explained what had happened. "A new book of spells arrived today. I was trying one, but I forgot to lock Theo out of the room. He's hard to stop when he gets curious, and he shoved the door open and came in at a crucial moment. I was turning marbles into cockroaches and my Theo got in the way. Now I have one extra cockroach and no boar."

"Why did you want to turn marbles into cockroaches?" Cory asked her.

"They make great party favors. I'm going to my friend Griselda's birthday party tonight and she asked me to bring them."

"Couldn't you turn all the cockroaches back into what they were originally?"

"Sure, if I had enough dried salamander spit, but I have only enough for one or two attempts. If I don't choose the right one, Theo is going to stay a cockroach for the rest of his life, which might not be long if I accidentally step on him."

"What do you want me to do?" asked Cory.

"Help me figure out which cockroach is really my boar. I met your friend Marjorie at your party and she told me what you did about the spiders that were taking over her house. I'll pay you back with a favor when you need it, if that's all right with you."

"That's fine," said Cory. "Although I don't really expect you to pay me back. You're my neighbor and I'd be happy to help you."

"Nope, one favor deserves another," Wanita declared as she opened the door to her house.

Although it had looked like a hovel at the edge of a swamp, it was actually quite comfortable inside. Even so, Cory noticed the musky smell right away. *So that's what a boar smells like,* she thought.

Wanita led the way to a round table with a large pink doily. A wooden box sat on the middle of the table. "Here we are. See, I put the cockroaches in the box. I'm going to lift the lid, so be sharp. I don't want them to get out."

Cory leaned over the table as the witch took the lid off the box. It was filled with a seething mass of shiny black cockroaches. "Maybe it's this one," said Wanita, reaching into the box. "He's bigger than the others."

She was fumbling around, trying to grab the bigger cockroach, when the rest discovered that the lid was off. They swarmed out of the box, darting across the table and falling to the floor in their haste to get away.

"Oh no, you don't!" Wanita exclaimed. Pointing a finger at them, she said something in a language that Cory didn't understand and they all froze in place. "Good! That should make it easier. Take a look and see which one you think is Theo."

Cory didn't know what to do. The cockroaches all looked alike, although some were a little bigger than others. Crinkling her nose in distaste, she picked one up and examined it. Still frozen, it didn't even wave its antennae, although she had a feeling that it was looking at her. She sighed and shook her head. "I don't know how to tell them apart. Unless … Can you unfreeze them one at a time?"

"Sure," said Wanita. "What do you have in mind?"

"Theo just turned into a cockroach, so he wouldn't know how to *be* a cockroach yet. He's used to being a boar, so wouldn't he move differently from the others?"

"Now why didn't I think of that?" Wanita said. "Let's give it a try. We can start with that one."

When she pointed her finger at the one Cory was holding, Cory hurried to set it down. As soon as the spell was lifted, the cockroach started to scurry away, but Wanita snatched it up and stuck it in the box, clapping the lid on tightly. "Not that one!" she said.

They had tried twenty or thirty cockroaches when the next one turned around and shambled toward

Wanita instead of running away. "That's got to be my Theo!" the witch cried. When she dusted him with powder, he turned back into the boar. Dropping to the floor, Wanita wrapped her arms around Theo and hugged him so hard that he grunted. "I thought I'd lost you, boy! It's good to have you back."

"I have to go now," Cory said, starting for the door. "I'm glad we found Theo!"

"Thanks to you!" Wanita called as she raised her face from the boar's side. "I won't forget about that favor."

E . D .   B A K E R is the author of the Tales of the Frog Princess series, the Wide-Awake Princess series, and many other delightful books for young readers, including *Fairy Wings, Fairy Lies, A Question of Magic, The Fairy-Tale Matchmaker,* and *The Perfect Match. The Frog Princess* was the inspiration for Disney's hit movie *The Princess and the Frog.* She lives with her family and their many animals in Maryland.

www.talesofedbaker.com

Enter the magical world of
E. D. Baker!

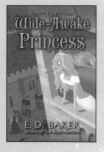

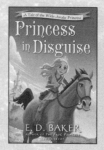

www.talesofedbaker.com

Read the entire
Frog Princess
series!

The Frog Princess — TALES OF THE FROG PRINCESS — E. D. BAKER

Dragon's Breath — TALES OF THE FROG PRINCESS — E. D. BAKER

Once Upon a Curse — TALES OF THE FROG PRINCESS — E. D. BAKER

No Place for Magic — TALES OF THE FROG PRINCESS — E. D. BAKER

The Salamander Spell — TALES OF THE FROG PRINCESS — E. D. BAKER

The Dragon Princess — TALES OF THE FROG PRINCESS — E. D. BAKER

Dragon Kiss — TALES OF THE FROG PRINCESS — E. D. BAKER

A Prince among Frogs — TALES OF THE FROG PRINCESS — E. D. BAKER

www.talesofedbaker.com

From dragons
to mysterious castles
to princesses . . .